Tortured Embrace

by

Julia Laque

Tortured Series

This is a work of fiction. Names, characters, places, and incidents are either the product of the author's imagination or are used fictitiously, and any resemblance to actual persons living or dead, business establishments, events, or locales, is entirely coincidental.

Tortured Embrace

Cover Art by *Diane Carlile*

The Wild Rose Press, Inc.
PO Box 708
Adams Basin, NY 14410-0708
Visit us at www.thewildrosepress.com

Publishing History
First Black Rose Edition, 2015
Print ISBN 978-1-62830-758-0
Digital ISBN 978-1-62830-759-7

Tortured Series
Published in the United States of America

Stepping in front of him, her head bent back. Jason balled his fists at his sides, demanding them not to move and caress her silken cheeks.

"Can't you feel how much I want you? You want me too, don't deny it." She moved ever closer, backing him up further against the door. In a second, he was going through the damn thing.

"Serena, stop." He shouldn't be here. He needed to leave, but he had a feeling she'd set off the fire alarm or bust a pipe just to get him to come running back.

"I need you, Jason."

Oh God...

"Stop fighting me. I know you want to touch me. Do it. My body burns for your touch. Show me what it's like to be caressed by a man."

The urgency in her gaze stunned him. She had no idea what her words were doing to him.

She glanced down, eyes blazing.

Okay...Guess she did know.

Serena reached for his chest, but he caught her wrists, holding them suspended in front of him. Staring for a moment at her delicate fingers, his control began to slip with every aching moment. God, he'd wanted to touch her for so long, really feel her in his hands...arms...

Very slowly, he brought his gaze to her breasts straining under her shirt, watching her chest rise and fall. How long had it been? He'd imagined this very moment, pictured him loving her, kissing her, moving inside her.

Damn it!

He had to try it, needed a taste of what he'd denied himself for so long.

Praise for *TORTURED SOUL*
Book One of the Tortured Series

"Truly and utterly brilliant. I was so sad it finished."

~Coco Diaz

~*~

"A great story, well written and I enjoyed from the first to the last page."

~Jenny P.

~*~

"Thrilling from beginning to end."

~Ary Figueroa

~*~

"It has mystery, action, suspense, steamy scenes, love, hardships, and it completely won me over."

~Jessica Mercedes

~*~

"I applaud Julia Laque and her wonderful debut novel."

~Kat in Chicago

~*~

"Looking forward to the next book!"

~Nicole K.

~*~

"This concupiscent love story has left me yearning for more!"

~Dedee Degante

Dedication

For Savannah,
my greatest accomplishment.
Love,
Mami

Acknowledgements

I'd like to thank my family and friends for the outpouring of love and support they've shown as I continue on with my writing career. I really could not do it without you.

A huge thank you to Lill Farrell for being such a wonderful editor and putting up with my constant need to toe the line.

Jesi, without your help I don't know where the Blacktails would be…

And, to Yani Sandoval, Diana Carlile, and Debbie Taylor for the coolest book cover I've ever seen. Well done!

Julia

Chapter One

1987

What the hell is she doing?

Light shone across the yard, illuminating the dark night as a door opened and a little girl stepped out from the back of her home. Jason Linus watched as the tiny figure carefully tiptoed out of the yard, taking anxious glances over her shoulder toward the house as she went.

It was only a matter of time, thought Jason. The shouts from within the house grew louder and before long, the seven-year-old sister of his best friend stopped looking over her shoulder and walked with determined strides around the house and down the street.

Coming out of the Midewin prairie where he'd positioned himself hours ago, Jason followed Serena Perez, curious as to where she thought she was going at one in the morning with just a backpack fixed on her shoulders.

Serena's gait slowed as she neared the park up ahead, and her tiny shoulders slumped as though all the energy had been knocked out of her.

Slowing as she did, Jason watched as she reached the secluded park and sat roughly on one of the three vacant swings. For a moment, he thought she was going to cry, but instead, Serena straightened her back, tucked a lock of her light brown hair behind her ear, then swung her bag in front of her and took out a book. Placing her bag at her feet, she opened the paperback and began reading, rocking herself gently on the swing, her shoes digging into the woodchips as she moved.

Jason stopped near the monkey bars and folded his arms. Leaning his shoulder on the cool metal, he gave her the space she needed.

Serena's brother, Adam, was in Chicago, managing his family's construction company. Over the years, Perez Construction had amassed to a lucrative business under Adam's careful administration. Serena's father, Xavier Perez, alpha of the Blacktail werewolf pack had been lax in his leadership in the company, causing Adam to pick up his father's slack.

Knowing his father's violent behavior, Adam asked Jason to keep an eye on things at his family's home in Wilmington, Illinois, while he was away. His best friend's concern was right on the mark. Moments ago, Xavier stumbled shit-faced into his home and not too long after, Jason heard a glass shatter and his alpha's voice raised at his wife.

The things Serena must see at home made him wince. She was so young and innocent. As far as they knew, Xavier had never put his hands on Serena, but he wasn't exactly kind to her either.

"I know you're there, Jason." Serena's tiny voice chimed as she turned the page, her eyes never leaving her book. Seeming at ease now, alone and away from her house she continued, "Mom said that my senses will be heightening now the closer I get to my transition and I can kind of smell you."

Jason smirked and pushed himself off the metal bar, striding slowly toward her, his broad arms swaying at his sides. "That bad, huh?"

She scratched her nose as she focused on the page in front of her. "No, you smell like the woods and aftershave."

That was pretty impressive for a werewolf her age, especially when she hadn't phased yet.

Taking a deep breath, she closed her book and stared down at the cover. "Adam told you to watch me, didn't he?"

There was no reason to lie to her. "Yes," he said, simply, and sat facing her on the low concrete wall surrounding the set of swings in a half circle. He clasped his hands in front of him and crossed his legs at the ankle.

Nodding, she peered up at him and in a small voice, asked, "What about Mom?" Her little shoulders heaved up and down, and he knew she was trying to control her nerves. As horrible as her father was, Serena maintained a calm and sweet persona. Not once had he seen her cry or throw a tantrum, and he'd been around since before she was born. Having grown up with her brother, he was as close to the Perez family as anyone could get.

After Serena's birth, Adam made it a point to stay close to home to watch over her and that included Jason. He'd do anything for his best friend and his kid sister but, unfortunately, he couldn't do much for her mother. She was married to his alpha, and there was no way Jason could go against him. He didn't want her to worry over her mother, but telling her this seemed insensitive.

His silence was answer enough for her. She let it go and they just sat there for a while, listening to the nighttime resonances of their quaint town.

"You don't talk much do you?" Serena asked after several minutes of just the sound of cicadas chirping their song.

He turned from his surveillance of the area, a bit startled by her stare. Had she been looking at him the whole time? "Uh...Not really..."

Before he could say anything else, she said in a low voice, "He scares me." Her dark brown eyes were not those of a seven-year-old. They were fearful and all too knowing for one so young.

At that moment, Jason felt cold hatred slip into his gut. His alpha didn't deserve his status. He didn't deserve his family.

He didn't deserve to live.

If it weren't for Adam and Serena, Jason would have been gone years ago. Sure, he loved his pack and would defend it to the death, but he couldn't stand the things Xavier put his family through.

"I don't want you to worry, little one." He shook himself, the gravity of her troubles weighing hard on his chest.

A tear slipped silently down her plump cheek. Her eyes round, she whispered, "You promise...you promise nothing bad will happen to me?"

Her words sent a jolt down his stomach, but not as much as his reply. "I promise, Serena." His voice was deep and measured as he vowed to protect her. "I will never, *ever* let anything bad happen to you. I'll always be here when you need me."

Serena's sweet face smiled.

****

Present Day

Jason shot up out of bed, instantly awake. A sheen of sweat covered his entire body as he gasped for air, jerking his head from side to side, looking anxiously around for…what?

His bedroom was pitch black except for the white glow of his alarm clock on the nightstand.

He froze in the act of his futile search and pinched his lids with trembling fingers. *Shit.* Did he really expect to see her there in his apartment?

Ripping the sheets off the lower part of his body, Jason stepped barefoot out of bed and headed to the bathroom in his boxers. Reaching the sink, he turned the knobs of the faucet, stuck his hands under the cool water, and splashed his face three times.

Taking a deep breath, he placed his hands on either side of the sink, the muscles of his arms rippling as he squeezed the porcelain that was sure to shatter in his tight grip. His shoulder-length hair, dripping with water, curtained his face as he tried to get a hold of himself.

Night after night Jason dreamed of her, Serena, as a kid in a ponytail, as a teenager with her nose stuck in a book, as a woman…

Fuck.

Pushing himself off the sink, he turned back into his room checking the clock. It was four A.M. *Great.* He didn't have to be on the construction site till six. He might as well go for a run. It had become a routine of sorts, a way to keep busy during the early morning hours. Every time he fell asleep or found himself sitting idle, images of her would creep into his mind and a cannon ball would erupt in his chest.

His best friend's sister had been missing for nearly

three months, and they were no closer to finding her now than they were back in July.

The Fighters, Blacktail members who protected the werewolf pack, had taken it in shifts to comb the area, but their efforts were fruitless. It was obvious she wasn't anywhere in or around Wilmington. There were five Fighters in town, including himself, and not one of them managed to find a trace. The six Fighters in Chicago were also hitting dead ends.

For a while, they were sure the Vampire King of North America had taken her. The pack had stirred up shit a couple months ago when Serena's brother Adam, now alpha of the pack, kidnapped the king's fiancée. To their utter disbelief, the piece of shit didn't have her.

Jason sat roughly on the edge of his bed, placing his head in his hand, elbows digging into his knees, waiting for the agonizing sting in his chest to subside.

Where the hell was she?

He knew she was still alive. Some inane part of him simply knew this fact because he refused to think the worse. There was no way she was…God could not be that cruel.

No. He'd promised her years ago he'd never let anything bad happen to her, a heavy promise to make to a little girl. Of course, he couldn't be sure she wouldn't get hurt emotionally, but he was sure he'd be around to protect her from physical harm.

He'd failed.

But as soon as she was back, safe and sound, he was going to spend the rest of his days making up for his failure.

She was alive. Of that, he was sure. He just hoped to God she wasn't hurt. So help the bastard who took her. If he hurt her…The headache he'd had the past several months returned, partly because he continued to bite down so hard on his molars. Trying to relax only stressed him out more though, so the grinding gave him something to do.

Jason sat in the dark, sparsely furnished room, letting the pain engulf him. Better for him to let his emotions run wild while he was alone and away from his pack. Although, werewolves, especially Fighters, were known to pick up each other's emotion from miles apart. He wouldn't be surprised if his pack members were up right at this moment, cursing him for waking them this way.

Sure enough, his phone rang, and he knew before he checked the caller ID it was Adam.

He answered instantly. When your alpha called, no matter how shitty you were feeling, you picked up. "Hey," Jason answered, his voice groggy from lack of use.

Adam's baritone rumbled on the other end. "Hey, J."

Serena's brother didn't say anything for a while, the two of them at a lost for words. Jason wasn't much of a talker as it was. Anyway, what would he say? *I'm fucking dying inside without her. I miss her so much.* Jason didn't even know how his alpha felt about his feelings for his sister. He really didn't want to go there now.

"Did you get any sleep?"

Jason cleared his throat. "Some…"

"Mmm…" Adam muttered. "Take the day off. Get some sleep. You can go on rotation after Nick."

"Can't," Jason replied.

7

"J, I know this is rough. I'm going out of my freaking mind too, but you're no good to me half dead on your feet."

Jason didn't respond, staring dejectedly at the hardwood floor of his room. As beta of the Blacktails, he had never disobeyed or refused an order from his alpha. A very small part of his brain wanted to apologize for being a hard head.

Instead, the image of Serena's parting smile the last time he saw her surfaced and the ache at his core was unbearable, crushing his insides like a meat grinder.

"Jesus, Jason…" Adam's voice was stunned, feeling the same ache Jason felt just then. He wouldn't be surprised if the entire Blacktail population was up right now.

"Sorry," Jason said, wearily. "Look, I need to keep busy. I won't go to the site, but I need to join you on rotation. I'm going for a run, and then I'll meet you at your place in an hour."

"Right," Adam said, morosely. "See you in a bit."

Jason punched the end button and tossed the phone on the bed. Getting swiftly to his feet, he marched back into the bathroom, running the shower icy cold. Slipping out of his boxers, he flung them on the floor and stepped into the standup.

He welcomed the cool water on his hot skin, letting the freezing shards of liquid sting his flesh. Whatever pain he inflicted was nothing compared to what his Serena was going through. He'd welcome a beat down if it would take away the suffering she must be enduring.

"Serena," he moaned, bracing his arms against the mosaic, hanging his head.

He'd fallen for her unexpectedly years ago. Realizing you were in love with your best friend's little sister was like getting hit by a semi. You see it coming at you, but you're powerless to stop it and know the outcome will be a complete disaster.

For years afterward, he'd kept his distance, or at least tried to. As a Fighter of the race, the alpha's sister was off limits. But he'd always kept an eye on her. It was hard not to. On occasion he'd run into her at her family's home or in town, content to just see her smile, hear her voice, anything.

He knew Serena had a soft spot for him too, which made their non-love affair even more depressing. Anytime he'd pick up on Serena's feelings for him, he'd keep his distance for a few months, hoping against hope she'd forget about him. But the instant he'd see her again, it was as if their feelings had grown stronger, sprouting more intense emotions they had no idea how to handle.

"Serena," he whispered again, aching to see her smile.

I'll find you, little one, he thought, squeezing his lids tight.

****

"Tuam sanquine, tuam sacramentum, tuam nomen, manifestum et natus a nocte walker…Tuam sanquine, tuam sacramentum, tuam nomen…"

The feeling of immense joy washed over Cassandra. Her spell, challenging though it may be, was working, and she fought the urge to rejoice. She stood amid her *convenio,* arms outstretched, palms up, chanting in the middle of the circle. Twelve witches surrounded her, reciting the incantation with her, again and again.

With dark, thick hair pulled back in a long braid and green piercing eyes, she let the magic consume her, her body swelling the stronger her spell became. It would not be long now. She watched as the heap of material atop the ancient sarcophagus began emanating a thick black smoke, rising high in the old ballroom of the Sweetin Home.

The wide room with its high ceiling was the only space in the house without windows, other than the convenient cells below.

The abandoned house in Hillview, Illinois, was the perfect venue for their assembly.

Sweetin had completed the home in 1862 with a natural stream running through the basement. It was left abandoned for years till Cassandra took up residence. The ruins of the house were now her home, providing ample space for thirteen souls and two prisoners to dwell.

Cassandra glanced up to where a man and woman hung naked, spread-eagle against the wall. Her devoted *convenio* had administered a serum to keep them from phasing. The man had his eyes shut, refusing to watch the orgy that would follow the chant. It was their common belief witches heightened and sustained their powers through group sex.

There was no need for the werewolves to worry, however. A real witch would never deign to lie with their breed; not like her forsaken great granddaughter, she thought derisively. Although, some of her *convenio* did like to play with the hostages and who was she to take away their fun?

Cassandra looked to the other wolf and grimaced.

She didn't like the way this one stared. The female's eyes were deadened, set deep in their sockets. She'd hardly eaten a thing for months. Her dark, vacant expression made Cassandra ill at ease. She knew, eventually, the girl would close her eyes, having been forced to witness all kinds of lewd behavior.

Now though, the girl's eyes latched onto each member of her *convenio*, as if committing each face to memory. She felt Cassandra's stare then, and their eyes met. Continuing to chant, she reached her senses out to gauge what the stupid girl was thinking and almost laughed. The girl promised herself repeatedly that it would be over soon. The poor fool. Hadn't she realized that it was her blood that worked better than the male's?

With that thought, Cassandra disengaged from the circle and headed for the curious female on the wall. More of her blood wouldn't hurt her spell. Besides, it'll teach this one to stare so openly at them again. She reached the female and stood quietly before her. Slipping her right hand in her robes, she took out her bejeweled dagger.

The girl sucked in a deep breath, knowing exactly what was coming.

"I don't like your stare, young lady. I think a lesson should be learned tonight, don't you agree?" Staring up into the girl's eyes, the dagger poised between them, she brought the tip of the blade up to her neck and began a teasing descent down her torso, around each mound, grazing her belly and lower…

"Leave her alone!" the male called. He had been watching, his face tight with anger.

Barely sparing him a glance, Cassandra lifted her dagger arm and sliced his cheek, making a gash from temple to chin.

The girl cried out, looking desperately at her fellow wolf.

"Not to worry, little fool. You'll get your turn." She bent and kissed the part of the female's thigh she was going to cut. The hot skin burned her lips. "This one bleeds so nicely." Cassandra stepped back, not liking the way her prisoner towered over her in this instance. She'd rather have the pups sprawled out on the floor, but hell if Cassandra would go on bended knee to do the deed.

Infuriated now, she stuck the blade into the indentation at her hip and cut deep, dragging the point down through succulent skin, watching with a heated urgency as her blood spilled.

Ignoring the female's shouts of pain and the male's groans of anguish, she stopped at the knee. Dropping the dagger quickly, she reached up and covered her palms in blood gushing profusely out of the gaping flesh. Turning to the sarcophagus, she ran her bloodied hands over the dead carcass and other gathered materials, which would bring her Nightwalkers to life.

In the circle, her *convenio's* chants grew louder as each opened their robes and slipped them to the floor, their bodies more than ready to complete the spell.

When Cassandra finished her ministrations, she turned, choosing to de-robe in front of her prisoners. She wanted to fornicate right in front of her innocent charges.

Cassandra leered at Serena Perez who no longer screamed or stared at the assembly around her. Her listless eyes gazed up at the faded mural adorning the high ceiling of the ballroom, her mind continuing to pray hopelessly.

I promise. It will be over soon. I promise.

Chapter Two

The jagged stone at her back made her skin itch, but refusing to move, she ignored it. It was nothing compared to the throbbing in her leg, and the smarting at her wrists and ankles from the prickly rope wound tight around them. It didn't compare to the emptiness inside her.

Pain was all she knew. In fact, as she stared upward at the cracked and worn ceiling, Serena couldn't remember feeling anything else. Things like laughing and smiling were foreign to her. She couldn't imagine how anyone could smile in this horrible world she lived in.

Angst wasn't really her thing. There had actually been a time when she was happy. After finishing school and traveling the world, she'd taken a position in Wilmington's quaint little library. Serena had been lucky to land the best job in the world for a peaceful girl like her, with access to so many books.

The day Serena told her brother about her new position, he'd bought her a car, thrilled to have his little sister stay in town. He'd taken her out to dinner, spoiling her as usual. They'd talked about the future, and she laughed at his dry jokes. She felt sorry for that girl now. The stupid, smiling idiot had no idea what was coming.

The acrid smell of the carcass on the sarcophagus

turned her stomach as the revolting couple in front of her cried out louder trying to get her attention. Refusing to watch, she focused on a washed-out impression of a cherub, oddly anticipating going back in the basement to her cold, damp room.

Being strung up was humiliating enough, but she couldn't stand being naked in front of these people. She should have been used to it by now, but it made her insides squirm every time one of them looked at her. And Ben. *God,* to have her boss see her this way was too much.

They usually avoided looking at each other when they were brought up, attempting to respect each other's privacy, but hated witnessing the other get hurt and eventually would take a cautionary glance to check on one another. The gash across his face looked like it would leave a significant scar. Though they normally healed quickly, there was only so much a werewolf's body could take. And they were weakening more now than ever.

Feeling the blood trickle down and around her calf was a reminder she could very well die tonight from blood loss. She didn't want to look at her leg. It was numb now, but the familiar agonizing sting would start in a minute, and then it would eventually heal by tomorrow night. She'd have a scar though, just like her other thigh. The more blood she lost, the weaker her ability to heal became.

The mural above her began to blur. She was going to pass out. Fighting the urge to close her eyes and let emptiness claim her, she continued to stare at the cherub, telling herself over and over again it could not last. It will all be over soon. Knowing the witch could read minds, she usually kept an ongoing prayer to keep her thoughts from giving too much away.

"Serena?" Ben's waning voice whispered to her.

This time she let her eyes close, refusing to look at him. He was taking this opportunity to talk to her while everyone else around them fornicated to punctuate their spell.

"Talk to me," he muttered and she knew he was barely moving his lips, not wanting to draw attention to them.

How in the world could she face him after what happened? And what did he want her to say? They were being held captive by witches, tortured by magic, and cut every other day by a psychotic bitch. Excuse her if she didn't feel like chatting.

"Are you okay? Please, just say something," he pleaded.

Serena opened her eyes, and she could feel his stare on her. "Don't look at me," she whispered under the countless sighs and moans on the ballroom floor.

From the corner of her eye she saw him turn to face downward, probably squeezing his eyes shut to avoiding the rutting witches on the floor. "How are you feeling? Have you been eating?"

She shook her head, then realized he couldn't see her. "No," she replied. The thought of food made her nauseous. Hesitating, Serena gave him the answer she knew he was looking for. "I...I...can't hold anything down."

Ben's head jerked her way. Reluctantly, she met his wide-eyed expression and grimaced. He didn't look good. Her boss had always been skinny, but he was all skin and bones now. Male werewolves were naturally big, but as a half-breed, Ben had only the height of a werewolf. A bookworm like herself, he had no interest in pumping iron to add muscle.

What a perfect catch they were for this sick lot. Serena and Ben were not Fighters, but simple Blacktail members who kept to themselves. Their potential to keep a low profile must have been why they were chosen for this experiment. They weren't trained in combat. Try as her brother might, she was never interested in learning self-defense.

Serena used to tell her brother sarcastically that she was a werewolf. If she ran into trouble, she would just morph and growl at her attacker. Who could guess her attacker would have a tranquilizer which kept them from phasing.

Serena gave Ben an apologetic look. "I'm sorry," she whispered a tear sliding down her cheek.

He understood her condition. Probably sensed it now and knew she suffered. Her inability to hold anything down worried her poor boss. She hadn't seen a mirror in months, but she was sure she looked worse than he did.

Ben shook his head. "Don't..." He seemed to get over his initial shock. "Just...please eat, okay?"

She nodded miserably.

The head witch, Cassandra became quiet, no doubt bringing their filthy act to an end at that very moment. Serena whispered frantically to Ben. "Don't think it. Clear your mind."

Ben nodded and shut his eyes again, his face tight as he focused on some unknown thought.

As she resumed her fixation on the cherub above, Serena heard him whisper, "It's going to be okay.

17

You're going to get out of here."

Dizzy from her brief panic of being overheard or worse, having her captor read their thoughts, Serena continued her prayer. She was slipping in and out of focus, the pain in her leg excruciating now. Desperately, she clung to consciousness, afraid of what her subconscious would reveal.

Her cherub's dark eyes lost their form, becoming tiny dots as the pain worsened. As her lids gave way, the chubby face no longer visible, the small dark spots turned a shimmering hazel. A man's piercing gaze interrupted her prayers.

Jason's eyes bored into hers, urging her to hang on. His strong face gave her hope and she held onto it as long as she could, until her world went dark.

****

Serena came to as a needle sank into her forearm. She was on her back on the floor of her empty, dark room. There were no windows, no bed, not even a blanket to lie on. Her captors had left only three bowls. One was for water, the other for the occasional slice of bread and cheese, and one bowl to conduct her business. The only male witches in the house changed them out every day. Aside from the woman, Cassandra, the other women didn't want to go near a werewolf.

The man kneeling over her paused a second to meet her glare then took out the syringe. She remembered his name was Leonardo, recognizing him as the male who had come down a week ago during the moon heat.

"Not such a big bad wolf after all, are ya?" Leonardo said with a leer. He dropped her arm and stood.

Staring at him with hatred in her eyes, Serena sat up gingerly, using her hands to pull herself to the back wall, dragging her injured legs across the filthy ground. She had never felt such violence toward another human being. "Get out," Serena said weakly, wondering why the hell he lingered. Usually the men just came in to switch the bowls or inject her with the serum, which kept her from phasing and left. They never hung around, except for a week ago she thought with mounting worry.

He laughed at her. "You're not exactly in a position to call shots now, are you?" Placing both hands on his hips, he continued to smirk at her. "By the way…" His eyes narrowed at her. "That was fun the other day, wasn't it?"

In spite of herself, she began to visibly tremble. She hated showing this man just how frightened she was. "You're sick," she whispered, nervous now beyond comprehension. He had touched her before, but only when she was brought to the ballroom and strung up. She had a feeling Cassandra had given them orders not to mess with the hostages when they were locked up. "How would your boss feel about what you did?"

Leonardo's face hardened and she knew she was right. "Cassandra wouldn't believe a stinking bitch over me," he said with a snort.

He could be insulting all he liked, but it was obvious he was scared now. Taking a step toward her, she jerked back, raising her knees up to cover herself.

Pointing a finger at her, he said, "You keep your filthy mouth shut, got it?" With that, he turned and left, slamming the door behind him. Serena watched through the thick square glass as he locked the door and stormed off.

Months ago, Leonardo and two other guys had completely altered her life. The day had been as normal as any other for a quiet girl like herself. After closing the library on North Water Street, she waved goodbye to the coordinator of children's services and walked to her car, stopping at an antique shop to look in the window at a new selection of Celtic jewelry.

The charming little shop was always inviting, but it was getting late, the sun having just set over the west woods, and she needed to get to the grocery store before it closed. The only thing in her fridge was string cheese, coffee grounds, and creamer…and she'd had that for breakfast.

Running off a list of things she needed in her head, she unlocked her Volkswagen Beetle and tossed her purse on the passenger seat.

Before she stepped into the car, she felt a sting in her upper arm as someone hissed rapidly in a foreign language in her ear. Her reaction instant, Serena spun on her heel, her hand over the strange tingle on her arm. Before she deduced what was happening, Serena felt her body become extremely limp. Her vision blurred, and the urge to lie down was overwhelming. A man in a leather jacket stood before her. For a moment, as he continued on in a different language, she wondered why he was wearing a leather jacket in the middle of the summer. The man finished his rant. Speaking in English he said, "You need to come with me."

His voice was soft and kind, but a logical side of her brain still in operation told her he was dangerous. Serena shook her head slowly. The act of speaking seemed too difficult.

"Yes. Benjamin's been in an accident around the corner. He's really hurt. He asked me to get you. Please…" The man took her arm gently.

Ben. No, he couldn't have. Her boss had left an hour ago. Serena shook her head. What was wrong with her? Why did she feel so strange? Just then, someone shouted her name.

"Ben," she mumbled, looking to the left. Her boss' voice had come from Canal Street. He really was in trouble. She shrugged the man off her arm and stumbled slightly around the corner. There were two cars there, but it didn't look like they'd been in an accident.

They were both parallel parked along the curb. Ben was in the first car, his head lolled out the window like he was going to be sick. Vaguely noticing it wasn't her boss' car, Serena started forward. Ben met her hazy gaze and mouthed the word, *No.*

Serena faltered.

Ben lifted his head with obvious difficulty, and called out as loud as he could, "Run, Serena!" His head was cocked back by a dark figure sitting in the car with him.

Before she could move, the muzzle of a gun met the small of her back. "You run or scream, I'll shoot. Get in the car."

The second car's back door opened, and she was pushed unceremoniously in. Her body, completely lax now, could not manage a single act of defiance. That small part of her mind still registering what was happening was the only thing panicking.

As someone drove, the man in black leather tied her wrists together. "Did anyone see you?" the driver asked.

"I don't think so," black leather responded.

Serena's head spun uncontrollably and she leaned back against the cushion. She met the driver's eyes in the rearview mirror. "How long will the incantation last? Shouldn't they have passed out by now?"

The man beside her looked her over and reaching up, slid his hand over her eyes to close her lids. "I don't think Cassandra's spell works so well on Weres. They both refused to come with me right after I enchanted them."

"You didn't do it right."

"I did it fine. We've got them, don't we?"

The driver was quiet for a moment as he sped off. Struggling to open her eyes with no luck, she tried to move away from the man beside her who reeked of stale cigarettes. "How long will the serum last? If she phases in the car, we're fucked."

"Relax. It's supposed to last twenty-four hours. She can't turn with the serum *and* under the enchantment. We're fine. Just drive. You're freaking me out."

Her captor's voices were the last thing she remembered before waking up in this cold room. The prison she'd been in for God knows how many days was made up of dark stone walls and a heavy wooden door with a small square glass at the top.

Outside her door, ruined bits of stone scattered around the dark hall along a stream, which must have kept the abandoned home cool over a hundred years ago. The stream's condensation maintained the cool dampness in the atmosphere, chilling her to the bone. There were a few other rooms, in one of which she knew Ben was being held.

The imposing thick walls around her were impenetrable. She'd pounded on them for days, trying as hard as she could to phase and bust the wooded door open, but the serum they injected in her worked to keep her wolf side from coming out.

Leonardo and the two other guys, she thought their names were Ken and Gary, were the only ones that injected her on a daily basis. Ken usually got her on the arm, right above her elbow, but Gary and Leonardo always stuck it in her vein on her forearm.

Perfect, she thought. Lifting her arm up to her mouth, Serena sucked as hard as she could at the puncture mark.

Days ago, Serena suggested this strategy to Ben and she thought it might be working. They didn't know if it could get the whole dosage out before it took effect, but it was worth a shot.

Squeezing her arm surrounding the area, Serena sucked as much of the disgusting stuff as she could. Releasing her arm, she bent over and spat it out on the floor. It might have been her imagination, but she thought she'd sucked in a lot more of the serum today. Could this mean she was gaining strength?

She looked at her leg. The wound had closed somewhat, but a long dark ugly line still marred her skin. Pulling the part of her thigh she could reach up to her lips, Serena licked as much of the wound as she could. When she was done, she sat back and stared. If that part healed faster than the rest she would know her ability to phase was returning.

If she could turn without being chained to the wall as they'd done during the full moon when the serum couldn't keep her wolf side in, then that little window didn't stand a chance.

Hope flared in her chest, the only decent feeling she'd had since arriving here. On the floor by the door were the bowls that held water and a couple pieces of what looked like cheddar cheese. Serena crawled over and taking a deep breath, ate every morsel. A wave of nausea washed over her, and she closed her eyes, fighting it. She had to keep this food down to give her body the energy it needed.

Her plan would work, and when they were out of here, she was going to see her brother again, going to sleep in her own bed, in her cozy house with all her books. She was going to see Jason.

After taking several sips of water, she lay down on the rough ground, quite acclimated to the moisture covering its surface. The cold floor against her cheek actually helped ease her queasiness.

As she lay, taking steady pulls of air, the Blacktail beta's eyes filled her mind again, warming her insides as they always did. The crush on her brother's friend had started years ago when she was a young girl. Unfortunately, Adam had soon picked up on it, the damn emotional bond giving her away when she was just a teenager. She could still hear her brother's scolding voice all those years ago.

"Are you out of your mind? He's old enough to be your father," Adam admonished.

Serena looked at her brother calmly while she did the dishes in their family's octagonal home. Aside from their cousin, Ramo, Adam and Serena were the only Perezes left, their parents having died three years previous. "You know age is nothing to Weres, Adam. He's too old now that I'm seventeen, but he's already stopped aging…" She paused, blushing at the look on her brother's face.

"Serena, you're my sister and he's my best friend. There are rules about this shi…stuff."

Rolling her eyes at him, she said, "I know you curse, Adam. I'm not a little girl anymore."

"Well, too bad because you will always be my little sister." He sat at the kitchen table, running his hands roughly over his face.

Her poor brother was so tired. Between his duties as the new alpha of the Blacktail pack and managing their family's construction company, there was little time for him to relax.

"Look…" he said, shifting uncomfortably in the chair he was too big to be sitting in. "Jason's a Fighter and beta of the pack, which puts him in dangerous situations. I don't want that kind of life for you. You'll spend half your time worrying for him."

Serena turned her back on her brother, scrubbing the dishes with frustration. "I didn't say I wanted to mate him, and I didn't say I wanted to marry him."

"Ugh…" Adam moaned, his head falling back on his neck. "Stop, please."

She almost giggled at the sound of his voice.

"Serena, you're going away to school in a couple of months. Focus on your studies. You'll have plenty of time for boyfriends when you're…forty."

This time she laughed out loud and turning, splashed water at him. "Sure, Ad, I'll start dating when I'm forty."

Adam laughed too. "Good. I'm glad we're in agreement."

It was too bad for her brother her feelings toward

his best friend had not dwindled in the slightest after four years of college, two years of grad school, and a year of traveling across the globe.

She returned to Wilmington seven years ago, to find Jason Linus more beautiful and mysterious as ever. And as much as he tried to hide it, she knew he felt something for her too.

Shuddering with anxiety, she hugged herself, pulling her knees in closer. The tears sprang again, falling into her knotted wisps of hair. What would her brother and Jason think of her now? What would they do when they learned of the innocent child growing inside her?

Chapter Three

Benjamin Michaels had never been in a fight in all his forty-two years. For goodness sake, he didn't curse, didn't feel the need to. He led a simple, average life in Wilmington. After graduating magna cum laude at Northwestern University, he moved back home and married his high school sweetheart. They lived in a two-bedroom house on Oak Street with their two girls. The biggest worry, up until three months ago, was which sport the girls would play in the fall.

As he paced his bleak prison, he tried to remember the last time he was seriously angry. It might have been when he received the outrageous gas bill last winter.

He continued to pace the small room, trying to work himself up. Usually it took the full moon for Ben to phase. He never felt the need to turn otherwise.

Until now.

Clenching his fists, Ben felt the heat flush his cheeks. How could this have happened? What they were doing to them was despicable. And Serena…She was definitely having a harder time. And she was a female, much smaller than he was.

Every time he watched that bitch cut her was pure torture, sickening him. He'd told the witch to leave her alone and just cut him, but apparently they liked Serena's blood better than his own.

They couldn't continue on this way. Serena's leg

had bled more this time. She was pale and thin, her brown eyes growing more deadened with every passing minute. He didn't know how much more her body could take.

And now...

Ben stepped to the wall and stopped, placing both hands on the wet stone, his head hanging off his shoulders.

She was pregnant.

That sick fuck Leonardo surprised him a week ago during the moon heat. The night before the full moon werewolves could not control their sexual appetites. The night the need to bury themselves into the opposite sex burned deep inside a were, overpowering their bodies, indicating it was time to mate.

Ben had had his wife to mate with on those days. Weres without a heat mate could take pills until the period ended.

The male witches were the only ones to witness Serena and Ben writhe in pain during their mating nights. They'd had to endure two heat nights already without pills, while the voyeurs watched through the glass windows, gawking as their bodies convulsed, aching to find release.

Last week, however, Leonardo had dragged him out of his room and threw him in with Serena so he could watch as they...

Never in his life had he felt so much remorse, such shame. They'd cried the entire time, but there was nothing they could do. It was their bodies' natural response, the innate thing to do on mating nights.

For as long as he lived, he will never forgive himself. He should have smashed his head on the damn wall, knocking himself out.

Jesus! It was bad enough he'd taken advantage of her, but he was also a married man with children and she was the sister of his alpha. Adam Perez will surely bring him up on charges or skip a trial all together and simply kill Ben himself.

Ben screwed up his face, fighting the tears. Hating his cowardice, he pushed himself off the wall, resuming the forceful march, back and forth.

He was going to get them out of here. Flinching, he thought of the brief conversation he'd had with Serena. It had been their only chance to talk and he had a feeling her plan was working. He felt stronger; the serum was leaving his body, and any moment he would be able to turn.

It was about time he manned up. If he wasn't so weak, he could have gotten them out of here a long time ago. Hell, if he wasn't such a pussy he would never have called out to her all those months ago, giving their captors a chance to get her in the car.

He would hate himself till the day he died for doing that. He should have let the fucker in the car shoot him in the head instead of jeopardizing her safety.

Hating himself was good. He was pissing himself off, and tiny shudders began to course down his back. As his body slowly swelled, he felt his vision change and his eyes turn bright.

****

Three days prior to Serena's abduction, Jason entered the Midewin Library, looking more out of place than a lion at a bake sale.

Hair whipped up in a ponytail, Serena knelt on the floor in between shelves in the nonfiction section, restacking books. She sensed him standing down the row before she even looked up, always irresistibly aware of him.

When she looked over, her heart leapt to her throat. In his usual garb of jeans and a t-shirt, his dark brown hair hung loose, his hazel eyes fixated in her direction. At six feet five inches tall, his head reached the top of the bookshelves. He didn't smile, hardly ever showing any sign of emotion, his expression always unreadable.

"Hi," Serena said nervously. She always felt like a giddy schoolgirl when he was around. Looking around and fumbling with the books in her hand, she tried to control her nerves, tried to be cool and natural, but there was no hope when he was near.

Coming forward, his enormous frame crowding the narrow aisle, he said, "Hey." Jason hardly ever spoke, but when he did, it always surprised her how such a powerful and colossal man could speak so smoothly. His quiet voice did strange things to her body, her heart rate quickening from the sound.

Her neck stretched back to look up at him. He was too imposing this way, so she stood up, clumsily.

Jason reached down to help her, grabbing her by the elbow, making her skin tingle. It was always this way for her. She could literally count the times he had ever touched her. Every time he did, she replayed the moment over and over again in her head.

This was the second time he'd touched her elbow. Once he'd lightly grazed her back, ushering her into her living room when she'd been wobbly after her first transformation. The last time he'd touched her was right before she'd left for college, chucking her under the chin in rare good humor.

Four times, she told herself. Lord, was she pathetic!

Standing now, she barely reached his pectorals, his body dwarfing her. It was a shared joke amongst the Fighters to tease her about her uncommonly small height. Blushing stupidly, she turned away, pretending to search for a spot to place the stack of books in her arms.

"What are you doing here?" Hoping her voice sounded casual, she stuffed a book in between two large volumes on microbiology. If it was in the wrong place, she'd fix it later.

Feeling him stare down at her, he answered, "Dropping off your car. Adam changed the oil and had it detailed."

Earlier today her brother had picked up her car. Perplexed she said, "Adam told me he needed to borrow it because his truck was being serviced."

A slight smirk appeared on his tanned face, making his high cheekbones more pronounced, making her lightheaded. "We can't fit in your car. He attached it to his truck, and I attached it to my pickup. He knew you wouldn't get it serviced till it was too late, so…" He held up her key to the Beetle between long, thick fingers.

Her brother knew her too well, but she'd wished he'd asked first. "You guys didn't have to do that." Taking the key, she put it in her pants pocket.

Jason shrugged, his golden face unsmiling again.

"Thank you." Despite feeling like a chided little girl, she was thankful, having been about a thousand miles overdue for an oil change.

He nodded, putting a hand in his pocket. Standing there with a tender look in his eyes, they stared mutely, letting the joy that came whenever they were near each other wrap around them. His hazel gaze roamed over her face, from her hair down to her lips, lingering for a moment.

Her boss chose that moment to round the corner and into their private aisle. "Serena, will you help this young lady? She's researching...Oh, excuse me."

Serena felt Jason's annoyance at Ben's interruption. Her boss undoubtedly did as well by the look of terror on his face when he noticed who she was conversing with. It wasn't every day the beta of the Blacktails entered his library.

"Mr. Linus," her boss stammered. "I apologize. I wasn't aware you were visiting today. May I help you with something?"

Jason had barely glanced in his direction, his focus solely on her. "Serena's helping me," he said simply.

Stifling a giggle, Serena gave her boss an apologetic smile.

"Of course," he replied, and ushered the woman behind him quickly along the aisle and out of sight.

Alone again, a painstaking feeling came over her knowing he was about to leave. Every time he left her she ached for him.

Jason tensed slightly, remaining where he was standing oh so close. Staring fixedly, his brow furrowed. "What's wrong?"

Darn! She had to learn to control her emotions, but how could she when it hurt so much to be away from him? "Nothing," she said, breathless. Pivoting, she walked along the aisle, focusing on the shelves.

It was so hard to be around him and not want to touch him, hold him, kiss…She shook herself. That wasn't going to happen. Her brother had made it clear, he didn't want this for her and after all he'd done for her, she didn't want to disappoint him. Not like Jason would ever lay a finger on her. He was too devoted to Adam to ever betray him.

His voice murmured low behind her and she jumped. "You were fine a second ago. Why are you sad?"

Motionless at his magnificent presence at her back, she refused to turn around, too cowardly to face him. Serena's breath caught as she inhaled his musky scent surrounding her, the fragrance she wished she could bottle up and keep with her forever. Chest throbbing, her shoulders heaved rapidly. His close proximity raised her heart rate to a million beats a second. In a small voice, she answered, "You know why."

She felt him stiffen.

The energy between them was palpable, closing in on them with every aching second. Serena closed her eyes, frozen in place, wishing, hoping he'd touch her again. How could this man make her body melt with wanting?

Reaching out, she brought a hand to the wooden shelf to keep her steady. She swallowed noisily, feeling his deep gaze burn the back of her head. "Why did you come? Why not Adam?" she uttered softly.

Then, she felt it.

The indescribable sense of yearning emanated from him. He wanted her as much as she did him. His longing for her filled her up, choking her with need, leaving her breathless.

Feeling him inch closer, his silky voice felt like ice running down her back, and her lids closed. "You know why," he murmured huskily.

Jason leaned down to her hair, inhaling deep and Serena heard the rapid pace of his heart beating wildly in his chest.

Her mouth opened to let in the air her lungs needed. How long could they fight this?

Bending lower, his breath tickling her ear, he whispered, "Be safe, little one." And he was gone.

Shivering on the spot, she stood where she was at a complete loss as to what she was supposed to be doing.

Turning, Serena walked down to the window facing the street, hugging the remaining books in her arms. She watched Jason get into the black pickup. Feeling her gaze, he looked over. Eyes soft, he winked at her.

Smiling, she winked back and turned away, reveling in the rush of desire coming out of the pickup.

****

Blacktail headquarters was stationed in Adam's octagonal house on Water Street, next to the Midewin prairie. The Fighters were assembled in the dining room, taking up every inch of the newly furnished room. Having recently mated, Adam's lady was busy decorating the place, painting every square inch and getting rid of the old furniture to give the house a more modern look than the Victorian setup Adam's late mother had left behind. Evangeline, Adam's mate and fiancée, still kept a few knickknacks here and there to mix the old with the new.

Jason shifted impatiently by the window when Adam finally stormed in running a hand through his disheveled black hair, a light blue receiving blanket thrown over his shoulder. They could all hear one of the twins crying in an upstairs bedroom as Evangeline hummed to him, pacing back and forth. "Sorry, had to help put the boys down for their nap."

Ramo, Adam's loudmouth cousin was leaning back in his chair, looking as exhausted as the rest of them. "Why didn't you tell us it was nap time? We're all sitting here twiddling our thumbs when we could have been at home napping?" Ramo's tired brown eyes twinkled with mirth, loving the way he annoyed everyone around him. His playful persona didn't match his appearance. Covered in tattoos and a lip ring, he looked like someone you didn't want to meet in a dark alley. Having been out all night, his crew cut was growing in as well as a morning shadow. Despite running on empty, he still had enough energy to run his mouth.

Adam glared at him mutely before addressing them all. "We're changing the rotation tonight. Nick, Alex, after you've rested, follow along the I-55 North. We've been looking at too many secluded areas. Hit every town you can in human form till you reach the city then turn back."

Nick nodded seriously, ever the devoted Fighter. Although they'd never say it to his face, Nick was the most standup guy they knew. Sitting next to Alex, they were as alike as night and day. The differences between the two were astounding. Nick was blonde and all angelic-like, and Alex…well…he looked like the devil reincarnate with black hair and eyes and full mustache and beard.

Adam turned to his cousin. "Ramo, I know you just got back from Indiana, so rest up and you can go at it again in the morning." He hesitated then turned to Jason. "I know you want to, but I can go it alone right now and you…"

"Don't start this shit again…" Jason interrupted.

"J, you just got back from Missouri. Take it…" Adam stopped at the look Jason gave him. "Fine, head southwest. Go slow, but I expect you back by midnight, got it?"

Jason just nodded, having no intention to come back so soon. He'd just tell his alpha he was following a lead. Serena had been gone way too long. There was no way he was slacking now.

"I'll continue to make calls to the east of us from here. Any questions?"

There was a collective murmur of *no* then Adam knocked his knuckles on the table and turned to go.

Jason grabbed his keys and phone from the windowsill and took a glance outside. His eyes fell on the front porch, and he paused, transported back to the time he'd watched Serena, as he stood in this very spot seven years ago. It was a bit brighter outside than it had been that night, but he could still picture exactly what she looked like at that moment, the moment his life had changed for good.

It had been cool for a May evening and all twelve Fighters, including the Chicago crew were joined together for a meeting. Once all topics were covered, they busted out the beers and started a few games of poker. Always the observer, Jason sat on the windowsill ready to smack Nick upside the head for anteing up with a shitty full house.

The Fighters had two games going, one with five players, and another with six. Tyson tossed two blue chips in the middle of the table. "Hey Adam, saw your sister today. When did she get back?"

There were mumbles of congratulations and genuine surprise that their alpha's sister, who they all doted upon, was back in Wilmington.

Adam grimaced. "She got back three days ago."

"Why the face?" Viola from Chicago asked, listening in on the conversation from the other game.

Adam answered with a look of disgust as he sorted through his hand. "Brought some guy with her to help move her things back in."

Jason stiffened by the window, an unusual feeling in his gut. He hadn't seen Serena in three years. Every time she'd come home to visit he'd been busy working or out of town. He guessed the funny sensation he had was due to the idea the young girl he watched grow up might have a boyfriend. Just felt weird.

"We could have handled it," Ramo said.

"I know, but you know how she is…doesn't want to impose…Anyway, he took her out to dinner tonight."

"Oh shit."

"Should we take care of him, boss?"

"Fuck…"

"I have my M4 in the trunk…"

As the male Fighters joked, or not joked, about all the things they could do to the guy Serena was out with, a weird sensation continued to build inside him. He shook it off, annoyed. Taking a swig of his beer, he turned his neck, cracking the tendons to loosen him up.

"Well, she looked good," Tyson said then raised a calming hand at the look Adam gave him. "Relax, I'm just saying I can tell she hit her peak, and that's great, right? Shows she had a normal transition and she's healthy."

"Wow, she stopped aging already? That's great." Nick said. "How old was she?"

Adam looked a bit calmer now they were talking about Serena's health. "She stopped last year at twenty-three."

"Nice," a few of them said. Werewolves usually stopped aging in their mid twenties. Those who continued to age a bit longer usually suffered some traumatic event. It was good to know Adam and Serena's rough upbringing hadn't had a lasting effect on her.

The sound of a car driving up in front of the house drew Jason's attention outside. They immediately knew who it was, smelling Serena's distinct scent even from the dining room.

"This could be fun…" one of them said, playfully.

Adam sighed. "She'd kill me if we interrupted. Let's leave them alone." His eyes swung to Jason, though. "J, watch him."

Standing, Jason just nodded, his eyes fixed on the blue Accord parked out front. He didn't know why, but he was anxious to see her again. It had been so long. He found himself wondering about the places she'd been. Did she enjoy herself? Was she careful?

Why the fuck were they still sitting in the car?

Just as Jason's hair began to rise, the passenger door opened, and Serena stepped out. Letting out a small breath of relief, a warm feeling washed over him as he watched her shut the car door, her dark jeans hugging her legs. Her hair was a little longer, just past her shoulder blades in layers that cascaded onto the short, brown leather jacket she wore.

It fit tight around her small frame, giving her a more urban look than he was used to her wearing. She looked all grown up, and he felt guilty as hell for staring at her for so long, but he couldn't look away.

He heard a second door slam and watched as a little pompous blond came around the car, step onto the curb next to Serena, and put his arm around her shoulder.

Alarm bells started ringing in his ears. Why the hell was he getting so heated up?

"What's happening?" he heard Ramo ask, leaning his chair back to try to look out the window.

Jason cleared his throat. "Walking her to the door."

"Aw shit," Adam moaned, then insisted, "Put up the music, please. I don't want to hear this."

Someone raised the volume, but it didn't drown out the resonating sound Jason heard. He stood stock still, watching the guy's every move. When they reached the top of the porch, they turned to look at each other and Jason had a clear, uninterrupted view of Serena's face. She was just as he'd remembered, but with subtle differences. Her face had lost all the roundness of her youth and she wore a little makeup. There was a glow about her now, a sense of confidence that had not been there before. This time, his hair stood on end for the things her face was doing to him. It was as though he was seeing her for the first time. Serena was a woman now, and unbelievably beautiful.

Vaguely, he noticed everyone behind him in the dining room had become silent, but they could have been screaming at him and he wouldn't have noticed, couldn't have torn his gaze from her face.

Serena smiled, her warm eyes sparkling at

something the blond said and making Jason's heart constrict.

Wow!

At the far end of a tunnel, he heard someone call out his name, but he ignored it, fixated on the beauty outside.

Then the blond fucker went in for the kill…right on her sweet mouth.

Explosions lit off inside him. The bottle in Jason's hand shattered to a million pieces, but he ignored the shards of glass digging into his skin. The urge to murder was so overpowering, he felt as though he would combust on the spot. The beast inside him snarled and before he knew it, his vision altered and he began to shake.

"What the…" someone said.

"Easy, J." Ramo came up beside him, peering out the window. He turned to Adam. "The guy's walking back to his car. It's fine."

Rooted to the spot, Jason waited for the thunderbolts to stop raging inside him. Jesus, the kiss had lasted all of two seconds. But in those awful moments, all he could think of was he, Jason, kissing her instead. He wanted to scream, *She's mine*, at the top of his lungs. He wanted to rip the fucker apart.

Jason turned to face the others, completely stunned, and found them all staring hard, a look of panic in their eyes.

Oh shit! They knew.

Everyone in the room had felt what he was going through. They sensed his desire for her, the jealousy, the… realization. The pitiful and anxious looks he was getting was like a neon sign.

His eyes, back to normal now, met his alpha's glare.

Adam's face was livid as he got up from his seat, slow and menacing. Snarling, he said to Jason, "Outside. Now."

Chapter Four

Serena awoke to an odd echoing sound. Sitting up, she felt the clammy walls tilt in on her and crawled quickly to the nearest bowl, retching what little was in her stomach. Reaching for the water bowl, she rinsed her mouth and spat it out on the floor.

The time of day was lost on her as well as the exact date on the calendar. At this point, she could only guess. She had been taken on July 27th, a Tuesday and since then she had endured three full moons.

Resting her back against the cool wall, she languidly tried to figure out how long she'd slept. Would they be bringing the morning meal soon or was it dinnertime?

Slipping into the endless void that was now her world, she wished she had some sort of hope, a positive focus. Staring numbly at the tattered ground, she had no exact thought in her mind. There was only a vague sense she should be praying for something, fighting for…

Waves of nausea assaulted her again and she grabbed for the soiled bowl, the sounds of her heaves echoing in the dilapidated room. Tears filled her eyes from the onslaught. *My God.* In her dazed state, she'd nearly forgotten about the baby. It was so easy to let the emptiness claim her since it was all she'd endured for so long.

Taking what was left of the water, she rinsed her mouth out again and drank the rest, afraid of getting too dehydrated.

She heard the weird echo again and for some reason it made the hair at her nape stand. Hazily, Serena got slowly to her feet, wincing at the pain in her leg. The cut had closed, but there was still a dark pink scar along the front of her thigh. Trying to determine if the side she'd licked hours ago looked different, the odd echo reached her ears again. It was much louder this time and vaguely familiar. What was it?

Angling her head back, Serena sniffed the air. Smelling the witch, Leonardo, she tensed. His scent came from the other end where Ben was being held.

She'd memorized the sound of the upstairs cellar door opening, the footsteps of each male witch, the familiar creaking of Ben's heavy cell door, but this sound was different.

Stepping to the glass on the door, she angled her head to try and catch a glimpse of something and felt... anger. Ben was....angry. She read his fury as if it were her own. Never having felt this from her boss before, it scared her. What was happening?

The creak of Ben's door opening echoed in the distance and a moment later she heard a distinct thud and the blessed familiar sound of a were's low growl as Ben's anger boiled over.

Heart racing beneath her bare, cool chest, Serena strained her neck to see what was happening. With trembling hands holding her steady against the door, she began to shake with anticipation.

He did it! He did it! Ben had managed to turn. The beautiful sound of her species was like a beacon, filling her with hope, something she hadn't felt in God knew how long.

Just then, Leonardo's face came into view through the glass and she pushed back from the door, knocking one of the bowls with her bare foot as she staggered to the far wall.

Oh no! Did he hurt Ben? Where was he?

Panting, she watched as the door to her prison was unlocked, and in came Leonardo, Ben's massive clawed hand wrapped tightly around his neck.

Joy like she never knew before filled her as she ran forward. She held the door open as Ben bent low to enter her cell behind the witch. In his wolf man form, he was close to seven feet tall. He had to angle in sideways to fit his wide shoulders through the doorway.

Lifting the struggling Leonardo off the ground, Ben hauled his arm back, and with a fierce thrust smashed his face into the wall. The witch's head pounded on the stone with a horrific thud, and he crumpled to the floor. Dead or not, Serena didn't care. She whispered, "Ben, let's go." For a moment, she thought her boss wanted to continue beating the witch senseless, but they could be discovered at any moment.

Nodding, he left the room with her, closing the door behind him. He motioned for Serena to turn the key in the lock. When the witch was shut in the cell, they turned to follow the opposite path the witches usually took them through. There had to be an exit out. That water flowed somewhere.

They walked along the stream in the dark, Ben's eyes as their guide. She had good vision, but in his wolf form, he could see perfectly in the dark. After several minutes, they reached a dead end. There were a couple more vacant rooms on either side of the wide passage, and the stream disappeared through a small arch-like opening. Ben stepped close and bent down, sniffing noisily in the small tunnel. Turning back to her, Serena sensed his relief and smiled, her skin stretching across her cheeks, a foreign feeling, as she hadn't performed the simple act in months.

They were free.

The stream led outside. Cassandra must have assumed her serum and the sturdy doors would hold because she couldn't hear or sense anyone else standing guard.

Ben reached out his arm, and she placed her hand in his. He helped her into the shallow stream, the cool water making her skin tingle. She crouched to look through the narrow tunnel that would lead them outside. "Ben, you're going to have to phase back. You won't fit." Her voice was a strained, scratchy whisper from screaming and vomiting. The sound of it was weird to her ears. She hadn't spoken much in so long.

In the far distance they could hear the cellar door opening at the top of the stairs. They both whipped their heads around, staring hard into the darkness they'd just come from.

"Ben, quick!" Serena whispered frantically.

Whirling around, Ben placed a hand on her head, pushing her down. She fell to her knees in the water, rocks digging into her shins. Serena felt his clawed hand shove at her, pushing her into the tunnel.

On her hands and knees, she made it inside, moving as quickly as she could. Twisting oddly, she looked back as her boss began to shift to human. He would be right behind her soon enough.

Resounding footsteps pounded in her ears as she made her way through, crawling on the jagged rocks. Someone was getting close. She wished Ben would hurry.

In her panic, she hardly felt the pain in her body, barely registered the numbness in her leg. She was running on pure adrenaline.

Up ahead, she saw the glowing light of a distant lamppost. The instant they were out, they could run like mad. There was no way a mere witch could outrun them. Hell, Ben could phase again and carry her. They'd be long gone in no time.

Several shots rang out, reverberating in the stone around her, stinging her ears. She jumped, a scream caught in her throat. Scrambling out of the tunnel onto dirt ground, she turned, shaking uncontrollably to find Ben.

They missed. He had to be in the tunnel already.

"Got him. Get him out of the way so we can get the girl," a man called out.

A dreadful pain stabbed through her heart as the witch's words echoed toward her. Wild shudders overcame her and for the first time in months, she felt the welcome aches of her body contorting, morphing into what she was born to be. As her eyes shifted, her vision became clearer.

At the far end of the tunnel, she saw Ben's lifeless form laying half inside the tunnel and half out, sprawled on his stomach. She homed in on his face, and her heart plummeted. Taking his last few gasps, his desperate eyes met hers.

Go! He mouthed.

Fighting the need to collapse in tears, Serena

nodded and took off.

Whirling in the first direction impulse led her, Serena hunched over and four-footed into a field of grass. Terror ran through every fiber of her being as she ran into the night. Her vision, while much sharper, shimmered blurrily as tears of grief and fear filled her eyes.

Suddenly, she met a strange resistance in the air, as if she'd hit an invisible wall of Jell-O. She felt her crouched body sucked into some sort of barrier, then pushed out like a cork, as if she'd been squeezed out of a bottle. It didn't matter, though. The peculiar feeling was gone and she could run through clear air again.

Sprinting as fast as her wolf legs could take her, she ran for her life, her freedom. She didn't know what direction she went in, and she didn't care. As long as she put a great distance between herself and that god-awful place, she would be safe.

A blinding pain threatened to overwhelm her, but she maintained, determined to survive. She would not let Ben down, knowing the blinding ache she felt was for him.

Oh God, she couldn't think of him right now. If she did, she would surely collapse. She focused on getting herself home. Paws hitting the ground with pounding force, Serena pressed on, even though her limbs threatened to crack with every thrashing step she took.

She had no idea how long she ran. Minutes…hours…time was not a concept she understood anymore. *Home*. She had to get home. The need to see Jason, to look upon his face pushed her on. If she could find her way to Wilmington, or a familiar town near her home, she could call out to her pack.

They would hear her and come in an instant. But she wouldn't dare howl now. They might be following her. She had no idea if witches could track, but she couldn't risk her captors discovering her location.

Hope and despair were only the few emotions raging inside her. The prospect of being tracked down by the witches or miraculously managing to make it home was making her heart pound in her ears.

As much as she wanted to continue her chant to the unborn baby growing inside her, she couldn't do it. There was no way to know if she or *they* would make it out of danger. She had no idea where the hell they were. *God.* The panic, the fear of the unknown was the most terrifying feeling she'd ever experienced.

Don't look back, she told herself. *Don't look back.*

Her leg began to throb, and she felt a rip on her thigh. Looking down briefly, she was shocked to see the pale coloring of her human skin. Without even realizing it, she was shifting back into her human form. The serum must still have some effect on her. Phasing, or her mad race to make it home, reopened the cut on her leg. Her weakening body continued forward as fast as she could, but at a much slower pace, her bare feet throbbing as they hit the dirt.

Doesn't matter. She was still faster than any human.

Run, goddamn it!

Tears stung her eyes as the memory of the countless cuts, the spells that made their bodies twist in agony, the cold cell, the humiliation, it all came rushing to the forefront. Her head swam with the images, blurring her vision. She tripped on something and hit the ground as if someone had lifted the earth and smacked it into her.

It happened all too fast for her to save any part of her body, her face receiving the most brutal hit of all. Her nose throbbed, the tears relentless now. The entire front of her body burned wildly, and she was only dimly aware she'd landed on gravel.

Cautiously, she turned her neck, placing her tender cheek on the little pebbles, trying desperately to see where she was. There were cornfields about five feet from her line of vision, and the longer she lay there, the roaring wind no longer in her ears, she could just make out the sounds of an expressway somewhere far off to the left.

Get up, she told herself. *You have to keep going.*

Every inch of her refused to cooperate with her brain. The fight had left her. There was no more energy inside her battered body. It was over. She could tell herself off all she liked, but there was no way she could move. Closing her eyes, she apologized to Ben, the baby, her brother. She apologized to the man she loved, for not having the courage before to tell him how she really felt. With his lasting image searing deep in her mind, she let the dark, traitorous world claim her.

****

It was two A.M. and as much as he didn't want to, Jason turned the Avalanche around, taking a different road back to Wilmington. Heading east on route 72, he thought about all the places they'd searched. He wondered if the Chicago crew looked hard enough. Perhaps he should take a trip up there tomorrow and make his own inquiries. *Again.* He could stay at his condo in the south loop for a few days.

Second-guessing himself for the umpteenth time,

he questioned if taking his pickup had been such a good idea. For weeks the pack had searched for Serena in their wolf forms, but they couldn't very well interview people that way, and the folks around here didn't take kindly to a naked man interrogating them. Tonight he'd driven all the way down to Quincy, stopping along the way at every shop, inn, motel, anything that remained open to ask questions, pushing a picture of Serena into every face he came across.

He drove slow, all senses on alert. His phone beeped next to him on the passenger seat. Glancing at it, he saw it was Adam, asking if he was home yet. As he was about to text him back, an overwhelming sadness blasted straight through his chest. All of a sudden, as though he'd just become someone else, he was filled with love, grief, and pain. Unimaginable pain.

The feeling expanded throughout his body, shocking him. Jason slammed on the brakes, his heart drumming in his chest, near to bursting, and pulled to the side of the road. His hands shook violently as the Avalanche squealed loudly, marking the road in its wake. He shot out of the truck, and stopped a moment, glancing in every direction, trying to find the source. It wasn't too far from where he stood and every fiber of his being told him it was Serena.

Contemplating phasing to sharpen his senses, he stepped into the cornfield and paused again as the faintest hint of her scent hit him. *Her hair*. He'd smelled it just before she went missing, and he'd recognize it anywhere. Forgoing the decision to change, he ran headlong into the tall ears of corn. He was close. The intensity of her emotions was weakening, but her scent grew stronger. His arms sliced through the high field, the sound echoing loudly, terrifying him to his very marrow.

Body shaking violently, Jason fought the impulse to phase. If she needed medical attention, he couldn't do shit with his claws. Up ahead, he saw an opening and knew he'd find her there. He raced into a clearing and stopped abruptly, crushing gravel beneath his shoes.

The world went silent, the drumming of his pulse the only sound beating wildly in his ears.

Sinking down to his knees, Jason's heart finally burst.

Serena's thin form lay motionless in front of him on the hard gravel, her face turned in his direction. *His precious girl.* Dear Lord, the sight of her was a blessing and a curse. He pushed a fist at the sting in his chest, holding his breath.

She lay face down, and he could see faint scratch marks on her back, as if she'd been rubbing against something rough. Other than deep cuts along her cheek, there were no other signs of injury. He bit down hard as he stared with shimmering eyes at her battered face. Did her attacker just do this? The cuts bled as though freshly inflicted.

In an instant, his hackles rose, sensing they were watched. Whipping his head to the side, his eyes locked on a gray animal entering the clearing. With its head bowed, shoulders raised, it poised to attack, lips curling over grimy teeth.

Snarling, Jason's eyes shifted as he pushed himself off the ground with his hands in a giant leap straight toward the jackal. Fear, rage, a maddening urge to kill everything and anything that dared to come close to Serena drove him to insanity. Not bothering to phase and without a thought to his safety, he reached for its neck as it leapt at him, and in a second, snapped it in a swift twist. The jackal's screech was cut short as it fell limp in his hands. He tossed it aside, his wolf eyes narrowing, surveying the field surrounding them. For whatever reason, the nasty beast had acted alone. He sensed nothing else.

He'd think about the strange attack later. Rushing quickly back to Serena, he knelt beside her, running shaky hands over his face.

For a moment, he just knelt there, frozen, as if touching her might make her disappear. He couldn't believe she was in front of him. And he was scared, scared shitless. He couldn't bear to see her hurt.

With trembling hands he reached for her and as gently as possible turned her over, laying her carefully in his arms and off the rocks.

Jason winced and bit down hard, his face contorting in anguish as he examined her, his vision gleaming in a blurry haze. Serena's entire body was bruised and there were marks all over her skin, old and new, the worst of which was the fifteen-inch cut running down her leg, pouring blood down the sides of her thigh.

She's alive, he told himself. Her body was still warm and he could hear a pulse, she was just unconscious. The tears sprung of their own accord, tears of relief, agony, and unequivocal love. Sliding her further into his arms, Jason embraced her tenderly, needing to feel her close to him, closer than he'd ever been. Rocking her slowly back and forth, he moaned in a wretched voice, "I'm so sorry, little one. I'm so sorry…I'm so sorry…" His body shook with grief as he held her tighter, his face buried deep in her tangled hair. "Oh God, Serena, I'm sorry. I've got you now. I've got you. Please forgive me. I've got you now."

He couldn't tell if he was consoling Serena or himself. Pressing his cheek against hers, he tried to calm his ragged breathing. He needed to focus now.

Getting up swiftly, he ran back toward the truck, trying as hard as he could not to disturb any part of her body. As he ran, his eyes darted back to her face, watching her closely. He kept his ears hard on her pulse, letting the subtle beats calm him into getting her safely back home.

When they reached the pickup, he slid her carefully inside. Reclining the passenger seat as far as it would go, he laid her out hoping to God she was comfortable. Examining her leg, he pulled his shirt over his head. Carefully, he wrapped it several times around her thigh, fashioning a quick tourniquet. Reaching into the backseat, he placed the jacket he kept there over her and ran around to the other side. Punching the call button on the steering wheel, he called Adam as he peeled back onto 72.

"Yeah," Adam answered, sleepily.

"I've got her!"

Silence.

With a shaky voice, he said again, "I've got her, man." He knew Adam was as stunned as he was. "We should be there in ten. Call Dr. Moros. Make him teleport right this second."

"She…she…" Adam stuttered.

"I think she's okay, but I'm not a doctor."

53

There was silence on the other end again, then, "You found her?" Adam asked quietly, still disbelieving.

Jason hesitated, his voice on the verge of cracking. He barely believed it himself. Serena was right next to him. He held onto her hand as if she might disappear at any moment. "Yeah," Jason answered, breathlessly.

On the other end, he could hear Evangeline in the background calling Dr. Moros from her phone, her vampire ears picking up the whole conversation. Thank God she was there. He and Adam were going to be no help at all.

"Hurry," Adam said. "I'll meet you outside."

Jason hung up and checked on Serena for the thousandth time. Her light brown hair was much longer and knotted all around her head. She was thinner. Too thin. Her cheekbones were more pronounced and her sweet lips were pale and dry.

"Can you hear me, Serena?" Jason tried, racing as fast as his truck could move, his left fist squeezing the life out of the steering wheel.

There was no reply. She was out cold. Jason's head reeled with panic. If the vampire doctor wasn't at the round house, he was taking her straight to Silver Cross Hospital. The doctors there were good enough, but they were nothing like Dr. Moros. He'd seen the guy in action.

Next to him, Serena gave a soft moan, her small frame shifting slightly on the seat. The sound of her voice, feeble as it was, felt like someone had gently hugged his heart.

"You're with me now, Serena. We're almost home." He brought her hand to his lips. "You're safe."

Chapter Five

Ramo dressed quickly, avoiding the woman's eyes as she slipped her feet into black pumps. Ordinarily he'd feel more relaxed after sex, in better spirits, but there was something about the way the girl looked at him that felt off. Why did she remind him of…

A hazy image of a dark-haired girl surfaced in the back of his mind, her dark eyes shiny and bright as she gazed at Ramo with naïve awe. *Shit!* He hated when his subconscious conjured up his estranged wife. Her face surfaced for just a moment before fading away. As it had been years since he'd seen her, he'd pretty much forgotten what she looked like exactly.

Guilt sliced through him, ruining the sex high he'd been hoping to bask in after his romp with the girl who was taking way too long to gather her things.

"I should go," the woman said hesitantly, running her fingers through her tousled hair. He glanced over, and her long thick hair fell behind her shoulder, reminding him again of his wife. He might not remember exactly how she looked like, but he couldn't forget her thick dark hair.

Making a mental note to steer clear of brunettes for a while, Ramo gave her a noncommittal smile. "I'll walk you to your car." *Damn.* He was feeling like crap because he couldn't remember her name.

The girl squared her shoulders. "No need." He felt

her embarrassment at his awkward behavior. "I know the way."

Before he could apologize for his rudeness, she was out the door. Running a hand over his face, he went to the kitchen for a beer, tossing it back in one long swallow. It must have been lack of sleep that had him out of sorts.

After a cold shower, he collapsed on the couch for a quick nap before it was his turn to go out searching again. The only sleep he got, however, was about three minutes.

He was the first to arrive at the round house minutes later. Having picked up Adam's elation seconds before he got the call, he'd shot out of bed, stark naked, throwing on just his jeans, jacket, and boots. He didn't bother with underwear or socks. They usually weren't necessary when you ran with a pack. You never knew when you'd have to phase in an instant.

Ramo stood next to his cousin now. Neither one uttered a word as they waited for Jason. For the first time in a while, Ramo kept any and all comments to himself. Even he knew when to shut up. His cousin's voice when he'd called a few minutes ago was unrecognizable. He doubted Adam would hear him anyway.

Ramo was, of course, itching to give his cousin a pat on the back or some sign he was thrilled Serena had been found, but the look on his alpha's face, said *Shut the fuck up*.

As far as he knew, Serena was okay, but she still needed medical attention.

Speak of the devil and the devil shall appear, or the

vamp doc anyway. Dr. George Moros teleported in front of Adam's octagonal home.

"Are they here, yet?" the Clark Kent look-alike asked.

Adam responded in a detached voice, his eyes hard off in the distance. "No."

Moros surveyed the house carefully then asked, "I'm not gonna get decapitated when I enter, will I?"

Ramo smirked, shaking his head. Before Evangeline's transition, his cousin's round house was like a landmine to vampires. Times had certainly changed, and Ramo couldn't help but think things were about to get even weirder.

Ramo answered for his cousin who'd stepped to the street, pacing now. "You're good, doc. Eva's setting up the master bedroom." He jerked his thumb toward the house. "Go on in, we'll bring her up as soon as they get here."

Moros took off into the house just as they heard J's car revving up Water Street. Alex and Nick arrived on foot seconds before Jason pulled up in front. They all stood to the side. While the others scanned the area around them, Ramo homed in on his cousin in the seat next to his beta, jaws clenched. Adam sped to the passenger side, wrenching the door open to gather Serena in his arms.

His cousin was wrapped in Jason's jacket and she didn't look good. Pale as hell, she was thin as a stick. Smelling her dried blood, Ramo felt deep vibrations wrack his body, aching for revenge.

They heard Jason growl low in his throat, stepping around the car, protesting anyone handling Serena, but him. Adam shot Jason a glare, responding with a snarl, reminding his beta who was boss.

Faltering, Jason shook himself then followed his alpha into the house with a maddening look in his eyes.

Ramo, Nick, and Alex all stared at each other. It was Ramo who spoke first. "I have a bad feeling about this."

The other two shifted uncomfortably. Nick asked, "Is the doctor here?"

"Yeah."

Nick nodded. "I have a feeling we're gonna have to break protocol tonight. Those two didn't look good," he said, referring to Adam and Jason.

Ramo knew what he was talking about. He remembered how Adam reacted to the vampire doctor when Evangeline was delivering the twins. Now the poor doc had Adam *and* Jason to deal with. The aching love their beta was emanating was enough to overwhelm any other feeling in the rest of the Fighters as though the emotional bond was a speeding train they were all on with Jason as the conductor.

Shit, he'd rather go toe to toe with a hundred vampires than watch his cousin and friend lose it.

For the second time that night, Ramo thought of the girl he'd married years ago. He'd never given his marriage a chance, having taken off minutes after the ceremony, but he figured he'd dodged a bullet. There was no way he wanted to be tied down that way, which was why Ramo found it necessary to shut down his emotions when he was around women. He couldn't imagine losing himself the way Adam and Jason did. That shit looked painful, and Ramo wasn't into it. He loved life, but guarded his heart like a motherfucker.

It was moments like this that reaffirmed his

decision to leave his wife. The girl was better off without him rather than suffering a werewolf's intense love.

****

Evangeline met Adam at the bedroom door, ushering him in with his sister's limp body in his arms. She was concerned for her soon to be sister-in-law, to be sure, but Evangeline was all too acquainted with her mate's temper and overbearing nature. She worried his presence in the room would not help Serena. And by the look on Jason's face, these two were going to be trouble.

Hustling in after Adam, Jason hovered over Serena as her brother placed her down on the bed. Adam sat by her side, smoothing her tangled hair out of her face, while Jason fumed on her other side, his brooding stance taking up half the room.

Dr. Moros gave Evangeline a knowing look. She responded with a brief nod, and then addressed her fiancé. "Babe..." she tried carefully. "Why don't you guys wait downstairs?"

Her mate gave her a crazed look. "No. She needs me. What if she wakes up?"

"I'll be here," Evangeline countered. "You know she's in good hands."

Adam thought for a moment, worry for his sister etched in his features, then spoke again, not meeting Evangeline's eyes. "We don't know what she's been through. If she wakes up and finds two vampires over her, she may flip out."

Ah. She hadn't expected that. New to this vampire life, it was almost easy to forget Evangeline and her werewolf fiancé were supposed to be enemies.

Nevertheless, Adam was just going to have to trust his sister would know she wasn't in any danger.

"Adam, the first thing she'll sense when she wakes up is our concern for her." She gestured toward the door. "At least stay put by the door, please."

Adam nodded and got up warily, but Jason stayed where he was.

"Jason…" Evangeline said, looking anxiously at her mate's best friend.

The beta's avid gaze was on Serena, his massive form generating all his power into protecting her. There were dark shadows under his eyes, his usual tanned skin a bit paler too.

Staring fiercely at Serena as though willing her to wake up, Jason looked like a man who'd gone to hell and back. Evangeline didn't need the werewolf bond to pick up the agony he was going through. The love coming off his expression melted her insides.

He spoke under his breath. "I can't leave her."

Evangeline bit her lip. "I know you can't. Please, Jason, just stand by the door."

When the doctor came around the bed, sitting at Serena's hip, Jason shut his eyes briefly, taking a deep breath in from his nose, then moved to the door.

Adam settled himself in the hallway, his back against the wall. She knew he couldn't really watch his little sister being worked on. Jason, however, couldn't keep his eyes off her. He stood staring into the room, taking up the entire doorframe. His imposing presence made even Evangeline nervous.

Dr. Moros looked at Evangeline, then over his shoulder at Serena's guard, muttering, "I might have to up my fee."

She smiled nervously, then turned her full attention on Serena.

Easing the oversized jacket off of her, Evangeline bit down hard at the smell of dried blood permeating her senses.

"Eva..." Adam called out sharply.

She reassured him quick. "I'm fine."

"You sure?"

Thanking the lovely people at the Transition Facility for Vampires, she answered, "Yep. Not breathing," she said, awkwardly. And as fast as she could, helped Dr. Moros clean her wounds, while he injected her with an IV. Once Serena's skin was fairly clean, she handed the good doctor various items he needed and arranged Serena's position on the bed for him as needed. She was sure Dr. Moros wanted to touch her as little as possible with the sentinel standing only a few feet behind him.

Every so often, she turned to check on Jason. He stood frozen in the same position, feet shoulder width apart, fists clenched at his sides. Several times she caught him trembling, especially when the doctor began stitching her leg. His low snarling made the doctor roll his eyes in frustration.

"He can't help it, George," Evangeline told him, apologetically.

"Right," he replied, drily.

Moros had barely finished when Serena came to. Evangeline moved swiftly, situating herself at Serena's side again. She put a cool palm over her forehead and gripped her hand with the other. "You're all right, honey." The girl, or woman, as Serena was older than her, stared wide-eyed for a moment. She didn't look

61

like Adam at all. Only their lips were kind of similar. "You're safe. You're in the round house, and Adam's just outside this door. Can you feel him?"

Serena looked around nervously, her body trembling. Wide-eyed, she looked to Dr. Moros, bandaging her leg, then around the room. Evangeline thought she saw recognition flit across her face.

"Yes, you're home." Evangeline smiled warmly. "You're going to be okay."

Serena's brown gaze met hers again, "Jason?" she whispered.

Adam's sister would feel the man's overpowering emotion at the door. Evangeline heard Jason behind her.

"I'm here," he replied, tenderly.

Before Serena could react, her body pitched forward, and she hugged herself tightly, screaming in pain. Evangeline grabbed for her shoulders as the doctor held onto her injured leg.

The rest of the Fighters came bounding up the stairs, their pounding footsteps echoing noisily around them.

Trying to keep her leg from bleeding out, Dr. Moros yelled, his face fuming, "If either one of you enters this room, I'm taking Serena out the window and away from here. I fucking mean it!"

They tried to soothe her, attempting to pull her out of her crouched position to see what was the matter, but Serena wouldn't let go, screaming harder now.

The doctor reached for his bag; about to give her something to sedate her when Serena came up, clutching her lower abdomen, her wild eyes pierced Evangeline's. "Please…save…save…" she whispered in a strained voice, then cried out in pain again.

Evangeline stiffened. Comprehension dawned at the same moment blood poured out of the girl's body.

Serena was miscarrying.

Evangeline shared a brief, shocked expression with Moros before racing to the door in a flash.

"Get out!" she shouted to all the Fighters, but Jason was the one front and center. His forehead tight, hazel eyes shimmering with unshed tears.

"What's going on?" Jason asked eagerly.

"You need to leave."

He looked to Evangeline, incredulously. "I'm not leaving her."

She saw Adam give her a questioning look over Jason's shoulder. "Please," she begged now, frantic.

Jason asked, "Why is she bleeding again? I can smell it."

Evangeline glanced back at the bed, thankful the doctor blocked their view.

There was no way Jason or her mate could handle this. Getting angry now, she said, "I swear to God, I will bite you all. Get out!" She unleashed her fangs for emphasis, and pushed at Jason's chest, but he wasn't even looking at her. He gripped the doorjamb with two hands, her new strength having had the power to move him a little.

Chest pumping, Jason's expression lost all control, his breath coming out short, he called, "Serena, what's happening? Talk to me!"

Serena's voice pleaded in between anguished wails, "Don't die...don't die...please..."

Jason called out, "You're not going to die, honey."

Serena thrashed on the bed, and they heard Dr. Moros curse under his breath. Evangeline needed to get

63

the men out of the house before they caught on to what was really happening.

Just then, Serena's cries ceased, and the entire house became deathly quiet until she moaned, painfully, "Please don't let the baby die!"

Even a human could hear a pin drop at that very moment.

Evangeline watched Serena's words register on Jason's face as it drained of all remaining color. She was reminded of the part in a movie where everything stands still and silent right before the big building blows up.

Jason and Adam's bodies contorted right before her eyes, and she saw Ramo grab for Adam, just as Nick and Alex helped Evangeline push Jason into the hallway.

In a rush, she shouted at them, stepping back into the room as Jason morphed into a seven and half foot tall wolf man. "Her attacker is not in this room. Settle yourselves before you even think about coming in here." With a determined thrust, she slammed the door in their faces.

****

Jason had gone momentarily deaf. The room and all its occupants spun around him, making him nauseous. The horrible drumming in his ear picked up again as a sharp pain slashed through his head and he wondered briefly if he was having an aneurysm.

Baby?

His mind ran like he was fast-forwarding a DVR. Serena had been missing for over three months. Werewolves only carried for about six weeks. If she was pregnant, then it must be her abductor's.

Rape.

Her cries for the baby she was carrying rang in his ears as though someone had just put the volume up in the room.

Shaking his head, Jason shouted, "NO! NO! NO!" Fists punched the sides of the door as three pairs of hands pulled him out into the hallway. Heaving uncontrollably, his body rocked, shooting up and out, phasing into a black and gray werewolf.

Evangeline yelled something at them and slammed the bedroom door. He looked around, aching to go back in, but he was blocked.

Adam had turned too, his arms braced on the far wall, his snout hung low, panting as he attempted to restrain himself.

"Don't do it." Ramo stood in front of him, with Alex and Nick at his sides. "You'll fuck up the whole room if you go in there. Let them do their thing."

Without a single thought, Jason crouched low; his lips curling back over his fangs and growled ferociously in Ramo's face, making the mirrors and scones in the hallway vibrate.

Ramo wiped his face. "Point taken." Moving himself in front of the closed bedroom door, he said, "Look, we're prepared to fight you two…"

Adam's deep snarl resounded in the hall for their insubordination, but he remained still. He was letting his Fighters tell him what to do, but his wolf side protested.

Nick held up his hands to reason with them. "You guys know what's best for her. Serena's dealing with her own drama right now. She doesn't need yours."

"A nice run might do you some good," Alex

drawled out.

Fuck these guys. Jason slammed Nick and Alex to the wall to get through. The round house was built with all the rooms on each floor surrounding a swirling staircase set in the center of the house. The winding stairs were placed so one could see all three levels except for the basement from every floor. Foregoing the stairs, Jason leapt over the railing and down to the first floor, charging through the open doorway.

He bounded toward the prairie, racing on all fours as fast and hard as he could. The wind in his ears now in sync with the echo of Serena's cries.

God. Not his Serena. Not his little one.

How could this happen to one so pure, so precious?

The rage inside him threatened to crumble Jason to the ground. He hoped to God no one else was out tonight. He'd murder the first person he saw.

Fuck!

Visions of some unknown piece of shit pushing over her as she tried to fight him off blurred his sight, and he skidded to a halt. Angling back, he let out the howl demanding to be freed. A few nearby birds took flight, flying out as far from the raging beast as possible.

Hunching over again, he paced around, not bothering to collect his bearings, but to focus on the *whys*. His ever-racing mind came to one conclusion.

He was to blame. He was a fucking curse!

Jason thought of his poor mother, retired in Florida and blissfully away from her son. The constant reminder that Jason was a product of rape didn't have to weigh her down anymore.

As soon as his mother had shared the story of his

origin, he offered to buy her a house in Naples, something she'd always wanted. The reason for his cold and isolated upbringing was now clear. His mother despised him.

He couldn't blame her though. Jason didn't look anything like his mother, so she'd had to endure raising a son on her own who resembled her rapist. He was surprised she hadn't left sooner.

From the day he found out about his wretched father, Jason, always subdued, became almost mute, speaking in low tones and only when he had to. His head bent low at all times, as though someone would recognize him as a rapist's son.

And now…his beautiful Serena suffered his mother's same fate. He was a goddamn curse.

Her abduction had to have something to do with the Fighters and by extension, him. His very existence was to blame. He should leave town and leave her in peace, but he knew it wasn't possible. If anything he would protect her even more, shadow her every move till the day one of them met their maker. But he would do so at a distance. Allowing them to get any closer was disaster waiting to happen.

Jason was aware she'd felt something for him before her disappearance, now though, he was sure she would hate him, hate him for not being there, hate him for not keeping his promise to her all those years ago, hate him for just being a man.

Good. It was better for her if she despised him too. No one else needed to endure the cloud he came under.

Before he appointed himself her silent protector, he needed answers because shit was about to go down, and the bastard that hurt her was going to pay.

Chapter Six

Serena slept amazingly peacefully, dreaming her body no longer burned in perpetual agony. She dreamed she actually lay on a bed and not a rock hard floor. Relieved God had finally taken her out of her misery, she delved further into the imaginary comforter, letting its warmth surround her.

A jolt stabbed through her heart.

If she was dead, then her baby was too.

Disgrace, the likes of which she'd never experience engulfed her. A sickening pain twisted her gut as a horrible sadness washed over her. Why couldn't she have hung on for the baby? In her selfish need to leave the world, she'd taken her unborn child as well.

A far off voice called to Serena and her heart leapt. She didn't think she'd ever hear that voice again. Although, if this was heaven, then Jason's voice was sure to be her commentator.

"Serena…"

Opening her eyes to face the afterlife, her gaze was met by a large ceiling fan, circling slowly over her. Tilting her head to the side, she squinted at the furnishings in the dark bedroom, a very familiar bedroom.

"You were having a bad dream. How do you feel?" the soft voice asked from the corner of the room.

Swinging her head around, her eyes fell on Jason's

large silhouette sitting on the floor with his back to the wall by the window, his knees bent. The room was dimly lit from an outside lamppost illuminating the street where she grew up.

She was alive and in her parents' home.

"Jason?" she called out, her throat scratchy and dry.

"Yes, it's me," his voice said in the darkness. "You should go back to sleep. You need rest."

Narrowing her eyes, she ached to see his face clearer and shook her head. "You found me." She breathed in heavily. "I knew you would find me."

Her savior said nothing, but she could feel his searing gaze. She stared, dazedly at his large dark form, barely trusting she was out of danger. The sound of his measured breaths was a kind of euphoria, easing the hurt away. She let the peace fill her for a blind moment until the memories came rushing back.

Gripping the sheets at her chest, every horrid detail hit her at once, the last of which resounding in the forefront of her mind.

Ben was dead, and she had lost the baby.

Tears flooded her eyes as she moaned in grief. Sinking into the mattress, she drove her hands over her face, her body jerking with every cry.

A warm hand covered her forearm. Jason's voice fought for control. "I'm...I'm so sorry."

Dropping her hands, Serena rose up off the bed and threw her arms over his shoulders, her sobs buried deep in his neck.

Stiffening, Jason knelt beside her, his arms frozen at his sides. It was the first time she'd ever held him, their only contact having been a light touch on the back or a graze of an elbow.

"Please, Jason. Don't do this to me now," she implored, her body wracking with grief. "I need you to hold me."

He inhaled sharply, thick arms sliding tenderly around her torso, warm and oh so wonderful. He held her for an eternity, letting her cry for all she'd lost, all she'd been through. She cried until there was nothing left in her and lay spent in his arms. As her breathing slowed, she felt his moist shirt at her cheek from her tears and squeezed him tighter to her, loving the way his hard body felt against her. Then she'd lose it again, weeping quietly once more.

And all the while, he held her.

Suddenly, the embrace wasn't about the horror she'd been through, but centered totally on them.

Jason's hold grew tighter and tighter, and she felt peace again, filling her, attempting to mold together the remnants of her decaying life. Their bodies had become one, clinging for all they were worth and their bittersweet reunion. Serena never wanted to let go.

A hand came up to grasp a knot of hair, and she heard Jason's deep intake of her scent and realized she was clean. Her hair had been washed, her skin no longer grimy, but smooth and warm.

Serena's voice shook. "Do you know about the...?" She couldn't get the word *baby* out. The thought of her weak body not being able to protect her child was too much.

There was silence before he answered, then she felt him nod at her shoulder. He pulled back to look her in the eye, and it was the first time in over three months she felt a ration of joy. Serena gripped his face with trembling hands, ran her fingers through his long hair, down his neck. His strong features were clearer now he was so close, closer than he's ever been before. She stared at the glossy whites of his eyes, wanting to lose herself in his gold flecks.

Jason's hand covered her cheek. "Who…You have to…" He cleared his throat. "Who was it?" Biting down on his molars, he waited for her to respond, his agonizing gaze hard on her.

"Witches," she said, still not believing she was in her family home, clean and warm and staring into the eyes that had given her strength to endure those long months.

Glaring, he waited for her to go on, placing both hands on either side of her hips on the bed.

Relaying the horrid details of her capture was inevitable. She wasn't quite sure she was ready to talk about it, but knowing the Fighters, they'd want to know immediately.

"Can you…?" Jason uttered, his eyes roaming all over her face. He swallowed hard, his jaw flexing on the right side of his cheek.

As much as she wanted to just bury herself in his arms again, she also knew this was something he needed as well. It occurred to her Jason and her brother must have thought the very worst of her disappearance. Of course they'd want to know immediately what had happened to her and who was responsible.

She nodded slowly. There was a great deal to tell. She'd have to start from the beginning. His presence must have given her strength; otherwise, there was no way she'd be able to talk about everything so soon. "It happened when I was leaving work." Looking away, the memory of that day became clearer. "Two witches put a spell on me to control my mind. Kind of like how a vampire compels. At the same time, they stuck a serum in my arm to keep me from phasing. After I got into the car I blacked out and woke up in this dark room, like an old cellar." It sort of helped to talk about it, but she'd rather be holding him again.

"Do you want me to get your brother?" Jason asked when she hesitated.

Shaking her head, she said, "I'd rather just tell this once, okay. I know the rest of the guys need to know, but I don't want to be there when they find out."

Jason bent his head low to catch her eye. "Would you prefer talking to Evangeline?"

"Who?"

"Your brother's mate."

Serena's brows shot up. "Mate? The vampire who took care of me?" Lord! What else had she missed?

He nodded. "It's a long story. I'll let your brother tell you, but you can trust Eva."

Sitting up straighter, Serena rubbed her injured thigh, amazed she didn't feel a thing and remembered the woman Evangeline holding her leg and belly right before she passed out.

Jason asked, "Are you okay?"

"Yeah," she answered, totally perplexed. "I feel a little weak, but other than that, I feel really good. It's odd. The things they did…I've been in this constant…" She stopped at the shudders beneath her.

Jason shook the bed as his body vibrated, his expression tensing as he stared. Serena brought her hands to his chest. His thick pectorals rippled beneath her palms. "Easy, Jason."

Hanging his head, he struggled with himself, taking deep shaky breaths.

"Maybe I shouldn't tell…"

"No." His eyes shot to hers. "I need to know everything. I'm sorry. It won't…it won't happen again." Pausing, he stared at her hands on his chest for a moment, then took her wrists and brought them down on her lap.

She frowned. Why did he still hold back? Didn't he realize she needed him more now than ever?

"The reason you're not in any pain is because Evangeline healed you. I wouldn't mention it to your brother, but she said it was all right to tell you." He licked his lips. "Eva is also a gifted witch, but again, I'll let Adam fill you in."

Serena froze, her eyes wide.

Jason shook his head. "Eva only realized she was a witch a couple weeks ago. Please, go on."

Taking a deep breath, she said, "They took all my clothes and kept us in separate cells." She hugged herself, hesitating, remembering how cold she'd been for so long. All of a sudden, saying the words out loud was too frightening. The horrible things they did to them would send Jason over the edge. Her chest rose up and down in quick succession. "I'm not sure I can talk about this right now."

His eyes narrowed, but he nodded.

They remained silent for quite awhile. Serena released her arms and sat staring at her hands in her lap, wondering when she'd have the courage to tell Jason and her brother all the gory details.

"You should get some rest," he whispered.

"I don't want you to leave," she said, woefully.

He exhaled a long breath. "I'll be right here."

Jason stood as she slipped under the covers again.

"Serena…" He paused and she knew he was dying for more information. "We don't want to pressure you, but eventually you'll need to tell us what happened. Anything you can tell us will help find who did this to you."

Resting on her side, she said, "I won't be able to tell you where they are, but you should know something."

He waited.

Swallowing hard, she forced herself to tell him, a tear slipping down her cheek. "It wasn't a witch who…I…I was carrying a wolf's baby."

A blast of anger and remorse shot through the room. Serena cringed at the onslaught his emotions were giving off.

"What?" Jason growled, looming over her. "How?"

Serena shut her eyes. Perhaps it was best to talk to someone else, a professional maybe or her brother's mate, someone who wasn't going to fly off the handle when she described the things they did to her in that god-awful place. Evangeline could let the Fighters know, but Serena felt Jason should hear about the baby from her own lips. She didn't know why, but she felt like she owed him this. "Could you not look at me when I say this?" she asked, peeking up at him nervously.

His hazel eyes pierced hers for a moment then he walked mechanically to the window, placing both hands on the sill. "Tell me," he demanded, frighteningly.

Sniffing, she said, "We had to go through a few moon heats without a mate, not like I ever had one, but obviously we didn't have pills either." Serena stared at his broad back, the muscles straining against his shirt.

Jason turned his head slightly to the side, his jaw twitched over his shoulder. "We? Do you mean Benjamin Michaels?"

Her voice shook as she spoke. "Yes. We were taken at the same time."

Jason's grip on the sill tightened, and she heard the sound of wood stretching. Pressing his forehead to the glass, she heard his deep inhales and exhales, his back expanding with every breath he took.

The tears were relentless now. She hated hurting him this way. "I'm sorry. I thought you should know."

He didn't move as the anguish poured out of him. The silence nearly killed her. Then Jason's voice uttered low, "Are you…do you…love this guy?"

"No," she said, immediately. "I didn't want this."

"What do you mean?" His voice was torn as he spoke through his teeth. "You mentioned separate cells. How did this happen?"

"We *were* kept separated. I only saw Ben when they brought us up to perform their spells until… this male witch thought it would be fun to watch us," she said, scornfully. "During the last moon heat, he brought Ben to my cell and I just couldn't…we couldn't…"

"Stop!"

Serena wiped her eyes on the sheets, listening to his heavy pants. "Jason, please. Tell me what you're thinking?"

There was a long pause before he spoke, the silence between them frightening her to her very core. "I know what the moon heat can do, but you wouldn't have done that with him under other circumstances, right?"

"Of course not. I never saw him that way. He was my boss."

"Exactly. It may not have been rape, but it was still against your will."

"Jason…"

He cut her off, his voice completely detached from his body. "You said you never had a heat mate. What do you mean?"

She bit down hard. When was all the hurt going to end?

"Serena…" he called.

"I…I'd never been with a man."

Hissing loudly, Jason's hands came up to grab the back of his head. "*Jesus Christ*!" he wailed, his voice cracking miserably.

There was nothing more she could say. If he reacted this way now, God knows what he'd do, if she told him everything.

"Can I turn around? I need to…I just need to see you," he said desperately.

"Yes," she whispered.

Jason turned to face her, his jaws locked.

Holding out a hand to him, she said, "Please come here."

He came to her, kneeling back beside the bed and gripped her hand, holding her knuckles to his lips. "You'll never know how deeply sorry I am this happened." Closing his eyes tight, he continued. "I made you a promise and I broke it. It will never happen again."

She smiled weakly at the memory of a seven-year old girl making a werewolf swear to protect her.

With taut features, he spoke in a low, tense voice. "I'm going to kill the bastard witch who put you in this position and your boss for good measure."

Her heart leapt. "No, Jason!"

He met her gaze. "Why not?"

Tears sprung to her eyes again. "Because Ben is dead. He died saving me."

****

Cassandra stared off into the distance from her balcony, fuming over what transpired down below. She'd lost a valuable tool. There was enough blood to create a few more of her pets, but they would need a hell of a lot more.

"You sent for me, mistress?" Leonardo's quivering voice asked from behind her.

Vengeance surged through her as she turned to face the idiot witch who let her precious wolf escape. His face was bloodied and bruised. Standing barefoot in only jeans in the middle of her room, he looked like he wanted nothing more than to bolt out the door. "Oh my. You do not look well, my Leonardo. Do you need medical attention?"

Caught off guard by her concerned tone, he said, "Uh, no. I'll be fine." He shifted uncomfortably. "Mistress...I tried..."

Cassandra held up her hand. "Speak only when I've addressed a question to you."

The anger raging inside her was at the boiling point. What was she going to do without her little wolf? They could plan a better abduction, but it wasn't going to be so easy this time. And strangely, she didn't want any other wolf, but Serena. Greed for the little dog's blood infuriated her, and her eyes blazed.

She watched Leo's reaction as her irises turned red. Very few witches could do this, and it pleased her he was so frightened.

"You will help me come up with a plan. My Nightwalkers are growing, but there aren't nearly enough. If you do not come up with a feasible plan within a few days, I will feed you to them. Is that understood?"

Eyes round, he said, "Yes, mistress."

Cassandra stepped closer. "You must be punished for your actions, Leo. I cannot abide such incompetence in my *convenio*." His quick breaths told her he was getting excited. In the past, her sisters would have their fun with Leonardo, but this time he was in for a surprise. She wiggled her forefinger in the air. "No, no. I said punish. You will not enjoy it." Circling him, she said. "Undress, please."

Leonardo did as he was told, tossing his jeans aside. The moron actually had an erection.

"Place your hands on the foot of the bed."

Once Leonardo gripped the bed frame, she conjured up ropes, which wound his wrists, and he stiffened. Her eyes were on the silky skin of his backside as she placed a spreader bar at his ankles to keep his legs from moving then gathered her leather flogger.

With fear in his eyes, she watched Leo struggle as Ken and Gary slipped inside. "What the…Cassandra, please…" Leo pleaded, his terrified gaze going from her flogger to the two men coming forward.

"Quiet! Continue to struggle, and I'll bring my pets to work on you as well." Raising her arm back, she made the first strike.

Chapter Seven

"They're called Nightwalkers. Serena says they're shaped like a jackal." Jason stood near the door next to Evangeline as she addressed Adam and the rest of the Fighters. The Chicago crew had come down for the meeting and all eleven of them listened as she relayed what Serena described. He was right. It was easier for Serena to talk to Evangeline than Jason or Adam. Neither one of them could control the growls now as Eva retold everything. They could all read Adam's mate very well, though, and she was leaving quite a bit out.

"Cassandra is building an army of these creatures to overthrow the wolf population. She kills the jackals first, then they're reborn from an incantation her *convenio* chants. According to Serena, the witches performed the same spell several times." Eva visually gulped before going on. "They'd use her blood along with other items to create them, which was why Ben and Serena were taken. Cassandra needs a were's blood to complete the spell. She also overheard Cassandra mention Tyson. She believes Tyson's blood was used to create the first of her Nightwalkers."

There were several hisses at this news. They'd lost one of their Fighters a few months ago, and believing a vampire had killed him, they'd retaliated. It was obvious now it was set up to look that way. While

Cassandra worked on her creatures, she had stirred up trouble between the vampires and werewolves. Hell, just a couple months ago they'd battled with the King's Coven in a warehouse. This witch bitch was on a mission.

"How would they take her blood?" Adam asked, his voice tight. He sat with the rest of the guys at the end of the dining room table, his face pale.

All the men in the room seethed as they honed in on Evangeline's fear. Jason's arms were crossed in front of him in a fierce grip, attempting to contain the wolf inside.

Evangeline placed her hand on her thigh. "Cassandra would take the blood from here…with a blade."

Several pack members hissed. Adam put his head in his hands, while Jason shook mightily.

"How often would they take her blood?" Adam asked low, looking down at the table.

Jason noticed Evangeline's hesitation. She glanced nervously at him before answering quietly. "Serena thinks it was about every other day,"

Jason shut his eyes, unimaginable rage coursing through him. *Why, God? Why? It should have been me. Why didn't they just take me?* He'd take a million cuts all over his body for Serena. It should have been him.

The room, which had been filled with low curses, was completely silent now. He opened his eyes to find everyone looking at him. His overpowering blast of pain and anger had washed all over the Fighters. The female Weres stared wide-eyed. Someone uttered under his breath, *"Fuck!"*

Danny Amato, a Chicago cop, spoke up. "We're all

glad she's safe and back home." He looked to Evangeline. "How is she?"

She gave him a small smile. "She's doing very well. All healed." Eva looked nervously at the top of Adam's head. "Once she regains her strength she'll be up and about. I left her with a big meal just now."

Danny nodded, glancing around at the rest of his crew. The guy definitely had alpha in him, but he would rather be a part of a pack than lead it. Adam put him in charge of the other five though. Since the twins were born, it was getting harder and harder to get up to the city.

The cop's job was easy. Make sure the boys were on rotation and keep shit running smooth. Danny was now making schedules for himself, Anthony Rourke, James Taylor, Viola Walters, Cameron O'Connell and Danny's sister, Samantha Amato.

"Why get involved now? They've left us alone for centuries. It doesn't make any sense," Viola Walters put in.

Nick said, "We outnumber them, I think. We breed like crazy. They might be afraid we'll turn on them eventually so they're beating us to the punch."

"Can she describe anything else about where she was being held?" Alex asked.

Evangeline shrugged. "Like I said, she was confined to her cell in a rundown basement. Said there were a few rooms like hers around her and stairs that would lead to a long hallway. The doors on either side were kept closed. They'd take Serena into a large ballroom where they performed the spells." She paused. "Oh, and she remembers the ceiling in the ballroom bore a fresco?"

"A what?" Ramo asked.

"Several paintings. She remembers a cherub, but that's all."

Cameron O'Connell spoke up. "Well, we've been fighting vampires, no offence…" he said to Evangeline, "…for centuries. We can take a piece-of-shit jackal."

Adam sat back in his chair, looking completely worn out. His eyes listless on the table, he said, "Their bite is poisonous to Weres."

The room went silent till someone asked, "How do you know?"

"I just know." Adam didn't dare meet Jason or Evangeline's eyes. "One bite and we're dead." Very few people knew of Eva's healing capabilities. Adam couldn't tell the rest of his pack his mate had saved his life when he'd been bitten back in August.

"Jesus," Samantha Amato sighed. "How many of these Nightwalkers has she made?"

Evangeline shook her head. "Serena could only speculate. She's guessing there are about fifty where she was being held, but who knows about other *convenios*. They may be teaming up. If she really is trying to eliminate *all* werewolves, she'll need a lot of help. Who knows…"

"Witches pulled this shit before and now look at us." Ramo put in, waving his hand in the air as if it were no big deal. Werewolves had originated several centuries back when the wolf curse was a witch's spell of choice. Eventually, the newly turned werewolves turned on the witches and began breeding like mad during the moon heat.

Adam sighed unsteadily. "All right. That's enough to go on for now. Each of us has to warn the other packs. We'll divide it up by regions."

"What? That's a lot of fucking packs," Ramo said.

"We're on rocky terms with some. What do we do about those?" James Taylor asked.

"I don't care. Just get a message to their headquarters. Let them know they are using were blood to create the Nightwalkers, and they are a threat to our race."

"Vampires too."

Every head swung to the doorway of the dining room. Serena stood, small and fragile, wrapped in Evangeline's purple robe, a hand on the wall to steady herself.

Jason raced to her side, gripping her arm gently for support. "Why are you out of bed?"

Serena craned her neck to look up at him and smiled warmly. "I wanted to walk." Her hair was much longer now, falling all around her in soft waves. For a moment he stared, completely mesmerized by her.

Stepping closer, she wound an arm around his waist and leaned her side into him.

Jason stiffened. They were both on display in front of the Fighters and Evangeline. He could feel Adam's watchful gaze as he approached his sister. They'd had their reunion earlier in the morning before she'd spilled all to Evangeline, so he simply held her chin between his fingers examining her closely.

"You got some color back, Rena. How do you feel?" Adam let go and stared hard. He was happy his sister looked better, but the way she held Jason was making him uncomfortable. His alpha was trying to contain the reproach itching to burst out.

So help him, but Jason couldn't let her go, even if

his boss commanded it. Last night was the first time she'd ever touched him, and he couldn't stop thinking about it. And now she held him again, and he was all too aware of her arm at his back, her small hand lightly gripping his side. Her touch was exhilarating, igniting his heart rate. He'd never felt so warm in his life.

"Much better, Ad." Then she tilted her head around him to look at Adam's mate.

Evangeline's eyes were wide. "What do you mean…vampires too?"

Serena said, "I'm sorry. I should have mentioned this, especially for your sake." She looked nervously at Adam. "Their main goal is to wipe out our population, but they hate vampires just as much as they hate us. I'm afraid they're targeting you too."

In a blink of an eye, Evangeline was at the doorway in one of her vampire flashes. She stopped abruptly with a look of confusion on her face.

Adam's voice murmured low and cool, "Where are you going, Eva?"

They all watched as Evangeline physically and mentally struggled with herself. Her back was to them, but she'd turned her head to gaze at her fiancé, her face frightened. "I'm sorry…I have to," she said pleadingly, inching closer out of the room in abrupt movements.

Jason instinctively pulled Serena closer to his side, knowing full well where Evangeline was headed. Her race was in danger too, and as the vampire king's ward, she was honor bound to warn him. Shit, the girl couldn't even decide for herself if she even wanted to go. Their blood bond was pulling her out the door.

His deep voice resonated throughout the room. "Do you have to go right this minute?"

Bending her head slightly, she gave him a sad smile and said, "I'm sorry, babe. I'll be back soon." And in a flash, she teleported on the spot, disappearing right before their eyes.

He felt Serena jump at his side, no doubt having never seen someone vanish into thin air.

Neither of them had to look at Adam to see the bitter betrayal on his face. Their alpha was humiliated in front of his pack, and he couldn't do a damn thing about it.

Sensing a couple Fighters' scornful attitude toward their alpha's choice of mate, Adam and Jason both spun their head around, sending the offenders warning looks, snarling. Viola and Cameron instantly bowed their heads in subservience, easing up.

"Take Serena back upstairs," Adam bit out, then whipped his arm up to grip Jason's shoulder. The look in his alpha's eyes, the raw warning oozing out of him gave him pause.

Jason just stared back, hard. "You know she's safe with me, right?" He was positive everyone could sense how much he cared for Serena. He could only guess his boss was being a prick because he was pissed at his mate.

Adam nodded and let him go.

"Wait," Serena said. Pulling away from him, she stepped to the table, her gaze scanning the Fighters. "I want to thank all of you for your hard efforts to find me. You're truly courageous, and the Blacktails are lucky to have you protecting us." She paused, an odd look spreading across her face, and he sensed her swift transition from gratitude to fear. "I'm not sure I've been much help, but I'm certain I'll... remember more soon.

I want to help in any way I can. Just give me some time." She gave them all a weak smile, then turned reaching automatically for Jason's arm.

Immense adoration for her radiated from him. It took a lot of courage to spill all to Evangeline, a stranger, but seeing her thank their pack after everything she'd been through broke his heart.

God, she was amazing.

He was dying to caress her cheek, run his fingers through her hair, but he wouldn't dare. Not here. Not ever. He may not be able to control his emotions, but he could control his actions.

As he led Serena up the spiral staircase, she pulled away from him, gripping the handrail. "I want to try this on my own. Coming down was easy enough, but I need to manage going up too."

Jason let go reluctantly, admiring her determination. He watched her frail back closely, her movements becoming stronger with every step she took.

She giggled, and the sound was the loveliest thing he'd ever heard.

"They're only stairs Jason. I'm not walking a plank." She glanced over her shoulder, noticing he was practically on top of her. She'd obviously felt his concern for her and was letting him know he could ease up.

He gave her a small nod and let her go ahead a few steps on her own, resisting the urge to pick her up and carry her wherever she wanted to go for the rest of her life.

They reached the bedroom, and she sank onto the bed, attempting to hide the fact she was still tired and weak.

Jason just stood in the doorway, not knowing whether he should stay or go back downstairs. For some reason, he couldn't bring himself to leave her. He stared at her pale skin. Her dark eyes seemed wider and there was a haunted look behind her gaze. He wanted to erase that look. He wanted to erase every memory of her ordeal.

"I'm gonna be okay, you know," she uttered.

"Stop." She wasn't fooling anyone, least of all him.

"What?" she asked, taken aback.

"Don't lie to me," he said, quietly.

Her brow furrowed. "What do you mean?"

He simply stared at her.

Serena angled her head to the side. "Still not much of a talker, are you?"

Jason lowered his gaze to the floor. What did she want him to say? There was no way she could be okay. This kind of thing stays with a person, eats you alive. She just didn't want him worrying. "Put up a front with someone else. Not with me," he said, flatly.

Her eyes roamed over his face. "Jason…"

His heart pulled at the sound of his name on her sweet lips.

"I know I'll be okay because…"

"What are you not telling us?" he asked, cutting her off. "What are you not telling *me*?"

Stiffening on the bed, her eyes widened at his brisk tone.

"There's more," he stated darkly.

She looked toward the window, her expression giving her away. And there it was…

Serena let out a profound sense of anger and

humiliation.

Blood boiling, Jason hissed at the sensation she was giving off. Seething, he asked, "What did they do?"

Serena squeezed her eyes shut.

"Jesus, Serena, please," he pleaded, his voice strained. Stepping further into the room, his eyes locked on her closed lids. His mind ran with the worst possibilities.

He should probably stop pressing her, but he just had to know. She didn't have to bear the pain alone. He wanted, no, *needed* to bear it for her. Perhaps then she'd begin to heal.

"They h..hurt me...they...tortured us with their spells..." She trailed off, her eyes still closed.

He bit down hard, bile rising in his throat. "Other than the moon heat...with your boss...did anyone..."

Her eyes shot open to meet his, and his stomach hit the floor. Anxiety laced through him.

She looked away, staring off toward the window again, her expression blank.

He'd never seen her face so devoid of life. It tore at his heart. "Ben was the only one," she paused, her face set in stone. "But the others liked to…touch..." She trailed off shakily.

"*No!*" he said, forcefully. It was like taking a bullet in the chest. Sirens rang in his ears. He felt his head throb and the room sway.

She flinched at the sound of his voice, dread washing over her.

The refusal just came out, as if it would make it not true. Every hair on his body rose. A blind, murderous rage filled him. He pictured what he was going to do with that entire *convenio*, letting the hate consume him.

His vision altered, he stared with his wolf eyes at her perfect face, her smooth skin, wanting to wipe away the feel of those fuckers' hands from her body. If she wasn't in the room he'd be tearing it apart, but Serena had been through enough violence to last a lifetime. There was no chance he was going to lose his temper around her. Containing it was doing a number on him though.

Body shaking with remorse, his arms at his sides vibrated with surging fury. He thought the veins might pop through his skin.

He almost went to her, aching to hold her, but he couldn't move. What if his mere presence made her uncomfortable? Why was he pressuring her like this? It was clear she was still hurting. Humility oozed out of her. "I'm sorry," he murmured softly. Those two words sounded meaningless. They wouldn't take away the pain she'd gone through. "Do you want me to leave?"

She shook her head, her somber gaze focused on the setting sun.

Nodding, he moved to the windowsill and sat down, facing her, no longer able to stand, his body still trembling. As much as he wanted to hold her, he couldn't bring himself to do it. His feelings for her were strong as it is, but when he touched her, every fiber of his being ran rampant.

He listened to her steady breaths, letting the sound calm his raging emotions.

Tensing impossibly more, he marveled at how empty she felt just then. He didn't like it. "What can I do?"

"This," she said automatically. Her eyes finally met his. "I can block it out. I will."

Taking a deep breath he said, "It may creep up on you." He swallowed the lump in his throat as he thought, *Why her, why her, why her…*

"Evangeline offered to compel me. You know…to forget everything." Her eyes shimmered in the sunlight as she spoke, staring out of the window again.

Jason's heart leaped. Why didn't he think of this? Although, if Serena had agreed, they'd be having a different conversation right now. "Why'd you refuse?" he asked, his voice grave.

Hesitating, she looked down and an overwhelming sorrow surrounded her. "I want to forget, really, but then I wouldn't remember Ben and what he did for me. I wouldn't remember the baby I lost. I don't think that's fair to them. Bearing this…whatever…will honor them in a way."

His brow furrowed at her explanation. Hell if he didn't get jealous again over the librarian. Jesus, the guy was dead. He wondered if he, Jason shouldn't be compelled. He didn't want to know she'd been with him. Regretted ever asking. Knowing what went down between them was drilling a hole in his head.

The urge to shout at her, *Please let Eva compel you*, made him shift uncomfortably. It wasn't his place, but he would give anything to erase those images in her head.

"Do I make you uncomfortable?" she asked. Her fingers played idling over the comforter.

Their eyes met. "No. Why?" He noticed the emptiness slipping away. She began to fill up with warmth the longer they gazed at one another.

"You're tense." Her eyes watched him carefully.

He noticed something new behind her stare as she

said, "I'm going to be okay because of you." Tilting her head to the side, her hair curtained her cheek. She was still pale and thin, but Serena's face was etched in his heart.

She was more beautiful to him than any living thing on earth. "I need to feel normal again. I know this is hard for you, but I don't want to talk about it anymore, so please don't ask. Just being with you calms me, even if we're not talking." Giving him a small smile she asked, "Can you let it go…for now?"

Could he? Could he really forget all she'd gone through when images of faceless monsters torturing her ran wildly in his head? *Absolutely not.* He knew he should be the one to try to bring her spirits up, to bring light back in her life, but he just wasn't built that way. Every detail of her ordeal would eat at him for the rest of his life. The question was, could she actually move on? His voice cracked as he replied, "I'll try."

Chapter Eight

Most of the King's Coven still slept at this hour. Cyrus Stewart, North American King of the vampires, however, awoke feeling exceptionally aroused. The dream he'd had still filled his mind as he'd had his way with the lovely Grace on his mahogany desk. He smiled, satiated, as Grace looked in the hanging mirror on his office wall putting her lipstick back on, her long red hair glistening down her back. It wasn't the exact shade he loved, but it was close.

A sudden current of anxiety struck his chest. It was odd. There was no reason to feel nervous. He shook it off, wondering if Grace would forget about dinner and join him in his suite instead so that he could have his *meal*. He moved toward her, his fangs tingling, intending on wrapping his arms around her to get her in the mood when the hairs on his neck stood on end. He faltered as he heard footsteps in the foyer. His head panned swiftly to the door, as his blood began to stir, humming with excitement, his body recognizing precisely whom had arrived.

My precious ward.

He moved away from her quickly. "I have a meeting," he blurted, a bit too sharply.

Grace straitened by the mirror, her hand frozen near her lips. She spoke to his reflection with a perturbed expression on her face. "I thought we were going to eat," she said.

He smiled nervously at her, his attention out in the hall as *her* presence grew stronger. "I'm sorry, my dear, but dinner will have to wait. Tomorrow perhaps." The insipid girl didn't move. It was like talking to a chimpanzee. "How about dinner at Carmichael's? You'll love it," he tacked on.

She beamed at him, then, ran to him and wrapped her arms around his neck, kissing him roughly on the mouth. He tensed as Evangeline drew nearer.

Gently, he pulled her arms from him, giving her an alluring grin. "I'll see you then." Giving her a quick peck, he then subtly pushed her away.

"Okay," she chimed and practically skipped to the door.

Cyrus rolled his eyes behind her as he righted his clothes. He didn't know how much more he could take of the girl. She was pretty with a big heart, but couldn't, for the life of her, think for herself. What did he expect? They couldn't all be like Evangeline.

Running a shaky hand through his dark blond hair, he glanced around the room hoping there were no signs of the activity he'd been engrossed in minutes before as Grace swung the door open.

Crap, he thought, his eyes shutting briefly as he imagined the scenario playing out at the entrance to his office.

If only Grace were vampire, she could have sped her ass out of the room, avoiding this confrontation. He tensed as he faced the door. Evangeline and Grace stood staring at one another in the doorway. The urge to laugh made him cough. The two women could be twins. Well… fraternal twins really. The longer he stared, the more their differences stood out. Grace couldn't hold a candle to his ward.

"Victor…" Cyrus called out, giving him a look that said, *Take care of this, will you?* His guardsmen stepped into view, gesturing for Grace to follow him.

Confused, she looked to Evangeline and back to Cyrus, her brow crinkling until Victor grabbed her elbow.

"This way, miss," he intoned.

Evangeline watched the girl leave, a curious look on her angelic face, until Victor closed the door. She looked to Cyrus, a perfectly arched eyebrow raised, "What? No introduction?"

Why did he feel like a teenage, idiot boy when she was around? "Hardly," he said.

Her head jerked back. "Why not?" she asked.

"It's inappropriate and unnecessary." He didn't want to go into details, but it just didn't seem right to introduce Evangeline to his lover; felt weird in fact, especially when the lover in question looked way too similar to his ward.

She stared, her green eyes somber.

He jerked his pants up, uncharacteristically frazzled, and walked around his desk. "This is a pleasant surprise," he said, looking everywhere but at her. Her admonishing expression irritated him. He shut his eyes exasperatedly. "Don't look at me like that!" Cyrus barked, his casual facade breaking.

Evangeline's brow furrowed more before she looked away.

Damn it! The last thing he wanted was for Evangeline to see he'd missed her, which led to his secret search for her double. He felt pathetic, but there you have it. He was in love with his ward, who in turn was in love with his enemy.

Shit happens.

"You know...there are a number of beautiful blondes in town..." she began, worry etched on her features.

"We are sooooo not discussing this, Eva." He sat down behind his desk and motioned for her to do the same.

She sat in one of the vacant armchairs facing him, her delicate nose crinkling as she glanced at the desk.

Letting out a sigh, he said, in a defeated voice, "I'm sorry."

"You don't owe me an apology," she said, seriously.

"I do. Had I known you were coming..."

"Cyrus, it's fine...really..."

"No. As my ward, you should be treated with the utmost respect and decorum." He gave her a halfhearted grin, unmistakably ashamed. Marveling at his contrition, he laced his fingers together on the desk. "Now...what can I do for you, love?"

Evangeline gave him a reproachful look at his endearment.

Before she could respond, he asked, pleased to have her here, "How are you doing at the Transition Facility? I've had great reports. They tell me you're a natural at teleportation." He paused, a sudden panic settling in his gut. Eyes narrowing, he asked, "How did you know you could teleport in the house? I didn't get a chance to tell you I lifted the ban for you." Vampires couldn't teleport in the King's Coven, unless the king himself allowed it.

Julia Laque

Looking momentarily confused, she said, "I didn't. I hadn't even thought about if I could or not. I just needed to see you." She shifted uncomfortably, her arms crossing in front of her. "The sire bond literally pulled me out of my house."

Anxiety laced through him. "What's happened?" he asked sternly, getting up to come around his desk, taking the empty seat next to her. The urge to reach for her hand was overpowering, so he clasped them together instead. *Christ!* He'd felt a slight panic a few moments ago with Grace, but ignored it, too busy to recognize his ward was troubled. *God.* If he hadn't lifted the ban, she would have been forced to teleport outside the coven during sunset. He shuddered to think of her skin being marred by the sun's rays. Would she have had the strength to teleport back? Would she have been able to if their blood bond was really pulling her to him? Cyrus cursed in his head. He had to do a better job as her sire.

His head reeling a bit, he focused on what she was saying. Evangeline explained what the alpha's sister relayed to the Fighters, her silken voice businesslike.

"What threat do these Nightwalkers pose to us? Do they have extraordinary strength?" he asked.

"I don't know about their strength. The jackal that attacked us last summer seemed to hold its own until the other Fighters showed up, but I do know their bite is poisonous to werewolves. If a creature a jackal's size can pierce a werewolf, they may be able to do us some serious damage."

"Is this all the information Serena gave on her whereabouts?" he asked, reaching over his desk to pick up the landline and dialing Florena, his assistant's extension.

"Yes."

He nodded then spoke in the receiver. "Meeting in five," he said, and hung up. He gazed warmly at Evangeline. "How would you like to attend your very first meeting in the King's Coven?"

****

"We need to talk," Adam told him, blocking his way into the kitchen.

Jason nodded his head noncommittally. When Adam said nothing, he raised his eyebrows at him.

"Not here. Take a walk with me," Adam said, stepping around him toward the door.

Alarm bells went off. He reached out and felt the tension his friend was radiating. "What about Serena? I don't feel comfortable leaving her."

Adam waved a hand toward the kitchen. "Ramo's here. She'll be fine," he said brusquely. The tension in his friend multiplied the instant he'd said Serena's name. It didn't take a genius to know what was coming.

Jason followed Adam out of the round house and down the street. They walked at a casual pace, neither one keen on being overheard by the occupants in the house.

Adam broke the silence after several awkward moments. "She's back," he muttered low, almost as if he still couldn't believe it.

Jason nodded again, his conversation with the woman in question still weighing on him. It felt as though he were crawling out of his skin.

They neared the park, and his eyes landed on the swing he'd watched a young Serena sit in as she'd read her book. He focused on the empty black seat as Adam went on.

"She's hiding something. So is Eva. And you know what? I don't want to know what it is." Adam's voice tight, he stared straight ahead, his eyes hooded. Jason knew he was fighting back tears. He didn't respond to his alpha, but he couldn't help the shot of remorse coursing through him.

Adam's head whipped around. "Fuck," he groaned. "Did she say…"

Jason shook his head, his gaze still on the swing. "Let's not do this. Neither of us is up for it," he said gruffly. He wished to God he didn't know. Still didn't, really. Serena had been pretty vague on the details, but he could only imagine what they'd done. He sure as hell wasn't going to put his friend through the agony he was going through. One crazy motherfucker was enough.

They passed the park, and Jason trained his eyes now on the ground. He saw Adam nod silently from the corner of his eye.

"Look," Adam began, his tone cautious. "Serena wasn't raped." He cleared his throat. "She was thrown in a room with Michaels during the moon heat."

A blast of jealousy ripped through the air. Clenching his teeth, Jason tried in vain to erase the horrid image in his head. Avoiding Adam's stunned expression, he walked on.

"She told you?" he asked, incredulously, his blue eyes narrowing at him.

Jason uttered through his teeth, "Yes."

The fact Serena would share something so intimate with him must have been the cause of Adam's stunned silence. Too late, Jason realized Serena wouldn't have said anything unless there was something between them.

"J, I know how you feel about her, and I'm sure you know she's had a thing for you since she was a teenager, but I didn't like it before, and I don't like it now. I don't think…"

"You don't think I'm right for her," Jason finished for him, his words coming out clipped. Trying to keep his emotions in check, Jason walked on waiting for the inevitable.

Adam coughed. "It's not that I don't think you're good enough for her. It's the life we lead. Especially after what's happened. You know the danger that surrounds us. Look what's happened to Eva. I nearly got her killed, and now she's a vampire." He shook his head, letting out a huff. "I'll never forgive myself for what I did to her."

"Yet you're still with her," Jason said without thinking.

Adam bristled at his words. "She's the mother of my children." He glanced at Jason before going on. "You and Serena…nothing's happened. You don't have a relationship or anything and you haven't mated so it shouldn't be too hard…"

Jason stopped and turned to face him, his arm muscles rippling at his sides. "Get to the point, Adam. You don't want us together, right? Got it. But don't presume to know what the fuck I'm feeling."

He'd never wanted to hit his alpha so much in his life. He knew he was bad for Serena, but having someone tell him to stay away from her was like being kicked in the head. He stared his master down, jaws tight.

Adam's upper lip curled back slightly at Jason's hostility. Narrowing his eyes, he pointed his finger at his chest. "You know what's best for her."

Jason cocked his head. "And you know what it feels like to live without the woman you love," he countered. *You've got some fucking nerve.*

Adam's expression faltered. He lowered his hand. "I'm sorry, but this is how it has to be," he said.

Jason looked away, letting out a deep exhale. "I know, man. Just hearing it…I don't want to be told what to do when it comes to her. It feels wrong." He passed a hand over his face, massaging his chin with agitated fingers. "Nothing's happened. Nothing will happen, but I can't leave her alone. I have to protect her, and that means I'll be around. You know I can't help it."

Adam nodded, but he looked worried, eyeing him mistrustfully. "Yeah, I know." He coughed. "Look…"

"Forget it," Jason uttered, edgy. He needed to put some distance between them before he said something he'd regret. He'd already toed the line by telling him to back off, but he seriously couldn't help it. They weren't mated, but to him, Serena was his.

Now he was being told not to get involved with her. God help him. The thought nearly killed him. Staring off toward the house, he gnawed on the inside of his cheek, dreading the one thing that finalized it. He squinted off into the distance. "Is this an order?" he asked, his chest stung as he waited.

"Yes."

Jason gave a clipped nod and walked away, leaving his alpha behind.

****

The moment she stepped outside, Serena felt as if a huge weight had been lifted. The cool fall day against her skin made her feel alive. Wrapping her favorite sweater tighter around her, she closed her eyes and let the sun's rays warm her cheeks.

"Are you okay?" her brother asked.

"Yeah," she assured, opening her eyes to give him a small smile.

Instantly alert, they both turned toward the north end of the street. Someone lurked in between the houses, watching them.

"Get back in the house," Adam ordered.

Serena shook her head, her gaze honed in the voyeur's direction. "No, Adam," she said calmly. Picking up on whoever skulked down the street, she couldn't feel any danger. Besides, it was going to take a lot more than some nosy passerby to frighten her now. "I love being here and spending time with my nephews, but I need to go back home."

"Serena, there is someone watching us right now. Do you think it's a coincidence?"

She looked over toward the meadow where she felt Jason's hackles raise as he too sensed their unknown company. "I've got you and Jason. Plus, you've added enough security measures it'll probably take forever to get into my house. I'll be fine. Besides, I don't recognize the scent. From what I can tell it's human." She squinted back down the row of houses. "It's probably some researcher, trying to get a look at the Blacktail alpha. Or better yet, his beauty of a mate." She smirked up at him, and he scowled back.

By the glow on her soon-to-be sister-in-law's face these past couple of days, Evangeline and Adam had made up when she returned from the King's Coven.

While she recuperated, Evangeline and Serena had had a long and interesting conversation as they played with the twins. She couldn't believe her brother actually kidnapped Eva. The brute. Poor girl must have been scared out of her mind. Although, the longer they talked the more she saw how in love Eva was with Adam. Serena liked her a lot and was very pleased to see her brother so happy with his new family.

An ache filled her chest at the thought of her nephews. She wanted to spend every waking hour with Daniel and David, but she had to get back to some semblance of her life. After spending four days in the roundhouse building her strength and playing with the boys, she was completely healed with just a few faint scars remaining on her thighs.

Her stomach tightened as a flash of a blade cutting into her skin filled her mind, momentarily blinding her.

"Serena?" Adam's voice severe, he watched her carefully.

Shaking her head, she conjured up an image of Daniel's expression as he'd spit up on Ramo yesterday. His little mouth had formed an O and big green eyes seemed to say, *Oops*. His chubby cheeks could cure anything.

Yes, going home and throwing herself into her work would take her mind off things. The longer she stayed with her brother, the longer they'd continue to treat her like a patient.

Ten minutes later, Adam was showing her how to work the added alarms to her bungalow. She tried to pay attention to what he was saying, but was too excited to be home. How she'd missed her little cozy house. It was small, which annoyed Adam, but she didn't need much space. The front door opened right into the living room/dining room facing a plush sectional taking up most of the area opposite an obnoxiously large flat screen her brother had bought her last Christmas. A small coffee table sat in front of the sofa where piles of books still lay. A throw was tossed haphazardly, and she thought of how late she'd been up the night before her abduction, reading.

"I'll send Maggie over. The place could use a good scrub," Adam said, referring to his cleaning lady.

"That's all right. I'll clean up." She took her sweater off, feeling quite hot. She didn't want to acknowledge how her skin itched at the feel of clothing, her jeans beginning to irritate her. The T-shirt she wore wasn't so bad, but her bra and underwear were suffocating. The minute her brother left, the jeans were coming off.

"What? You're going to clean now?" Adam asked.

"No time like the present."

He followed her into the tiny kitchen where a small table for two sat just under the back window, providing a panoramic view of her backyard. Looking out, she saw the wretched state of her rose bushes and froze, a sudden overwhelming sadness flooded through her, stinging her chest.

The red buds had shriveled to a dry chalky black. The crispy petals which managed to hang on drooped from crusty vines with cracked leaves. The sight was disturbingly haunting. Her throat swelled, and she felt her lungs cut off. It wasn't until a brown paper bag was shoved in her face that she realized she was hyperventilating.

On her knees in the middle of the tiled floor, Serena took long exaggerated pulls of air as her brother rubbed her back, trying to calm her in a hushed tone. The tears relentless, she couldn't control her ragged breaths. She kept lifting the bag from her face, sobbing hysterically.

"My roses, Adam! My roses!" she cried in a high-pitched voice, rocking back and forth. Dizzied with panic, Serena blinked profusely at her blurred vision. The stabbing pain in her chest was unbearable. Anxious, she vaguely wondered what was happening. She had no idea what had come over her, but her kitchen seemed to be closing in on her, her heart beating loudly in her ears.

"Breathe, Serena…" he hummed.

"No…my…" She took a deep breath. "…My…" she spluttered.

"It's okay, Rena. Next year, honey. I'll help you. You'll have your roses. I promise."

A howling cut off his words of comfort far off to the east.

Sniffing shakily, she stiffened.

Adam's hand stilled at her back as they both listened to the prolonged wail echoing around her house.

Serena closed her eyes and slowed her breathing, taking deep inhales and exhales… in and out…in and out, letting the sound of her wolf's agonizing howls slip inside her soul, easing the pain.

She was all right. She was home. Her brother was here, and Jason was just outside, comforting her as he called out. Just hearing him suffer for her, was enough to pull her back. She was okay. There was no need to panic. *I'm okay*, she thought, knowing he'd sense she was on the mend. Her heaving shoulders slowed, her breathing easing up.

Taking one last long breath into the bag, she removed it from her face, dropping her hands in her lap. Opening her eyes, she stared listlessly at the legs of the kitchen table. Her chest swelled as she calmed, but evenly now. "I'm sorry," she said, a numbing sensation paralyzing her on the floor. Strangely, she liked the feel of the cool tile beneath her.

Adam kissed the top of her head. "Don't apologize," he said thickly.

She didn't know how long they sat there, but a strange calm had settled inside her. The cold, hollow pain in her chest still lingered though, and she wondered if she'd ever feel right again.

God, what was that? Why had she reacted in such way to a bush? It was fall. Of course her roses would be dead by now. She hated to admit it, but perhaps it would be best if she'd talk to someone, other than Jason and Evangeline. She wasn't sure it would do her much good, but it was worth a try. There was no way she wanted another episode like this to happen. People would think she was out of her damn mind.

"I don't want to leave you alone. I know you want to be home, but can I send Eva over to stay with you for a while?"

"No. The boys need her more than I do. It's okay Adam. I'm feeling much better."

Her brother still looked worried as he helped her up. His mouth thin, he bit down hard before he spoke. "Okay. Let's get started."

She looked at him. "What?"

Heading for the cabinet under the sink he said, "I'll help you clean, and then we'll order a pizza and catch up on the soaps." Trying futilely to sound like a bad ass as he took out supplies and gossiped about her favorite soap opera, he said, "Sonny's getting on my nerves…"

Serena listened to her brother ramble on, her throat closing up as the tears began, unbelievably thankful for his presence. A small smile lifted her cheeks as she watched her enormous brother shake out a can of Pledge as he chatted on about the new girl on the show. Serena was to blame for his little soap addiction. He'd had no choice but to watch every episode with her when she was growing up.

Taking a deep breath and some serious control on her emotions, she headed for the pantry to take out the broom, determined to make a fresh start.

Chapter Nine

By the time Adam left the previous evening it was nearly midnight. After cleaning, stuffing their faces with pizza and hot wings, and their soap opera marathon, she went straight to bed.

Serena passed a fitful night, though. Several times she awoke in a panic, expecting to see the black stone wall of the prison, not the beige coloring of her bedroom. She stared inertly now at the espresso wood dresser across the foot of her queen-sized bed. The white floral duvet always comfortable, now suffocated her.

Turning roughly onto her side, she tried to go back to sleep. Feeling disorientated frustrated the hell out of her. And if she was honest with herself, it scared her as well. The wretched notion she could still be back in the damp cellar, fighting the pain drove her insane. She found it difficult to separate the past from the present, to distinguish reality from horrifying memory.

No matter how hard she tried to forget, she lived in a perpetual state of fear. She was afraid of being alone, and even worse, of being physically hurt again that it was odd to feel healthy.

At five in the morning her eyes shot open again when she heard the familiar sounds of footfalls on stone stairs, but it was only her warped imagination. She wiped the sweat off her brow and yanked the covers off, her hands immediately going to her thighs, but there were no open wounds. They moved automatically to her forearms, searching for a needle imbedded in her vein, but none was there.

I'm home. I'm safe, she told herself. Why couldn't she feel safe?

The lamp beside her was still on, having no desire to wake in the dark thanks to her imprisonment. She could now add *must sleep with the light on* to the pile of her dysfunctional traits.

Forcing herself out of her musings, she got out of bed and headed to her dresser. Rummaging through her drawers, she found the only workout gear she owned. She'd never really had the inclination to work out. Runs during the full moon were exercise enough, but Evangeline bought her several yoga videos, insisting they'd ease the tension in her body and help her relax.

Still uncomfortable with a lot of clothing on, she glanced up at her reflection in the mirror to gaze at her bare body. She was still too thin. Serena had always been around hundred and twenty pounds, but she must have dropped about forty. She'd put on a few at her brother's with all the food Evangeline and Adam made her eat. She obliged them, even though the food tasted like sawdust in her mouth.

Knowing Jason thought her too fragile, she was resolved to build her strength, to prove to him she could get better, and filling up was just the beginning. Determined to thicken up, she thought pancakes might be in order, knowing this was probably the only item left in the cupboard she could fix herself.

She turned to the side. The way her bones stood out on her hips and ribs made her cringe. Her breasts appeared smaller too, but a few days of burgers would remedy this.

Her hands fell over her belly, but before she could fall into a state of depression over her unborn child, she straightened and immediately got dressed. Throwing on black stretch pants and a V-neck, Serena headed into the living room barefoot. She took a quick glance outside, peering through white wood blinds as she wrapped her too long hair in a ponytail.

It was still dark out, her street softly illuminated by two lampposts. There were only a few cars out since everyone on her block had garages. Looking further down the street her eyes landed on a familiar pickup. Her heart rate escalated. This is why she'd glanced out the window, her wolf instincts telling her someone was out there in the quiet night. From where she stood, she could clearly make out Jason's silhouette in the driver's seat. Had he been there all night? She hoped he'd gone home to rest. He'd run himself ragged if he kept this up.

She felt a sudden awareness, a tingle at her nape and knew he'd spotted her watching him. His dark head moved a fraction of an inch, and she found herself wishing she could see his face. An eternity passed as they gazed toward each other before she withdrew from the window.

When they'd last spoken, she'd sensed his distance. Where do they go from here? He worried for her constantly and as thoughtful as it was, she didn't want him to see her as a poor battered woman he needed to take care of. She wanted him to see her alluring, attractive, strong enough to handle all the things that came with his life.

The last three months were horrid, but it also made

her realize how precious and short life was. Having cared for the beta for most of her life, it was high time she did something about it. She thought of his arms around her, the feel of his body pressed against hers, the heady smell of him, and she closed her eyes feeling as though she were in his embrace right now.

She didn't know how, but Serena was going to make it clear to him there was no way she was letting him go.

He cared for her. Of this, she was certain. Now she had to figure out how to make it work before he slipped away.

After her workout and hearty breakfast, Adam accompanied Serena to Ben's family home before dropping her off at work. Together they relayed all the details of their capture, and Ben's heroic role in her escape. There was no need to tell her about the moon heat and the baby they'd lost. Ben's wife and children had enough grief to deal with.

They watched with heavy hearts as Ben's wife tried to remain strong in front of them, until the woman succumbed to the pain and finally broke down. Serena went to her, gathering Ben's wife in her arms. She loathed leaving the widow alone, and held her for several long minutes. She told herself she was comforting the woman, but Serena knew it was the woman's embrace that gave her solace.

Sometime later, with swollen eyes and a hole in heart, Serena returned to work. The employees at the library welcomed her back with open arms and, thankfully, with no inquiries as to where she'd been. She suspected her brother had something to do with their lack of questions. It was odd going back to her normal routine at the library. Having felt disoriented all day, she'd made about ten different mistakes. She supposed it would take time to adjust to a common workday, just like everything else.

There were moments when she felt together, calm, content, and suddenly another horrific image would assault her, the cold panic constricting her lungs. Several times she'd run to the bathroom to take deep breaths, fighting the tears, fighting the memories.

When she returned home later that evening, she forced a cheeseburger and fries she'd picked up at a drive-thru down her throat, then curled up on the couch, fully clothed. In an instant, she was out.

The next few days followed the same pattern, yoga, work, yoga, work… She continued to wake in the night, but after the fifth day back home, she was waking less and less.

Dr. Moros came to visit for a check-up and referred her to a psychologist he held in high esteem. She met with him once and after an hour of reliving all the details of her abduction, Serena walked out of the session uncertain as to how she felt about it.

He'd given her a few breathing exercises to do at home and encouraged her to get back into the normal swing of things, but wasn't she doing this already? Before she judged the whole therapy session unhelpful, she'd give it a couple more times.

Her nerves still troubled her though. The anxious knots in her stomach, however, were not because of the witches' torture, but due to the fact she had not seen Jason.

Serena knew he was never far, but she hadn't actually seen his face. It was frustrating to know he was so close, but she couldn't see him, talk to him, touch him…

Walking up her front steps a week later, Serena felt a familiar presence lurking nearby.

Squinting to the right, she reached out her senses, homing in on the human who had spied on them by Adam's round house. What was he or she doing here? Initially she'd thought they were spying on her brother, but now she felt the stranger's attention on her.

Alarmed now, she fumbled with the key pad, entering the wrong code a few times, her eyes never leaving the direction the human…

Her hand froze as a number of emotions ran through her. All at once she was, thrilled, worried, angry, and sad. It was this melancholy that gave her pause, the wretched feeling overpowering anything else, only it wasn't her, it was *him*. Yes, the human was definitely male. She picked up the smell of Old Spice coming from his direction.

Who was he? And what did he want? Why was he lurking about feeling so distraught?

She sensed sudden dismay and panic, then felt him slip away, glimpsing his shadow as he rounded the corner at a fast pace.

Curious, she opened her front door and stepped inside her living room. She hung up her jacket on the coat rack on the wall and dropped her purse on the small console table. Serena wondered if she should be afraid, but there hadn't been any hostile feelings from the man. Besides, after everything she'd been through, a human spying on her was just a drop in the bucket. Though, something would have to be done.

Heading into the kitchen to pop a frozen dinner in

the microwave, she was about to call her brother's cell when an intriguing thought entered her mind. She stopped scrolling for his number and just stared at her phone, the corner of her mouth curling up. Before she could think any further, she typed a text to Jason: *Hi Jason. Are you on patrol tonight? The human from the other day is spying in my neighborhood. It's a man. Gonna get a closer look. Serena.*

Barely containing a smile, she tossed her dinner in the microwave and leaned back against the counter, waiting.

It took seven seconds to receive the following text—*Stay n the house! Don't move. Lock doors and set alarm. Don't leave ur house Serena. I MEAN IT!*—two minutes to pick up Jason's fear and anger nearby and by the time her microwave dinged four minutes later, he was at her door.

Biting her lip nervously, she fidgeted as she entered the living room, taking a quick glance at the round mirror above the console. She'd gotten a haircut two days ago, and it fell in soft layers around her face, cascading a few inches past her shoulder blades. No longer pale, Serena thought her cheeks looked less gaunt. They were fuller and rosy with excitement. Her eyes weren't so wide anymore, although a slight gloom still lurked in their depths.

She adjusted the black turtleneck she wore, tucking it into her skirt, somewhat pleased with her appearance. With a deep breath, she opened the door.

Her heart leapt at the sight of him. His dark brown hair windblown, yellow eyes glowing, Jason stood, panting slightly in a tattered black t-shirt and holey jeans with splashes of spackle and varnish.

A white dusting of some kind covered him in splotches, his forearms, hair, on his left cheek... My God, Jason never looked so appealing to her than he did right now. She pictured him hard at work on a construction site, his strong hands handling a tool as his muscles rippled with the physical effort.

Serena had known Jason all her life, but every encounter still made her light-headed. The teenage crush that began years ago only intensified day after day.

"You didn't set the alarm," he stated harshly, his thick arms throbbed right before her eyes, his shoulders heaving from his race here.

Mouth slightly open, Serena stared. *He's so big*, she thought. Had he always been so...

"Serena?" he said loudly.

Shaking herself, she said, "You didn't give me a chance to." She smiled then, ecstatic he was here. "Come in." Stepping to the side, she held the door wider for him.

Jason didn't move at first, his brow furrowing as his eyes turned back to hazel. Hesitantly, he stepped into her living room, ducking a little through the door and looked around awkwardly. He seemed oddly nervous now as if he would knock into something since he dominated the small room.

She realized this was the first time he'd ever entered her home. Turning to close the door, Serena hid her blush. As she pivoted back around too quickly, her face banged into his chest. Jason gripped her elbow to steady her, then let go. Chills went down her arm at his touch.

He hovered over her, his posture tense. "I didn't

see the human. I smelled him about three houses down. What happened?"

Trembling slightly at his close proximity, she stammered, "Nothing. I caught wind of him staring, and then he took off."

"Why the hell were you going to approach him?" he demanded, his massive shoulders looming over her.

Smiling in spite of herself, she gazed at the gold flecks in his eyes, tempted to caress his hard jaw, twitching in irritation. Would he pull away if she tried to wipe clean the dust on his cheek? She held her hands in check, clasping them tightly together at her midriff. Breathless, she answered, "I wasn't going to."

He jerked, but thank God, he remained ever so close. "You said you were…" Jason paused as he picked up her jitters from the ploy she'd made. Watching her carefully, his gaze darted back and forth from her left eye to the right.

She couldn't move, his powerful frame doing a number on her body.

Jason stared for a long while, his features registering, cottoning on to the real reason she'd texted him. Helpless to contain it, Serena's heart swelled with the love she felt for him, her body heated from his incredible scent.

He was so close. It was torture not to reach out and touch his magnificent chest, those pectorals expanding with every measured breath he took. She could quite literally reach up slightly and press her lips to them, but he'd only pull away and she wanted him right where he was.

Inhaling deeply, his pulse quickened as he read her emotions.

Hazel eyes drifted over her face, lingering on her mouth. If he kissed her now, she would surely faint. How could she handle it? It was too much as it is to be so near him. What if she had another panic attack? Oh God. How embarrassing would that be?

Glancing down at her chest, he said gently, "Easy."

Serena placed a hand on her racing heart, her eyes roaming over his shoulders, arms, chest, abdomen, back to his shimmering eyes…"I can't help it," she whispered.

The silence ensued. Minutes, maybe an hour went by as they stood frozen in the middle of her living room, soaking up the precious moment. It was what they both needed, a chance to come together and wrap themselves in the love they shared. It was better than therapy. Jason was the only one who could cure her soul.

As heartwarming as it was, this was the only intimacy he would allow. It was beautiful and agonizing, and she didn't dare move. Her elbow still tingled from his touch, she couldn't imagine what would happen if he pulled her to him. How wonderful would it feel to be in his arms again? It would be different now. The pain of the past had somewhat dwindled. Their next embrace could truly be about them. But in this instant, Jason's visual caress was far stronger than any physical contact.

The house quiet, the only sound was the occasional car passing and their ragged breaths. And yet, his gaze never left hers. His expression struggled between solemnity and warmth, agony and love. Serena would give anything to know what he was thinking at this very moment.

Sensing how much he cared for her, she also felt restraint, as though he were fighting an internal battle. She watched his handsome jaw clench several times, his breathing labored as if at any second he could crack.

Memories of Jason flooded her mind, and she thought of the very first time she no longer saw him as just her brother's friend, but as a stunning, attractive man, the moment her feelings had truly begun to grow.

She'd always thought he was handsome, but growing up with him watching over her, Serena's schoolgirl crush had been innocent, until the day she spied him shirtless coming out of the meadow by the round house after a run with Adam. She'd faltered at the kitchen window, mouth agape.

Serena watched him playfully punch her brother on the arm as they laughed at something Adam said. It was the few times she had seen him smile, relaxed and invigorated after his run. His smile could make the fiercest nun blush. It was mesmerizing.

He slung his shirt over his shoulder and meandered barefoot toward the house, his body tanned and perfectly muscled with perspiration running down his chest.

Adam had caught her staring from the window and picked up her embarrassing arousal. Mortified, she'd been helpless to hide her flushed cheeks when her brother walked into the house, which had led to their argument in the kitchen that evening.

My God, how those feelings had multiplied. It was a wonder they had managed to stay apart for so long, particularly since, seven years ago, standing on her brother's porch with her ex-boyfriend, she'd realized Jason returned her affections. On that very night, she vowed to remain faithful to only Jason.

The man standing before her, melting her with his searing gaze was the love of her life. And the possession in those hazel eyes told her she was his.

It was a long while before they spoke, Jason's deep tenor breaking the silence. "You look well."

Serena gave him a small smile, not trusting her voice just yet.

"Please tell me you're okay," he asked softly.

Angling her head as she continued to gaze at her amazing man, she said, "I'm better."

Nodding slowly, his jaw flexed. He was going to leave. She felt his regret and an incredible sadness laced through her.

Jason closed his eyes, his expression tight, massive shoulders moving up and down. "I have to go, Serena," he murmured.

Her throat closed, unable to speak, she tried to put on a brave face. *Say something, dummy. Make him stay.* Staring mutely, she couldn't help herself. A hand moved in slow motion to the left side of his face, her thumb made contact first as she brushed away the white dust on his perfectly sculpted cheekbone in slow, agonizing strokes.

Jason flinched slightly, but didn't move, eyes still shut. Waves of arousal drowned them, a cyclone of heat building between them. Her breath caught at the look on his face. All too soon, he opened his eyes, his focus steady on her as he took her palm lightly from his cheek. Turning it over, he wiped the debris from her fingers. He held her hand gently between his thick fingers, his thumb moving slowly across the center of her palm.

A curious sensation ran through her, straight to her very core.

Jason froze the moment he sensed it, then let go of her hand. Taking a deep breath, his features less tense now, he gave her a soft smile, the same smile that had done her in.

Her heart completely shattered.

"Goodbye, Serena."

She drew in an unsteady breath. "Goodbye, Jason."

****

Kevin Goode stepped into his room at the Knights Inn in Wilmington. Shoving off his jacket, he tossed it onto the bed and plopped down with a heavy sigh.

Removing his glasses, he rubbed his tired eyes with calloused palms. At sixty-five, he no longer traveled much, not that he ever did a lot of traveling. The last time he'd been away from home for longer than a week was during the war. He figured there was no reason to leave the comfort of his home to learn about different places when you could simply read about them.

Massaging his aching shoulder, he stared morosely at the room he occupied. He hadn't slept in a bed that wasn't his in ages. The town of Wilmington was nice enough, but the impromptu trip was beginning to affect him in ways he'd never imagined.

Wondering if it was a mistake to make the short drive down from Chicago, he debated going home. Kevin had recently retired from an old Chicago plumbing company after forty-three years of labor. It felt odd to have so much time on his hands. He wasn't used to it yet. When you lived a life of solitude, work was the only thing you had.

Standing, he bent down by the dresser to pick up

his duffel and felt a small pop in his right shoulder.

His doctor had been pressuring Kevin to have surgery for years, but it was too much of a bother. Besides, the thought of recuperating in a hospital alone with no visitors, no one sitting vigil at his side, depressed him.

He doubted his son would fly from the west coast to visit him in the hospital. He was lucky if his son returned his calls at all. Every time Kevin mentioned taking a trip out west on the rare occasions he'd reached his cell, his son would find an excuse to refuse him.

It wasn't his son's fault, really. Kevin's ex-wife cut the line of communication as soon as they'd divorced thirty years ago.

Now, he was a stranger to his own son. He'd never even met his grandson.

Rummaging through his bag, he took out the photo he'd printed off the Internet, and his heart nearly stopped.

The girl in the picture had brown hair and brown eyes. She was seated at a desk, holding a book open, as if she were about to read it to the photographer, smiling playfully at the camera. He had found it on the Wilmington Library website. Bending, he placed it upright against the mirror on the dresser.

It wasn't fair.

Life, love, loss... Not. Fair.

He hated how his thoughts turned morbid, but what else could he focus on, but the girl in the photo?

No. He wasn't going anywhere. The trip to this town had been a must.

Looking away, he idly pulled the revolver from his duffel, staring at it a long while as he turned it over and over in his hands. What he was doing was wrong, but he couldn't help it. Fisting the handle, he stepped to the window.

Yeah, he'd have to man up and get it over with, he thought, his hands trembling slightly.

Serena Perez was in for the shock of her life.

Chapter Ten

Serena left work late the following evening, having no desire to sit alone in her living room daydreaming of Jason, or eating alone gazing out of her gaping window in the kitchen…daydreaming of Jason. She couldn't step into the living room now without her heart squeezing from the memory of him consuming the tiny room.

Feeling exceptionally irritated tonight, she entered her bedroom to undress. A quick glance at the electronic calendar on the dresser told her it was almost the full moon. Although, she wasn't certain the moon's effect was the reason for her agitation. She'd been edgy all day. No matter what she did, everything felt off. Her morning coffee made her nauseous; her tasks at work stressed her out more than usual, her walk during lunch made her anxious.

Throwing her clothes in the hamper, she sat on the bed in a pajama t-shirt reaching just above her knees to work on her breathing exercises, taking deep inhales in, and exaggerated exhales out. While this helped some, she couldn't clear her mind to focus, not when Jason's image continued to live in her head.

It was almost sickening how much she thought of him. It hurt to know he was so close, yet so irritatingly far. It wasn't fair. Why did he keep her at arm's length?

Anger began to course through her. The idea of

never being with Jason was going to drive her mad. What the hell were they doing? Why wasn't he here right now holding her? Why couldn't they have the life she felt in her bones they were destined to have?

Picturing the two of them snuggled on the couch after devouring peanut butter and jelly sandwiches, his favorite, made her want to scream. The tension in her body increased. Breathing exercises be damned. There was nothing that could heal the wounds in her life better than Jason's mere presence.

Enough was enough. Sick and tired of denying them the happiness she knew was as easily attainable as breathing air, she decided to take matters into her own hands. Life was too short to walk on eggshells. Being alone for so long and enduring the witches' torture put a lot in perspective. *Hell.* It wasn't just a smack in the face. It was a kick, punch, and elbow to the gut.

Getting up from the bed a bit more composed than before with her new plan in mind, she walked to the living room, knowing with all her heart Jason was just outside. She felt a prickle at the back of her neck, sensing the impending storm about to rain down on Wilmington. Opening the door, she stepped outside, stood on the front porch, and paused for a second in her long T, her arms still at her sides, the sensory light illuminating her in the darkness. Then, gracefully, she turned in his direction.

The Avalanche was parked down the block, facing the house. The instant he spotted her, thunder cracked deafeningly in the air as it began to pour. Sheets of rain blurred her street. The raging clatter coincided with the roaring in her heart. The short awning above her porch protected her from the buckets cascading down from the sky.

Feeling his concern for her, she knew he wondered what she was doing out in the rain, late at night.

Straining over the rumble of thunder, she searched for the sound of his pulse, finding the rapid pace beating wildly in his chest as he stared avidly at her through the hazy windshield of fog and rain. His fiery gaze caused her blood to boil. The rise and fall of his shoulders made her as breathless as he was.

Serena didn't care how odd she looked standing here. This was a message to him, a calling. With a trembling hand she reached up to unclip her hair, letting it fall over her shoulders. Her face humorless, she played softly with her tresses, running her fingers lightly through the thick strands over her shoulder.

With a lasting look, she strode purposefully back into the house leaving the front door wide open. It was a silent yet clear invitation for him to come in. She knew he would as the temperature had dropped immensely the instant it began to pour and he wouldn't want her to get cold, which was why she loved him with every fiber of her being.

****

The door is open.
Damn it!

Jason clenched and unclenched his fists on the steering wheel, watching the veins on his hands ripple with every squeeze. The creaking sound of vinyl echoed loudly with the pounding rain. It was getting stuffy sitting in the cabin of his truck with the engine off and in his John Varvatos officer's jacket. He'd only put the thing on to cover up the mess he'd made of his arms at the site today. With his mind solely on Serena, he'd been clumsy with some flammables. Luckily, no one but him got hurt, and he'd heal faster than the humans on the site.

Why was she doing this to him?

Staring dazedly at the ripples of water on the windshield, he chewed on the inside of his mouth. He'd watched with bated breath as a scantily clad Serena stepped onto the porch and faced him with a determination that scared the hell out of him. He'd never seen his sweet Serena so stern. The thoughtful look in her eyes, the controlled stance, what did it mean?

The door is open, he thought again, stupidly.

Letting go of the wheel, he dropped his hands in his lap and leaned his head back. God, the way she'd looked at him made him go hard in his jeans. It was getting increasingly uncomfortable in the seat of his truck, but he couldn't go in there like this.

Willing the shit to go down, he maneuvered awkwardly out of the driver's side and stepped into the rain. His gait was slow, and he half hoped she'd come to her senses and close the damn door in his face, knowing full well she'd left it open for him on purpose. Taking a deep breath, he walked up the front porch and into the house.

Serena sat with her legs tucked under her on the sofa, her elbow on the arm of the sectional, her head leaning adorably in her hand. They stared for a moment, their muted greeting a routine of sorts. They'd never felt the need for mundane pleasantries. His stomach knotted at the sight of her, so lush, so exquisite. What he wouldn't give to lay her out on the couch and…

Thunder sliced through the silence as the rain continued to run down heavily.

"It's getting a bit drafty in here. Can you shut the door?" she asked, serenely.

His heart leapt. Biting down the urge to curse, he asked, "What are you doing?"

Shrugging, she said, "I thought you might want to come in from the rain." She glanced at the door. "Could you?"

Pursing his lips, he turned to close the door then leaned his shoulder against it.

"Would you like to sit down?" she asked, motioning to the seat next to her.

Jason shook his head, digging his hands in his pockets, because hell if he knew what to do with them. *Well*...No. Shit. What the fuck was wrong with him?

She smirked. "You're just going to stand there in your jacket?"

Staring at this new cool and casual Serena, he nodded. What was going on?

"I feel odd conversing this way. It looks as though you're about to bolt through the door."

"I am," he answered, lowly.

Jerking, she let her hand fall from her head, straightening on the couch.

"I'm dripping wet, Serena." He lifted his elbows slightly to indicate his sodden clothes. "I don't want to mess up the floor. What are you doing?" he repeated.

She relaxed a bit. "I thought we could talk for awhile. Seems silly to sit in your car alone when I'm in here...alone."

The way she said the last word made him go hard again. Shrugging a shoulder, he deftly shifted his jacket to conceal himself. "Okay."

Eyes roaming everywhere around the room but in her direction, Jason felt a peculiar sensation in his gut. Neither of them said anything for several minutes, and a loud warning seemed to ring in his ears. She was up to something, but all he felt from her was a placid composure. There was definitely something she was hiding, though, something underneath the façade. Yes, her cool and collected persona was just for show. Hiding beneath the surface was a current just waiting to wash over him, and drown the ever-loving life out of him.

"I'm making you uncomfortable again. Why?" she asked, her sparkling brown eyes narrowing at him.

Shaking his head, he looked further away from her, peering down the hall toward the kitchen, the bedroom.

Fuck!

Before he could stop himself he muttered, "Maybe you should go put some clothes on."

She gave a short laugh. "I have clothes on."

He shot her a wry look. The twinkle in her eyes, that blushing smile drove him wild.

Peering up at him through her lashes, she said in a small voice, "It's not like you haven't seen me, Jason."

All the breath in his lungs shot out. Looking away again, he focused on the coffee table. "I didn't really...I couldn't look..." Damn, he could barely speak around her.

She was quiet for a moment as he fought not to look in her direction, his eyes searing into the cover of one of her novels. "You averted your eyes, didn't you?" she asked, sweetly.

"Of course."

Serena let out a long breath. "Wow."

His gaze wondered to the wall behind the couch where she had a weird abstract painting of what looked like two people...*Oh crap!* Shrugging his hand out of his pocket, he ran it roughly down his face. Then, when he couldn't resist any longer, his eyes landed on her.

Meeting his stare head on, she sat serenely before him then unfolded her legs leisurely in front of her, stretching them out on the chaise side of the sectional. The only noise beating in his ears was the sound of her skin sliding over the couch, their slow rhythmic breathing, and the thick rain pelting noisily on the windows.

His chest tightened at the sight of her smooth skin, her delicate bare feet just aching for his touch. The desire to run his hands over each calf, massage the arch of her foot, kiss every part of her skin made him go momentarily blind.

"You're staring," she said, her voice husky.

Glancing up, he saw her watching him ogle her with her head slightly tilted. Her eyes heated, asking for something he was sure she wasn't aware of. "Why are you doing this?" he uttered.

Sternly, she answered, "Because I want you and you want me."

He froze. A deer in freaking headlights.

Her delicate chin lifted. "If you even think to deny it, I'll scream. If you tell me to stop, I'll scream. If you utter one word which sounds like a rebuttal, I swear I will start throwing things."

In her tirade, her cheeks had flushed, and it took every ounce of control not to go to her. Shit, he had to get out of here, but he was too scared to move a muscle.

What if she made do on her threat? He'd never seen Serena lose it, and quite frankly, the notion terrified him.

"Why do you continue to fight this? Us?" she asked, her eyes growing sad.

Closing his lids briefly, he loosened his stance and pushed off the door, running a hand through his damp hair. "Serena... I can't. We can't."

"Why?" her voice shook, her shimmering brown eyes earnest on his.

She was killing him, seriously, *killing* him. "I don't want to hurt you." Shit. He wasn't good at this, didn't know how to express himself. What could he say that wouldn't hurt her? Struggling for the right words, he said, "If we were together, I'd end up hurting you someway."

"You can't possibly know..."

"Yes, I do. I'm beta, Serena. What if something were to happen to me? I don't want you to bear such a thing. Aside from the danger that comes with my life, I'm never around. If I'm not working, I'm on rotation and..."

"... outside my door," she interjected.

Letting out a harsh breath, he said nothing.

"Do you honestly think just because we're not officially together, I wouldn't mourn if something were to happen to you?" Sitting up, she went on. "It doesn't matter how much time passes, or if we go months, years without seeing each other, I'm yours, Jason."

"God, Serena," he whispered, his gaze riveted on her.

Nodding she repeated, "Yes. I'm yours." Licking her lips, her heart rate kicking up, she said, "And you're mine."

Jason turned away and slumped back against the door. *"Fuck."* This conversation would be his undoing. Never in his career of loving this woman had he ever wanted her more than he did right now.

Leaning his head back, he shut his eyes again. If he looked at her, he'd go to her and do things they would both regret.

"You want to kiss me now, don't you?" he heard her ask sweetly.

Eyes firmly shut, he nodded, gritting down on his molars.

"I don't know what's more intense, just being close to you or when you hold me."

Slowly, he opened his eyes. How right she was! It didn't matter if they were inches, feet, miles apart, as long as they were near each other, a powerful force bound them together. Lowering his head, he turned to his left to stare avidly at her perfect face.

Breathing heavily, her chest rising and falling, she said, "I can feel you, though. Even when you're not touching me, I can still feel you."

"You have to stop saying everything that comes to mind," he uttered, breathlessly.

"You have to start," she disputed.

Smirking, he said, "Touché, little one."

Biting her lower lip, her eyes widened at him. "I love it when you smile at me," she whispered, standing gracefully to her feet.

He stiffened.

"Jason?"

"Mmm?"

"I want you to be my *first* and *only* lover."

"Jesus, Serena." He didn't know whether to come in his pants or pass out.

"Don't…"

"No! We can't, Serena. You have no idea what you're asking." The only thing holding him up right now was the goddamn door at his back. Focusing on the hallway, he refused to look at her, though he watched her every move through his left peripheral.

"Yes, I do," she said coolly.

He shook his head. "No, you don't." Taking a deep breath he went on carefully. "After everything you've been through, I could never take advantage of you." Glancing at her, he saw those glorious brown eyes blaze at him and stiffened.

"Don't presume to know what I can or cannot handle."

Mouth agape, he stared. This convo was getting way out of hand. Jason treaded cautiously. "Serena…if you and I…" He swallowed. "If you had even the slightest hesitation, a moment where you felt…uncomfortable, I'd never forgive myself." His hand rested on his abdomen. "Please, honey, don't do this."

"I could never feel uncomfortable with you."

"You don't know that. You don't know how a man can get…" Jason lips tightened in a hard line, looking away. Refusing to think of Benjamin, he finished angrily, "You don't know how *I* can get."

Her heart leapt excitedly, and he cursed.

Shaking his head, he said, "I'd never hurt you, but I don't think I'd be able to restrain myself with you. It may…frighten you," he trailed off, quietly.

Serena's expression took on a whole new emotion,

one all too new for her. For emphasis, lightning struck the night's sky, illuminating the hungry look in her eyes. Gently, she said, "I'm done talking, Jason."

His aching shaft twitched, straining for release. "No," he said in a small voice.

Stepping in front of him, her head bent back. Jason balled his fists at his sides, demanding them not to move and caress her silken cheeks.

"Can't you feel how much I want you? You want me too, don't deny it." She moved ever closer, backing him up further against the door. In a second, he was going through the damn thing.

"Serena, stop." He shouldn't be here. He needed to leave, but he had a feeling she'd set off the fire alarm or bust a pipe just to get him to come running back.

"I need you, Jason."

Oh God...

"Stop fighting me. I know you want to touch me. Do it. My body burns for your touch. Show me what it's like to be caressed by a man."

The urgency in her gaze stunned him. She had no idea what her words were doing to him.

She glanced down, eyes blazing.

Okay...Guess she did know.

Serena reached for his chest, but he caught her wrists, holding them suspended in front of him. Staring for a moment at her delicate fingers, his control began to slip with every aching moment. God, he'd wanted to touch her for so long, really feel her in his hands…arms…

Very slowly, he brought his gaze to her breasts straining under her shirt, watching her chest rise and fall. How long had it been? He'd imagined this very moment, pictured him loving her, kissing her, moving inside her.

Damn it!

He had to try it, needed a taste of what he'd denied himself for so long.

When his eyes met hers, the last of his restraint crumbled. Pulling her toward him roughly, he hugged her to him in a fierce embrace. She clung to him, arms wound tight around him, her hands squeezing the back of his jacket.

Serena felt incredible. Her breasts against his chest sent his hardened soul afire. The feel of her legs pressed up along his, her arms enfolding him…it was so right. This is where they belonged, in each other's arms.

A light lit inside him, and suddenly, his mind had no control over his body. Jason pulled back to look at her, not her face, but the body he craved. Hands began roaming of their own accord, clasping her waist, her hips, eyes following with a raw intensity. He tested every curve, massaging her skin, reveling in the feel of her. With a savage need, he reached behind her and grabbed her sweet backside, molding his fingers over her glorious mounds.

Noticing how she watched him, a small part of him thought he should slow down. Was he scaring her with his forcefulness? So help him, he couldn't stop. He needed to feel every single inch of her. Turning her around, he brought her ass up against his swollen sex, sliding his hands over her thighs, stomach, winding his arms around her to squeeze her to him again and again. A hand came up to her throat and ran possessively down her sternum, in between her mounds, pulling her shirt down to expose her breasts. Bending his head

Julia Laque

lower for a closer look, he murmured deep in her ear, "Let me see you."

Serena arched her back to give him a better view.

"God, you're beautiful."

Her hands moved to grip the sides of his thighs, her heavy panting mingled with the sound of the storm clouded his mind. He was out of control.

Laying her head back against his chest, Serena squirmed further into him.

"*Ah, Serena,*" he moaned. The death grip on her shirt released, his hands sliding down her rib cage to the tops of her thighs, lifting the hem of her shirt straight up over her head. His vision altered at the sight of her sinuous form, resting bare before him, her nipples hardening from the cool exposure. Growling low, his hand wondered up to feel one of her luscious breasts.

Pausing, he hovered a moment over her skin as reality hit him in the face. Any second now, he'd have Serena's breast in his hand, and a part of him registered this was a bad idea. This was Adam's sister, the woman he'd loved for years, but she was off limits, forbidden fruit.

As he was about to drop his hand, Serena nimbly clasped him and brought him to her silken breast.

"*Oh God,*" he whispered, his thick length throbbing, digging into her back as his hips thrust into her, his other hand held her belly, rocking her into him. His mouth found the curve of her shoulder, the smell of her skin tantalizing his senses. Tasting her, he ran his tongue up the side of her neck, nibbled impatiently at her ear lobe. "Tell me to stop," he whispered.

"No," she moaned, squeezing his jeans at his thighs.

"Mmm…" Jason's hand at her belly moved automatically to the juncture of her legs. "*Ah,*" he uttered, excited at the feel of bare skin. Gently caressing over her entrance, he paused a second. Jesus. Was this for real? His body quaked at the notion of being inside her, and his fingers tightened as if the muscles in his hand were as anxious as he was. "Are you wet for me, honey?" Before she could answer, he slid his middle finger in between the folds. "*Yesss,*" he hissed. Making his movements smooth, he glided deep, dipping his finger in the hot moisture, then back up to encircle her swollen jewel, all the while playing with her nipple between his forefinger and thumb, gently plucking at the luscious bud. He rocked her into him, over an over.

Her nails dug into his skin through denim as she moaned in a sexy voice he'd never heard come out of her. "*Jason.*"

Sucking in a deep breath through his teeth, he came hard at the sound of his name. Pumping into her as the spasms wracked his body, Jason's head reeled.

"Oh God….is this…I think…I'm…" Serena orgasmed, her body tightening in his embrace, then shuddering hard, her stomach muscles quaking beneath his arm.

Continuing to strum her like a guitar, Jason let the waves of release settle, their weighted breaths outshining the sound of the showering rain until she fell limp in his arms.

They stood there, her tiny body lying atop his, her head tilted to the side, trying to catch her breath.

Savoring this moment, he watched her nipples rise with every breath, desperate to taste them. A savage need unlike any he'd every felt laced through him. He wasn't nearly done. The urge to be inside her overwhelmed him. Turning her around he held her at arm's length, drinking in the sight of her spent body, naked for him. His Serena. His love.

With heavy lidded eyes, she gave him a small encouraging smile. "Kiss me," she demanded.

Crushing her to him, his lips found hers, fusing together in a deep, penetrating kiss. Good God, she tasted wonderful. Her lips fit perfectly with his, meeting his every move with executed skill as though they'd rehearsed this first kiss a million times. Their tongues met at the same time, molding together effortlessly.

Fingers slid into his hair, pulling him closer, squeezing him at the base of his neck, painfully. "Damn it, Serena, you're gonna make me come again," he uttered, taking a breath, but she pulled him back greedily, crushing her lips on his. His hands ran up and down her back. God, they couldn't get enough.

Spinning her around, he pressed her up against the door. Gripping her wrists, he brought them up over her head, pinning them to the door as his knee spread her legs.

She hitched in a quick breath, her eyes widening.

He froze.

And sure as fuck, he'd rue the day he ever let her talk him into this.

"GODDAMNIT!" he shouted and pushed off the door roughly, moving as far away from her as possible. With shaky hands, he ran them up and down his face, his back to her. He was a motherfucking pig! How the hell could he do that?

"Jason…"

"Don't say a word, Serena," he uttered, icily.

"It's okay, I'm fine."

"Jesus Christ, I mean it. Not a word." Visibly shaking, he tried to get some control, but couldn't.

She'd panicked. What he'd been most afraid of had actually happened. She'd fucking *panicked* because of him. Because he was a lousy, fucking pervert.

"FUCK!"

The sound of fabric behind him told him she was getting dressed, sniffling in the process.

Serena was crying.

"Ah hell." His chest ached, a painful sting as though he'd been pierced through the heart with an arrow. "Are you okay?" he asked, his voice unsteady as he stared at the dinning room table.

"I told you, I'm fine. Please look at me," she wailed.

"I can't. Damn it, Serena I told you this would happen." Great. Now he was throwing it in her face. Real classy, dumb shit.

"I'm sorry. I don't know why…it was just for a second and then it was gone. Please look at me," she pleaded.

Turning, his head low, he peered at her. "Why are you crying?"

"Because you stopped," she said, instantly.

He let out a sharp breath. "It was too fast. I couldn't…I can't control myself with you. Don't you understand? I want you too damn much, it's wrong. I'm not right for you." Biting down hard, he screwed up his face, whispering dreadfully, "I fucking scared you." Chest heaving, his vision grew cloudy as his throat closed up. "I scared you, little one."

Shaking her head vigorously, she mumbled, "No." Swiping at her cheeks, she said, "It's you, Jason. I could never be scared with you."

Forlornly, he responded, "Then why were you?"

Chapter Eleven

The bang of metal rung stridently in the air the instant she shut the cage. Only twenty of her creatures fit the average-sized room in individual kennels. There were another twenty in the adjacent bedroom, as well as twenty in the vacant cellar. Cassandra kept two in her own suite to remind her *convenio* as to who controlled her Nightwalkers.

Bending at the knee she stroked the snout of a gray. Before conducting her spells, the creatures were quite aggressive, especially when they detected their impending demise. It almost saddened her to think of the carcasses in the closet, but the enchantment could not be performed with a living jackal, they needed to be reborn under her care to grow into the beasts she needed. Now they were subservient to her alone as, for all intents and purposes, she was their new mother.

The gray nudged her hand the moment it stilled, encouraging her affections. Flinching at the doe-eyed creature, she said, "No, no, my sweet. Never beg." Now that they'd undergone the change, she wanted to rear them to be aggressive canines once more.

Standing, she smirked at how large this one had become, impatient to see just what they can do. As crepuscular animals, jackals were most active between dawn and dusk, which put a minor kink in her plan since they were now only useful at night. It hardly mattered, though. After meeting with the other *convenios*, they came to the consensus the creatures were to be only used nocturnally as the daylight hours would cause too much exposure. Her litter would be shot dead by the next season's hunting party were they to operate so openly.

The door behind her creaked, and a spineless voice echoed in the room. "Excuse me, mistress, but…"

"Leonardo," she called, her nostrils flaring at the very thought of the idiot letting the wolves slip away. "I trust you have good reason for interrupting my bonding time?" she asked, practicing her silent hand gestures to the female gray. Bending her elbow, she raised her palm in the air. The female sat on her haunches. Lowering her hand, the Nightwalker immediately fell to the down position.

She smiled.

"Yes. I've had an idea. I've been watching her closely, and I'm pretty confident this will work."

Pointing a finger at the female, her eyes gleamed as the hairs rose hostilely on the creature. "Pretty confident doesn't work for me, Leo."

"Quite confident," he reiterated.

"Mmmm," she hummed, not sure she wanted to hear the fool's plan. Having established her next move, she wondered if his surveillance could prove helpful. She guessed it couldn't hurt to hear the boy out, but not while in here. Her pets needed her undivided attention. "Come here, Leo."

Silence met her demand then the sound of shuffling feet approached. Pausing at her side, Leonardo's battered body tensed.

"Take one pigeon and place it in the cage, just

beyond her reach." Cassandra gestured to the basket of dead birds at their feet.

Stiffening at her request, Leonardo looked to her.

She raised an eyebrow at him, waiting for him to comply.

Swallowing, he flushed as he bent to the basket and retrieved one foul-smelling pigeon. Glancing at her nervously, he set it quickly in between the bars on the floor.

"Leave it," she demanded fast as the gray inched foward. The Nightwalker stilled, hackles raising ever more, waiting for Cassandra's permission to take her reward.

Leo wiped his hands on his jeans, stepping back.

"Thank you. Now…take it back," she said.

His head snapped in her direction. "What?"

"You know how I hate to repeat myself. Take the bird away," she mouthed, exaggerating her words. If she was going to keep the stupid witch, he should damn well do something useful, and angering this lot was one way to ensure her beasts became the violent weapons they were born to be.

"She'll bite my hand off. Their fangs are made to pierce a Were. My skin won't stand a chance." Sweating now, Leo looked from her to the Nightwalker, eyes wide.

"Then be quick about it."

He let out a shaky breath. The poor boy looked like he was going to soil himself. Leo lowered himself on unsteady legs, his eyes didn't blink as he watched the gray, just waiting for an attack. The minute he reached his arm out, the female curled her lips, snarling at Leo's threatening hand.

Smiling bright, Cassandra nodded swiftly at her pet the instant Leo made contact with the carcass. At her consent, the female leapt, snipping at the witch's hand. Leo cried out in pain. The Nightwalker managed to nip a piece of skin when she seized her prize.

Letting out a sharp laugh, Cassandra threw her head back, unable to contain her enjoyment. "Good girl," she chuckled, ignoring Leo's whimpers at her side. "Oh my darling…you just might be my favorite," she cooed, as her Nightwalker devoured her reward.

****

Fuck you, moon heat.

Jason parked the truck in front of the library, and resumed his sit and watch position he'd taken since Serena's return. His ass and legs had fallen asleep so many times it was a wonder he could still walk.

This time, however, he wouldn't have to wait too long. Serena was leaving work early today. On moon heat days, werewolves were required to leave the work place at a decent hour to prepare for the night's…exertions. Even if they were on pills to suppress the urges, one could never be too careful.

Grabbing the prescription on the seat next to him, he stared at the tiny pills through the orange plastic. He'd taken two of his own bottle already, even though it was only two in the afternoon. The way his body had been since last night, he might have to take the entire bottle by dusk.

This bottle was for Serena. *God*, to have endured three moon heats without pills or a heat mate… Slamming his head back, he cursed. Why did his mind always go there?

There was no way he was taking a chance on

Serena going through agony again. Tonight she'd have enough pills to mellow her out. Once he made sure she was home safe, he'd pop a few more and call it a night.

The glass door of the library opened, and Serena stepped out, a black tote slung over her right shoulder. She wore a black trench coat reaching just above her knees and gray pants. Her hair was loose, the afternoon sun highlighting the deep brown to a brilliant mahogany.

A cell in hand, she was distracted as she walked out slowly, texting as she went. No doubt telling her brother she was leaving the library as her brother had instructed her to do, or, and his stomach tightened at the thought, messaging a potential heat mate telling him she was on her way.

Damn it.

Now he felt like an ass. His preemptive trip to drop off pills to her seemed stupid now. Having no claim on her, he had no right to shove pills at her.

No. Serena didn't have a heat mate. She couldn't. She wouldn't do…

What was wrong with him? He had to stop. Adam had been pretty damn clear the other day, and wasn't he always telling himself he was no good for her? Then why did he have this incredible urge to know who the hell she was texting?

His stomach rumbled. This moon heat was going to be a bitch. Not only did Weres suffer from hunger pangs during the hours leading up to night, he was already feeling agitated; another clue he had to get the hell home. Whoever Serena texted was none of his damn business.

He jerked the car door open, the sound jolting

Serena from her cell phone. Her head shot up, faltering mid-step. "Hi," she said, cheerily.

Slamming the door, he stepped to the curb, glancing at her phone. "You shouldn't text and walk at the same time. You need to be more alert."

Her face fell as he felt his phone vibrate in his jean pocket.

"I…I just texted you."

I'm a douche bag.

He gave her a half-hearted grin. "Sorry."

Straightening, she threw her phone in her jacket pocket and asked, less joyfully, "What are you doing here?"

Before he could stop himself, he blurted, "Where are you going?"

Flinching at his harsh tone, she answered, "Home." Her eyes narrowed at him. "Why?"

He shook his head, at a loss. Reminding himself he had no right to question her, he held out the pills. "I brought these…"

Shifting her weight to her right leg, she crossed her arms in front of her chest, her delicate brow furrowing. She glanced at the bottle. "Did you think I was going to meet up a heat mate?"

Taking a deep breath through his nose, he clamped his mouth shut. He knew not to touch this one.

Shaking her head at him, she said, "You're unbelievable."

"Serena…"

"No. Do you honestly think I want anyone other than you?" She unfurled her arms and pointed at his pocket. "Check your message."

"I'm sorry. I don't know why…" He searched the

street around them for some kind of help. All he got was passing cars. "Look, I just came here to give you these. I wanted to make sure you had enough." He held the bottle out to her.

Folding her arms again, she said, "I'm not taking those."

"What?"

"You heard me." Her eyes softened at him. "I'm not taking pills tonight."

A growl escaped him, and he stepped toward her, menacingly. "You said there was no one else," he said, angrily.

Serena's eyes gleamed as a corner of her mouth perked up, seductively. "I don't know why you fight it. You want me, Jason Linus. And tonight…I intend to have you."

He jerked back, feeling stupid again for jumping to the wrong conclusion. "Stop. You know we can't. I won't do it. Just please, take these."

Pursing her lips, she glared at him. "Fine." Taking the bottle from him, she walked around him toward her car.

Jason's eyes followed her.

When she stepped off the curb she turned to face him, a devilish grin on her face. Popping the lid off, she spilled the contents of the bottle down the sewer.

"Serena!"

Spinning on her heel, she called back, "Check your text message, Jason," and hopped into her Beetle.

****

You have no idea how sorry and embarrassed I am for reacting the way I did. I'm okay. Really. I need you,

Jason. Tonight.

    Serena. We can't. Please.

She hadn't responded to Jason's last text, knowing full well he'd continue to argue with her.

She was playing with fire, to be sure, but it was the only way they could be together. Serena was determined to show him just how "okay" she was.

It was a half hour until nightfall as she stepped onto the fourth floor landing of his apartment building. Having never entered his home, Serena followed his scent to his door.

Pausing in the hallway, she tightened the belt of her trench coat with shaky hands. Never in her life did she ever imagine doing something like this. She wasn't the gutsy type. Thinking back, she couldn't recall doing anything exciting. When she traveled, she stuck to walking tours with large groups, avoiding boats because she wasn't a good swimmer, and bicycles because she couldn't ride one. Hell, she even hated roller coasters. But now…now…she was about to embark on the biggest ride of her life.

Shifting uncomfortably in the one of the few pairs of heels she owned, she moved to the door. Just before she could knock, it swung open.

Jason's large frame filled the doorway, looming over her, even with her added high heel height of four inches. His long hair damp from a recent shower, he stood before her in just a pair of jeans, his tanned, masculine feet bare on the hardwood floor, his chest still tantalizingly moist.

Speechless, she could only stare.

Abruptly, he reached for her, grabbing her by the arm and hauling her inside, slamming the door shut as he shoved her against the wall.

"What the hell are you doing here!" he hissed, his breath warm on her face.

Oh no. He was not going to intimidate her. Swallowing loudly, she inched her chin up. "You know why I'm here." His lips tensed, and she had to control the urge to run her tongue over them. *God, he smelled good.*

Gripping her arm tighter, he said through gritted teeth, "Do you have any idea what time it is? Do you want to be caught by some sick human, looking to take advantage of innocent werewolves like yourself?"

Hesitating, she thought for a moment. "There are people who do…"

He huffed. "The fact you don't know such things is the reason why you shouldn't be here," he snapped.

Gathering her courage, she shoved him away from her.

Startled, he let go, stepping back a couple feet.

"Tell me you don't want me here and I'll go."

"God…that's not…" He let out a harsh breath, placing his hands on his hips.

Her eyes drew down to his waistband where a light patch of hair receded low into his jeans.

"Serena…" he scolded. "Look at me." Jason scrutinized her with his eyes. "Tell me you took some pills."

"I didn't take a thing." With that, she opened her trench coat and rested her hands on her hips, revealing the black lace bra and thong she picked up earlier.

Dumbstruck, Jason's eyes grew bright, traveling over her body. "Jesus Christ!" he uttered. Turning away from her, he stepped to the window in the living room, his fists clenched at his sides.

It was the first time she noticed her surroundings. The apartment was small, with the kitchen overlooking the living room. Only one armchair faced a flat screen on the wall and two stools at the kitchen counter. It looked to her as though no one lived here.

"I can't do it, honey. I can't," he said to the windowpane. "Jesus, if I scare you, I'll never forgive myself. You can't do this to us. There will be no *us*. Do you understand?" His voice strained, he added, "I don't know what to call what we have, but this could ruin it."

"That's not true. I know this will make us stronger." His back muscles tensed. What could she say to persuade him? This constant fight he put up was waning on her nerves. "Look at me, Jason."

Bowing his head, he muttered, "Close your coat."

"No," she responded simply.

Turning slowly, he stepped back closer to the window, his eyes roaming over her body, from head to heel. His mouth tight, he took a deep breath and said in a steady voice, "Please, Serena. We have a few more minutes. Let me take you home right now."

Bringing herself to her full height, she raised her chin, trying to hide her nerves, "Either you take me right now, or I walk home." Hesitating, she added mindlessly, "Isn't Nick medicated and on patrol tonight? I thought I saw him. Maybe he could take me home…"

A threatening growl blasted her back against the wall, as a crack sliced through the room. She stared wide-eyed at the piece of white wood he'd just ripped off the wall behind him, gripping it tightly in his hand.

Tamping down a giggle, she said, "Oh, Jason, your

windowsill. I hope you can replace it. Wouldn't want you to lose your deposit."

Eyes flashing yellow, he charged her, his thick long legs stretching his jeans as he pounded toward her. Within a second they were nose to nose. "I own the building," he said. "And if you ever threaten me with another man, Serena Perez, you'll be sorry."

"Why? You said we shouldn't be together. Fine. Why not someone like Nick?"

Jason growled in her face, and her body reacted at once. She felt the stirrings of heat, a flicker of light deep inside her…very…deep…

"No," he said deeply. "Anyone, but him." A brief look of shame flashed over his face and she felt his jealousy, his envy for his pack member.

Her mouth fell open, feeling instantly guilty for using Nick to work him up. "I feel nothing for Nick and you know it."

His brow tight, he said in a tense voice, "He'd be a helluva lot better for you." Unsettled, he whispered, "And that kills me."

"No, he's not. Dammit, Jason, when will you stop fighting me?" she cried, her body heating with every passing second.

Wolf eyes moved over her face, his cheekbones more pronounced now that he was so close. "I'm not a monster. Taking you tonight would make me feel like one. Look at what happened last time. I lost control and all you were doing was standing in front of me. If you were naked in my bed, I won't be able to hold back."

Taking a deep breath, she inhaled the sweet heady smell of him. The skin of his chest was so close to her mouth she could almost taste it. His scent clouding her mind, she barely heard a word he'd said.

A familiar daze was coming over her as she gazed at his thick neck. The heat at her center began to tingle, sprouting from her core, branching out through every limb, filling her from within. She'd read a few years ago, some side effects of the moon heat were akin to taking ecstasy. Touch played a huge role, but the need for sexual gratification overruled everything else.

Every inch of her skin, even her fingertips rivaled for stimulation, vibrating with extreme sensitivity. Without realizing it, she rubbed her belly with one hand, her thigh with the other, her eyes traveling down the sides of his neck to his shoulder, her chest panting embarrassingly. "It's happening," she whispered, ignoring whatever he'd said to her.

Eyes flaring, he jerked his head back.

"Don't move," she said breathlessly. Desire surged through her, enflaming her to her very core. A burning need to touch him made her eyes shift, and she thrust forward, gripping his waist roughly, digging her nails into his skin.

Startled, he watched with arms firmly at his sides completely transfixed as her shoulders heaved, and a light sheen of perspiration doused her skin. "Serena," he said low.

"*Jason, please,*" she said, squeezing her legs together as her hands roamed over his skin…chest, abs, shoulders…He was so beautiful. Hot moisture poured out of her, and she moaned. She was on the precipice of a mind-shattering orgasm, and he wasn't in her.

Aching, a blazing fire lit deep inside her, her sex pulsating, begging for release. Biting down on her molars, she shrugged off her coat, letting it fall to the floor, and gripped him with trembling hands. Reaching behind him, she lifted his thigh between her legs, nestling him against her hot center. "*Ah...*" she cried shakily, as she rubbed against his jeans. Jason staggered forward, bracing a hand on the wall behind her.

Gripping his thigh to her sex greedily, she stretched an arm out and held onto his neck as she leaned back, rocking his leg, hard. Her torso convulsing, she rode the thick muscles of his thigh eagerly, feeling the sparks ignite inside her. Closing her eyes, she leaned her head back, biting her lip as she came.

"*God almighty,*" Jason whispered.

As she spiraled down, she lowered her head and pinned him with blazing eyes. "Not. Enough," she said, heatedly.

Barely registering his mingled expression of astonishment, arousal, and a touch of terror, she grasped the front of his jeans, unbuttoning fluidly. "Wait, Serena…" he began, staying her hands at his fly. He flinched at the look she shot him. "The bedroom," he said, sweetly. And lifting her off the floor, he brought her lips to his as she straddled his hips.

Moving down the narrow hall, their lips worked urgently, tongues fusing as if they could not get enough. With her legs wound tight around him, she moved against him wildly, feeling his hard length rub up and down the thin, damp lace of her thong. She arched back, her arms reaching out to grab the doorjamb, stalling them from entering his bedroom as another wave rode through her. "*Oh God, Jason.*"

This time, she heard him growl as he watched her come a second time, waiting patiently as she pumped her hips to his, riding the final aching seconds of release, loving the feel of him between her thighs, his hands supporting her backside.

"I need you inside me," she moaned, agonizingly.

"Soon, my love," he soothed, and moved them inside.

Gently, he laid her out over a thick coverlet, making the skin at her back tingle delightfully. Standing over her, Jason gazed at her body, writhing on the bed. Even in her sex-driven mind, she would never forget the look on his face at that very moment. Jaws throbbing, head bent over his wide chest, expanding with every deep breath he took. A hand caressed her thigh as he stood before her, his other hand hesitating at the front of his waistband.

Before she could reach down and rip her underwear off, he moved languidly and gently moved her hand away, lightly kissing her fingertips by way of an apology. With ease, he slid her thong down her legs. Leaning his head to the side, he paused again to gaze between her legs, his hands roaming over her outer thighs, inner thighs, down her hamstrings in a slow, torturous caress.

The fiery ache building again, she squirmed on the bed. "*Jason.*"

A hint of a smirk crossed his features as he reached a hand behind her to unclasp her bra, tossing it onto the floor then went for his zipper. Avidly, she stared as he stood over her, unzipping his jeans. He watched her reaction as her eyes fell to his beautiful arousal sprung finally free.

A frenzied rush came over her. "*Now, Jason. Now!*" She gripped the cover beneath her, needing his thick long member inside her as if she'd die without it.

Reaching up, she seized his shoulders, not letting him take off his jeans completely. Hell, she didn't even let him on the bed. Bending, he rested his knees at the edge, and reached between them to guide his long length to her heated flesh. With a soft kiss to her temple, he entered her, filling her to the hilt.

"*Ah*," he moaned, bracing his hands on either side of her head, he cocked his head back as his body began moving rhythmically inside her. His expression strained, eyes closed, he uttered, "*You feel so good.*"

Serena gripped his wide shoulders, mesmerized by the sight of her Jason moving within her. It was too much. Her other hand slid low beneath his jeans, grabbing his ass, urging him to go faster. "*Don't stop, Jason. Oh God.*" She met every thrust, lifting her hips off the bed to drive him deeper, crying out as another orgasm racked her body.

"Come for me, Serena. That's it," Jason murmured, plunging faster, harder.

The turbulent sensations plaguing her were enough to drive her mad. She could not get enough of him and worry that he would stop drove her to grip him tighter and tighter. She felt almost violent.

Sliding her fingers through his hair, she yanked his head back, clenching her teeth together till they nearly cracked, trying to satiate the fierce need overpowering her body.

"*Fuck, Serena*," he whispered, his eyes falling back in his head. He slowed his pace, pulling in and out of her in slow, agonizing moves.

"*No*," she moaned.

"I won't, honey." Moving fast again, he uttered, "Tell me when."

She knew he had to finish, but the thought of him stopping was unthinkable. As a werewolf, he could keep going, but he'd need to slow down again. "One more okay. Just…just once more…then you…" Damn, she was being selfish. His feet were still on the floor.

"Anything you want, my love," he said deeply, pumping his sex roughly into her, just the way she wanted.

Love for this incredible man stung her heart. Kissing him fiercely, she whispered against his lips, "*Come with me.*"

Pulling back, Jason stared as another orgasm came over her, just as she felt his arousal peak. Right before he filled her, he pulled out and palmed his thick length, spending himself onto her belly. Gripping the sheets, her body convulsed again, coming severely at the sight of him pleasuring himself, the moans escaping his deep throat, his clenched eyes, the feel of him against her hot skin. It was the most erotic moment of her life.

****

Jason flipped the light off and stepped out of the bathroom, a cloth in hand, his jeans hanging loose around his hips. He waited for the regret to hit, but none came. The only thing on his mind was Serena. *His Serena.* As soon as the heat hit her, he made it his goal in life to service her. She'd needed him, still did, and he couldn't be more happy to do anything she asked of him.

It was as if a light bulb lit over his head the second he sensed the moon affecting her. Sure, it had terrified him a bit. He'd never seen Serena so goddamn alluring, but he'd also never witnessed a woman during the moon heat when he wasn't himself going through it. *It was fucking amazing!*

As he approached, he sensed a tad of shyness from Serena underneath the sexual tension. She reached for the towel, her face flushed. Jason's hand paused in the air. "May I?" he asked, seductively.

Blushing profusely, Serena nodded.

Jason perched on the side of the bed and slowly wiped her chest gently with the towel, sliding it carefully down and around her stomach, wiping the remnants of their lovemaking from her smooth skin.

He felt her watching his expression carefully, studying the intensity on his features. He imagined what she saw, and guessed he looked like an artist would, gazing, mesmerized by his masterpiece.

"How do you feel?" he asked, voice heady. Folding the towel, he looked her over as the hairs rose on his neck, sensing her fierce urgency.

"I can't...get enough..." she stammered, twisting the cover beneath her. "I feel so stu..."

"Don't, little one," he said automatically. Rising from the bed, he tossed the towel on the floor and kicked off his jeans to join her, pulling her to him. "You are so beautiful, and it is my honor to fulfill you this night."

A tear slipped down her cheek as she squeezed his arms, struggling with something other than her desire. Turning her face away, she closed her eyes as her thighs rubbed together. "I wanted it to be you. I cried the whole night, imagining you," she wailed.

Oh God.

Anger sliced through him, and he looked away, biting down the urge to curse. Gathering his strength, he took a deep breath. Licking his lips, he said comfortingly, "Shh…it doesn't matter, Serena. It doesn't matter." Refusing to let those horrid images fill his brain, he raised himself over her. "Look at me." When she did, his throat closed. "We're together right now. I'm here," he murmured.

Eyes moist, she nodded, bringing her hands to his chest. "Come inside me."

Jason shook his head. "Not tonight. We'll talk about it later."

Nodding, she lifted her hips to him, beginning a slow rhythm. "I need you now."

"Anything," he said, kissing her passionately, then pulled away. "I'm yours, Serena. Let me take care of you."

Sliding down her body, Jason's heart pounded in his chest, his thick hardness grazing down her leg. He knew she needed to find release fast; it rivaled his need to taste her. Pausing at her breast, he lapped at her nipple, his swollen staff twitching at the intensity of her smooth skin in his mouth. Eyes shifting, he tested the tiny bud with the tip of his tongue, gently teasing it between his teeth. The moan she gave dizzied him. "*Mmmm…you like that?*" he groaned, lifting his head to watch her heated eyes glaze over.

Wriggling underneath him, she moaned, running her hands over his shoulders. He felt like a king at that moment, gazing at the kingdom he'd just conquered.

He bent lower, rubbing himself between her thighs and whispered in her ear, "I need to taste you."

Her eyes shot open, and he heard her heart leap. "What?"

Smiling, he gave her a peck on the tip of her nose. "You'll see." Descending down her body, Jason kissed every inch of her stomach, nipping gently here and there, as he made his way between her legs.

Resting on an elbow on his side, he spread her wider, staring fervently at her folds. Her sex was swollen from his ministrations, and he gazed. Loving how she looked because of him, he distended a finger to test the engorged nub, still wet and waiting for attention. The instant he did, she came. He gazed, enthralled as her body pulsed right before his eyes. As she climaxed, he stuck his forefinger in to feel her sex clench around him, hot and wet.

"Jason!"

Moving slowly, he brought his tongue to her flesh, clasping her jewel with his mouth, sucking as she cried out again. Thrilled every time she called out his name, he continued his probing. This time, he wanted to taste her on his tongue. "Come for me, Serena," he hummed, deeply. Purring against her moist sex as his tongue explored every fold.

"*Yes, Jason! Yes!*" she cried.

The vibrations of his hum brought her over the edge, wet moisture filled his mouth, and he sighed. Pulling up on his knees, his smoldering eyes leveling hers as he came over her, bringing his lips to hers, kissing her fervidly. "*Mmmmmmm…*" he moaned, whispering naughtily in her ear.

Her mouth fell open at his words as her head kicked back into the mattress, moaning loudly as shudders ran through her.

Chuckling softly, he said, "And you say I never speak…"

Lifting her hips to his, she gasped at the contact as he deftly filled her. "Keep talking," she ordered.

And he did.

Jason whispered in her ear all night. Some words were heartwarming; others made her blush down to her very toes. When the sun came up, he bathed her gently and laid her back onto clean sheets. Gathering her in his arms, he whispered his last sentiment before sleep claimed them, "I love you, Serena. God, how I love you."

Chapter Twelve

"Jason!"

Loud banging at the door woke them out of a deep sleep. Jason sat up fast, his eyes immediately checking on Serena. Awake and on her stomach, her eyes grew wide as her heart rate spiked. He placed a calming hand at her back, rubbing gently.

Christ!

His alpha continued to pound on his door. Running a hand over his face, Jason cursed. He had to face him sooner or later, but hell, he didn't think he'd have to deal with Serena's brother while she still lay in his bed.

Wincing as he got up, Adam called out from the hallway, "Open this fucking door, J, before I bust it down!"

Jason's head swung from side to side, searching for his clothes. As he threw on his jeans and a t-shirt, he thought of what to say. How could he explain to Adam how he couldn't resist his sister? Violating a direct order from your alpha had repercussions. He wondered if there was any way they could keep Serena out of it.

"What..." she began, sitting up in bed, holding the sheet to her chest, her hair adorably ruffled around her face.

He quieted her quickly, placing a finger over his lips, then pointed to the floor, signaling for her to stay put in the room.

Worry crossed her features, but she nodded.

Exhaling roughly through his nostrils, he opened the door, shutting it firmly behind him and traipsed into the living room to let his alpha in.

Adam stormed through the door. Gripping his car keys in a tight fist, he panned the room for any evidence of his sister's presence.

Shutting the door quietly to not alert anymore of his neighbors of the drama on the top floor, he crossed his arms in front of him and waited for the onslaught.

Adam sniffed. "Is she here?" he asked menacingly, his eyes searing a deep navy blue, his face flushed. The vein on his buddy's forehead threatened to break skin.

Biting the side of his cheek, he didn't respond, couldn't even look him in the face. Ashamed, he stared at the floor.

"I can smell her all over you. I'll ask…"

"Yes."

Serena's scent was all over him and coming from the bedroom, but Adam still flinched as if he couldn't believe it. "You son of a bitch," he whispered.

Jason met his scowl. The look on Adam's face would haunt him for years. Never in his life did he think he'd betray his friend this way, in any way. Adam was his best friend, and he'd outright done the one thing Adam asked him not to do.

They stared for a moment, as the reality of the situation washed over them both. Jason never felt more uncomfortable in his entire life. He'd rather be chatting it up with a room full of vampires at a tea party than facing his girl's brother after what they'd done.

Adam's cheek twitched as the bitter sense of hurt and betrayal filled the room. "You took advantage of an innocent during the moon heat? After what she's been through? What kind of man are you?"

Shutting his eyes, he let Adam's words sink in. That's exactly what he'd done. As soon as the heat struck, he'd become a different person. Not being able to control his urges made him a sorry excuse of a man, but what could he say? She'd refused pills, and he'd taken the last of his last night, nearly overdosing.

Practically reading his mind as it was clear that Serena had come to him, Adam said, "You should have refused her. You should have sent her home. Nick was on patrol, he could have…"

Growling, Jason's eyes shot to his, shoulders hunkering down.

Leaning his head back, Adam pinned him with a glare and waited for the rumble to pass, jaws tight. "Despite how you feel, you were given a direct order."

Jason opened his mouth to speak.

"What order?" Serena asked.

Adam's head swung to the hallway where a scantly clad Serena stood in one of Jason's t-shirts, skirting the tops of her knees.

Jason groaned in his head, aching to be inside her again, and wondering if Adam would kill him here in front of her or have the decency to wait until she left.

Her brother grimaced at her appearance then asked through gritted teeth, "Are you okay?"

"I'm fine. I asked you a question, Adam. What order?" she queried again, her cheeks turning a bright red as she sensed her brother's answer.

Looking away from her, Adam spoke to the room at large. "He was given orders not to get involved with you. Moon heat or not, he disobeyed them last night."

Julia Laque

"How could you do that?" she asked, aghast. "Who do you think you are?"

"Serena…" Adam tried, but she cut him off.

"No!" she shouted, her expression fierce. She moved closer to her brother, pointing a delicate finger at his chest. "You don't run my life, Adam. I'm an adult, and I can and will do whatever I damn well please."

"We've discussed this, Serena. This is not the life…"

"Screw all your excuses, Adam. Enough is enough. I choose what is best for me. And for your information, Jason didn't disobey you. I came here unmedicated to be with him. He had two options; let me writhe in pain in front of him or mate."

Scowling, Adam growled down at her, "You should have been home."

Leaning closer to her brother she uttered, her voice shaking, "My. Life."

They glared at each other before Jason spoke up. "I love her, Adam." Sister and brother snapped out of their staring contest and looked to him. "And I'm not sorry for what I did. She's mine and I'm hers. I'll face the consequences for my defiance. Just name the date and time."

"No!" Serena shouted, her expression panicked.

His eyes soft, Jason looked to her and gently said, "It's okay, little one. It has to be done."

She rounded on her brother again. "What are going to do? I swear, if you hurt him…"

His alpha was actually at a loss for words. He looked everywhere but at them, his fierce expression had vanished, replaced with turmoil and regret. Shame

162

for what he had to do oozed out of him. Shaking his head, he uttered, "Damn you, J. *Damn you.*"

"When?" Jason asked, quietly.

"Tonight."

****

Kevin marched the last few steps in a huff. Breathless, he took out his handkerchief and dabbed at his forehead. By the names on the mailboxes downstairs, he'd found the Blacktail beta's apartment. He wondered why the Fighters of the pack lived so out in the open.

Weren't they concerned their enemies would find them? It had been so easy to procure an address it was almost laughable. What he hadn't expected, though, was the two Glocks aimed at his face the second he'd reached the top landing.

"Whoa, whoa, whoa," Kevin uttered, gruffly. Old age and his years of smoking cigars had roughened his vocal chords. Holding up his empty hands, he managed to take his eyes off the two barrels. He looked up, way up to find two of the most frightening men he'd ever met.

They stood shoulder to shoulder in t-shirts which threatened to tear at any moment under gargantuan arms. One had long brown hair, the other short and black, but they both had the same fierce amber eyes glowing bright, their teeth bared as they snarled threateningly.

Arms outstretched, the dark haired male spoke. "Stupid game you're playing, human. Two choices. One, speak real fast and get the hell out, or two..." he cocked his gun, smiling devilishly.

"Okay, fellas. No need for that. I don't want any

trouble," Kevin said, arching his shoulders back to appear bigger than he was. Years ago he stood at five feet ten inches, but now he hunched a bit. Not wanting to show these two beasts he was out of his league, he stood straighter and cleared his throat. "I'm assuming you're the beta," he said, looking at the long-haired male.

Choosing to ignore this inquiry the guy asked, "If you don't want any trouble, then why the hell are you packing, old man?"

Guess these two either smelled the metal in his pocket or he wasn't concealing it as well as he thought. "I've got a license to carry a weapon, and it's my damn right," he admonished. "Now you two boys need to lower your weapons. I told you I didn't come here for trouble. Feel my emotions, why don't you. I just came here to talk to the beta."

For a moment, the two men stared blankly at him as if he'd just given them a math problem they couldn't figure out without pencil and paper.

The dark one spoke again. "Weapons stay until you state your business. You've been lurking around too much for our liking, and now you're way too close for comfort. What do you want?"

Kevin winced slightly, feeling stupid to try and spy on a pack of werewolves. "I take it you've noticed my presence there, huh?"

They just stared back mutely, waiting for an explanation.

Linking his hands behind him in military fashion, a position he'd taken when addressing a man of superior rank, he surveyed the men. These guys weren't military, but the way they carried themselves made

Kevin feel like he was a lieutenant speaking to his captain. "I wanted to introduce myself to the Blacktail beta. I'd hoped he could arrange a meeting with you, sir." Kevin nodded his head at the dark one, assuming he was the alpha of the pack.

Both men seemed to relax some, their yellow eyes fading back to their normal color.

As he'd been looking at the alpha, he immediately noticed the brilliant hue of his blue eyes and froze, remembering just who this man was. "Adam, is it?" he asked, a small smile escaping his lips.

"There are better ways to approach us," he said, his scowl still in place.

Kevin shook himself. "I understand, but under the circumstances, I felt I had to be…cautious."

"If you're going to continue to be cryptic, these weapons are staying right where they are," Adam Perez said.

"My apologies," he said, then shot a nervous glance at his feet. "Look, I don't know how else to say this, but I need to meet your sister."

Both men tensed again, the Glocks getting closer to his face as the beta growled low.

Adam spoke through tight lips, "Not a chance in hell, grandpa. You can say what you have to say to me, then get out and stay as far away from Wilmington as possible. Got it?"

Clearing his throat, he jerked his chin up at the man. "No," he said as strongly as he could.

"You got a death wish, old man?"

Kevin blinked, his throat closing up. "Not anymore, sir. My only wish is to meet my daughter, Serena."

****

Serena stared apprehensively at the man before her. The older man stood in the middle of Jason's living room shifting anxiously from foot to foot. With etched lines near his eyes and graying hair, he looked to be in his sixties.

As they'd all picked up on the familiar Old Spice scent at the same time a few minutes ago, Jason and Adam had hustled her into the bedroom the instant the man ascended the stairs. Curious of course, she'd listened to their entire exchange out in the hall.

Serena and the man continued to stare, dumbfounded.

Daughter?

At first she thought the man must have been crazy the second she heard his announcement, but then she felt recognition wash over her brother and Jason, then pure astonishment. Shocked, she heard Adam utter the words, "Dear God," and before she knew it, they were ushering the man through the door.

Before she'd left the bedroom, she threw her coat on over Jason's shirt not wanting to greet the man so scantily clad. He didn't seem to notice how awkward she looked in a black trench coat and bare feet.

He gazed openly at her now, his misty eyes shimmering, and she couldn't help but feel the joy and agony he experienced. His emotions were doing a number on her. It was heartbreaking. The need to cry was overwhelming, but she wasn't sure whose need was greater, his or hers.

"Hi there," he said, twisting a handkerchief through trembling fingers. "My name's Kevin Goode." He coughed through a fist. Glancing nervously at Adam, he said, "It's lovely to meet you, Serena." He hesitated, repeating her name as though testing the sound, "Serena." He gave her a small smile. "You have no idea…"

"I know who you are," she said pointedly, cutting him off.

Kevin jerked slightly, "What…how could…"

"I can hear quite well," she answered, pointing distractedly toward the hall.

He let out a nervous laugh, coughing again. "Ah, right." Looking down at the floor, he hesitated, his eyes somber as she felt worry lace through him. Meeting her avid gaze again, he asked timidly, "You believe me?"

Serena couldn't speak for a long while, her eyes roaming over his every facial feature. Understanding as to why her brother and Jason had let him in hit the instant she'd laid eyes on his.

Those *eyes*. God, they were the exact same brown as hers. Even his nose was a larger image of her own and what hair wasn't covered in gray was the same shade as hers too.

She let out a sharp breath, staggering slightly. Before she could lose her balance, Jason's hand was at her elbow, holding her steady, yet still giving her space to process what was happening right now.

Shaking her head, she stuttered at the man, "How…how…"

Kevin gave her a sad smile, tilting his head. "I'd love to explain everything, my dear. But, please, just give me a moment to look at you." Gazing mesmerized, he added softly, "You have no idea how happy I am." He laid a hand over his heart. "I wish to God I knew…" Shuddering, he rubbed his eyes.

They all stood quietly taking it all in until Adam uttered the words she could not manage to speak. "How did you know our mother?"

Serena drew in a shaky breath, her heart racing as she waited for him to answer.

Kevin stuck his hand in his pocket, taking out a tattered card. Taking her eyes off his face for a second, Serena realized it was a photo. Dazedly, she took it from him when he held it out to her.

Sitting in an armchair near a window, the sun's rays cast a woman in an ethereal glow. The woman in the photo smiled sultrily at the camera with a white coffee cup in her right hand, her legs tucked underneath her. A pang shot through Serena's chest.

Her mother was absolutely stunning.

Longing for her stung her eyes, but it was the smile she wore that truly broke her heart. Never in all the years she'd spent with her mother had she ever smiled so beautifully. Even though it was just a photo, Serena could feel how relaxed her mother felt at that exact moment. Her brother realized it too as she sensed the uncontrollable sorrow run through him.

"We met through mutual friends," Kevin began, but Serena couldn't take her eyes off the photo. "Your mother had gone to Chicago for a funeral." Gesturing to Adam with a nod, he added, "Perhaps you remember. Danny and Samantha Amato's father had passed that year, and your mother came up to take care of their mother, Gina. Gina's parents and mine were old chums. We grew up together in Lincoln Square."

Hanging on to every word, Serena dragged her tear-stung eyes from her mother's photo to face her...*father*.

"I met your mother at the funeral, and we…" he smiled adoringly, remembering some secret memory. "Well…hell…she stole my heart the second I saw her."

The tears were now relentless. Serena laughed as though she too was there at their first meeting. She didn't know what overcame her, but for some oddly wonderful reason this news made her happy, happy to know her mother who'd suffered for so long with her wretched, abusive father had, for a short time, found the carefree love she deserved.

She didn't need to know the whole story to know this man had truly loved her mother and if she was not mistaken, Kevin had taken this photo of her to capture the love she'd held for him.

Kevin stared open-mouthed, "Oh wow. You've got her smile, my dear."

Serena smiled even brighter at his words. Turning to beam at her brother, he relaxed a bit, watching her carefully. "You okay, Rena?"

Nodding vigorously, she looked to Kevin. "Where have you been? I can tell you're stunned so you obviously didn't know about me. So…how did you find me?"

"I ran into Danny a couple weeks ago. The night you returned, I believe." His lips stiffened, anger boiling through him. "Told me he was on his way here. He'd been excited you were finally found and told me who you were."

Shaking his head as if he still couldn't believe it, he continued, "Your mother told me she was married and had a son. We only had those few days, but we spent every possible minute together."

He swallowed visibly before continuing, "We

fantasized about starting a family of our own, and she told me how much she'd always wanted a girl. We even talked about names, and I...I said I'd love to call our daughter Serena."

Serena's hand went to her throat, trying to control the sobs aching to burst out of her.

"The instant Danny mentioned your name I knew. I knew you had to be *mine*."

Chapter Thirteen

Ramo waltzed right into his cousin's house without a knock, wiping his boots on the mat, noisily. He knew it seriously irritated his cousin when he let himself in, which was why he did it. Besides, Eva didn't seem to mind. He assumed the lady of the house was still in bed after enduring the moon heat with her mate since she didn't come out to greet him.

Moving along the circular house with an extra spring in his step from *his* heat mate's services the previous night, he went in search of the guys. The minute he stepped into the archway of the dining room he felt a heavy sense of dread filling the room. He stopped in his tracks.

"What?" he asked seriously. "What's wrong?"

Only Nick looked his way, shaking his head.

Ramo's eyes panned to Adam standing at the window where Jason usually stood. It was *him*. Adam was the one filling the room with anxiety. His pack members' fear stemmed from him. His cousin had something to tell them, and it filled him with such trepidation he was pale in the face.

Standing with his arms crossed, shoulders tight, the Blacktail alpha bowed his head, staring dejected at the hardwood floor. "I call…" Adam cleared his throat. "I call this meeting to order…"

"Where's J?" Ramo asked, not taking a seat, but

remaining where he was by the door, confused. The alpha didn't call a meeting without his beta. And why was he being all formal? Old packs "called meetings to order," but the Blacktails didn't give a shit about propriety. What the hell was going on?

"…to address the insubordination of Jason Linus, beta to the Blacktails."

Ramo stiffened as growls reverberated around the room. The rumble was instinctive, each member reacting to Jason's betrayal *and* the fear of what might happen to him.

Jason was not just their pack member, he was their friend, no, a brother to each of them. He was stunned. "What did he do?" Ramo asked quietly, hardly recognizing his subdued tone.

Adam remained silent for a while, his jaws twitching. His brow screwed up tight, he squeezed the life out of his bicep.

Sitting up straighter in his chair, Alex asked, "What happened, boss?"

Adam chewed the inside of his mouth for a second then said, "I gave Jason orders not to get involved with my sister. Last night, he disobeyed me."

Ramo sucked in a deep breath through his teeth. *Damn*, he thought, although, he couldn't help but silently applaud the guy. It was about freaking time. He'd only been in love with the girl for-fucking-ever.

Picking up his elation for Jason, Adam's focus from the floor moved to him. "You got something to say, Ram?" his cousin bit out.

"Yeah, actually I do," he answered, snidely. Stepping closer into the room, he addressed his cousin. "Before you finish your statement, I'm telling you now,

I won't inflict pain on my pack member. I don't care what he did. We weren't aware of the order so I think we should be exempt from the punishment."

Ramo's face filled with anger as he spoke, nervous for what was coming and for his alpha's stupid order. He continued his rant. "You know how much Jason loves her, why the hell would you give such a command?"

"Serena has gone through enough…" Adam shouted, before Ramo cut in again.

"She's *fine*. Better every time she's around Jason and you know it. I'm telling you, I won't do it. I won't." He looked around at Alex and Nick for some support. "Tell me you wouldn't hurt your beta? Tell me!" he ordered.

Lifting a calming hand to Ramo, Alex addressed their alpha. "We haven't had a punishment for years. Certainly not under your reign, nor your father's. You're aware of what must be done. Are you up for this?"

"No," Adam said, immediately. "But it has to be done. It's stated in our laws. I can't let this go just because he's our friend. What will the other Blacktails think?"

"Who gives a shit what they think?" Ramo spat out. "They don't even know you gave the order."

"They will," he responded low.

"How?" Ramo asked, incredulously, his palms up.

"I documented it," was all he replied.

Ramo threw his hands in the air. "Oh come on! Seriously? Wasn't it bad enough you gave the verbal order, you had to write that shit down in our laws?"

Adam pinned him with a hard glare. "She's not

your sister so I don't expect you to understand, but you need to lower your voice and remember who you're talking to," Adam growled.

Ramo felt his alpha's force lower his head in obedience. Pissed beyond belief, he snatched the nearest vacant chair, and sat down roughly.

Alex rubbed his beard, his dark eyes contemplating. "We understand the punishment must be brought out. Have you thought of the devices…"

"*Jesus*," Ramo uttered, shaking his head.

Alex went on, "…because I agree with Ram, I won't be a part of torturing my beta with physical pain. If that is his punishment, you can count me out as well. I *will* disobey that order."

Adam started to snarl, but stopped himself, his body trembling to withhold the reprimand. When he calmed some, he spoke carefully, but in a stern voice. "All of you can feel how much I don't want to do this. Jason has accepted his punishment and as alpha and his friend, *I* will carry it out."

They stared frozen in their seats at their master's words. Despite how furious they were, they couldn't help but feel admiration for Adam. It took a strong amount of valor to carry out such a painful deed. But what would become of them? Something like this could kill their friendship, the Fighters as a whole.

Fact was, they all knew it had to happen. The sense of trepidation practically stifled the room. How would he carry it out though? Thinking of the old torture methods, Ramo cringed. Images of the iron maiden and the rack filled his mind, and he felt nauseous. The formal punishments for disobedience dated back centuries.

Adapting to the world they were born into, werewolves took on these harsh forms to sustain power throughout the pack. As time went by, they became illegal in the human world, but as few werewolves ever deceived their alpha, these penalties withstood.

"Alone?" Nick asked quietly, his face drawn.

Adam nodded. "I would not put this on your shoulders." He straightened, placing his hands on his hips. "Notices will be sent out to the rest of the pack, but I don't want a crowd so…"

A pop resounded throughout the room, startling the men. Evangeline had teleported from the upstairs to the dining room in her robe, her face fuming with anger and centered on her mate. Her icy voice came out slow and clear.

"Adam Perez, listen carefully because these are the last words you will hear from me if you lay a finger on that man." Adam's stunning mate visibly shook before them. "Need I remind you, if it weren't for Jason, I'd be decaying in the middle of the woods right now."

His alpha stared, open-mouthed at his fiancé.

"What's more, had it not been for Jason's helping hand, you, dear alpha," she stated mockingly, "would not have two healthy-born sons."

"Evangeline…" Adam started.

"Save it." Storming toward the door, she waved her hand at him, rolling her eyes."

"Goddamnit, Evangeline, you…"

Evangeline spun around and addressed Nick. "When your *true* alpha returns will you tell him I've taken the boys to my parent's house." With that, she left the room in a vampire dash.

Adam shut his eyes in defeat. "I keep forgetting

she can fucking hear everything."

This was met with two heavy pounding thumps from the upstairs, letting them know she heard that too.

They watched Adam flinch at his mate's fury. Battling with himself, they felt his urge to console Evangeline and the self-loathing for what he had to do to their friend tearing him apart.

Ramo couldn't be a part of it, but he was beginning to feel guilty letting his cousin bear this weight on his own. He addressed him evenly. "How Adam?"

Straightening, Adam walked toward the door, faltered on his feet as if he'd had one too many, and stilled. Then said gravely, "The pillory."

****

Jason pulled Serena in tighter, bringing her closer to his side. Feeling her arm close around his torso, he shut his eyes, basking in the afterglow of the moon heat. Sure it had been tainted with Adam's visit, then jerked awake by Kevin Goode's announcement, but here she was, with him. Sensing her worry for him didn't sit well of course. He wished she wouldn't fret so much about the order or his looming punishment. He'd endure a hundred beat downs if it meant an eternity with her.

"Please stop worrying, Serena. It'll be fine, I promise."

Her voice vibrating against his chest, she said quietly, "You don't know that."

"It's no big deal. You're getting yourself worked up for nothing. It'll be over and done with before you know it."

Her emotions were going haywire. How much would his love have to endure? She'd been kidnaped, tortured, pregnant, miscarried, and now that she'd given herself to him, Serena would have to lie in wait while he paid the price for their union and to top it off, a father she never knew she had popped into her life to stir the pot.

Jesus!

Serena and Kevin had made arrangements to meet the following afternoon for lunch to get better acquainted. Despite the shock, he knew Serena was looking forward to getting to know him. Jason had to admit, Kevin was a standup guy and he and Adam approved of their meeting as long as one of the Fighters accompanied her at a safe distance. They really didn't expect the guy to harm Serena, but it was all a bit much for her, and he and Adam wanted to make sure she didn't get too overwhelmed.

Lifting her head, Serena rested her chin on his chest and regarded him. Melting in her beautiful brown eyes, he ran his fingers through her hair, repeating the gentle glides as goose bumps rose all over her.

"How are you feeling?" he asked, smoothly.

Her cheeks flushed adorably, knowing he referred to their vigorous "workout" the previous night. "I feel amazing."

Smiling, he licked his lips, completely enamored with her as he continued his caresses.

"*You're* amazing," she added.

Now it was his turn to blush.

Tilting her head, she asked hesitantly, "Why didn't you stay inside me? Why did you…you know…"

He looked away, taking a deep breath, knowing they had to discuss this at some point in time. "I know you don't want to talk about it, but after what you've been through…it just didn't seem right. What if I got you pregnant?" Jason heard her heart rate increase as joy washed over her, and he froze, gazing admiringly at her.

"You'd make me the happiest woman in the world," she said, warmly.

Chest expanding, he brought her to his lips, molding them to his in a searing kiss, his head swimming from her delicious scent. The idea of having a family with Serena was a dream he dared not think of before. Now, well…*could it possibly happen for them?*

Pulling back, she smiled. "I understand why you felt the need to be cautious, but it's not the moon heat now," she said, suggestively.

A low growl escaped him as he gripped her waist, bringing her atop him in an effortless move. Serena sat straddling his waist, her hair draped around her shoulders as she gazed down at him with wide eyes. "You look beautiful up there," he said, biting his bottom lip.

Giggling, she brought her hands to his chest and his skin tingled at her touch. "I don't know what to do," she said, shyly, wriggling a bit over him.

"*Ah, Serena.* You're already doing it."

She gasped as his thick length grew under her, nudging against her warm sex.

"See?" he teased. In a swift move, he lifted his t-shirt over her head and tossed it to the floor. "Wow," he whispered. Seeing her this way, so delectably shy, sexy, and naked over him was going to give him a heart attack. His toes curled, his leg muscles tightening up as his breathing changed. Running the back of his knuckles over a nipple, she arched back slightly, sighing. "I'm not going to go as rough as I did last night. You're in charge."

With her lips slightly parted, she gazed thoughtfully for a spell before lifting her hips. Her hand reached down between her legs as she moved to clasp his arousal.

Hissing, he grabbed her thighs, squeezing them softly. He nearly closed his eyes, but he wanted to watch her every move. God, the feel of her sweet hand around him drove him wild.

Serena brought the tip of his length to her entrance and sat down right on him. Damn, she was so tight. "*Oh,*" she moaned, and began to move, her hips rocking slowly back and forth, her stomach undulating in waves. He didn't know whether to stare at her heaving breasts or her belly, rolling beautifully before him.

Meeting every aching thrust, Jason's hands glided over her hips, up her sides… He couldn't resist. Sitting up, he brought his mouth over her breast, laving at the hardened bud that tasted so damn good. Lying back against the pillows he watched her progress, a surge of love and possession running through him as his gorgeous girl had her way with him.

Her movements grew stronger and stronger, yet she maintained her unhurried pace, her rhythm smooth and oh so wonderful. Serena's head fell back, and he stared transfixed at her swollen lips and the sweet moan she uttered with every stroke. "*God, you're so deep,*" she whispered, breathlessly.

Smirking in spite of himself, Jason felt the shudders begin as she climaxed, her body trembling as he felt her throb around him. Gripping her bottom tight, he bit down hard, finding his own release. Only this time, he stayed deep inside her, filling her up with his hot seed. His head jerked back at the intensity of riding out his orgasm still warm and enveloped in her sweet body. *"Oh, God, Serena…"* he sighed.

The moment he stilled, she fell to his chest, completely spent. Soft breaths tickled his neck as she regained her strength. He held her to him, loving that they were still connected.

"Are you okay," he asked, rubbing her back.

Nodding, she uttered, meekly, "Yes." Then, "I love you, Jason."

Chest constricting, he responded in kind. "I love you."

Several blissful seconds later, her heavy pants turned to slow rhythmic breaths as she drifted off to sleep. He let her stay on top of him, loving the feel of her warm body draped against his, hoping and praying she would sleep the rest of the evening and into the night, blissfully unaware of his impending torture.

Chapter Fourteen

The darkening sky hovered over Jason as he made his way through the Midewin woods. The sound of his footsteps disturbed the quiet as though he were an intruder, an outcast. Usually the forest seemed to greet him like an old friend coming home after a long absence, but all those cozy feelings had somehow dissipated. She was now cold, distant, as if every tree and brush wanted to punish him too.

He'd be lying if he said he wasn't a bit nervous, but every time he thought of what he did, he almost chuckled. Hell, yeah, he'd do it again. Whatever was coming was so worth it. Serena still lay in his bed, exhausted from their lovemaking.

The love of his life in *his* bed.

Bring on the pain.

Entering a small clearing, Jason saw Adam waiting, tall and solemn amidst the towering dreary trees, which seemed to stare ominously at him. They were both barefoot and shirtless since in a short time the moon would turn them into wolves for the rest of the night. He'd been looking at his best friend's somber face for so long when he suddenly noticed what was behind him.

"Are you kidding me?" Jason asked, aghast.

Adam moved aside, his head hung low to reveal a wooden apparatus. The pillory consisted of a thick

Julia Laque

stake onto which two parallel wooden boards clasped together with holes for the head and arms. Once a person was locked in the holes, there was no way to escape. It was meant to humiliate, just really uncomfortable, not painful.

Of all the torture devices, his alpha chose the one that was least harmful. He didn't know whether to be grateful or offended. He stared at Adam, forcing him to meet his eyes. "Tell me you're going to kick my ass first before putting me in there?"

Brow tight, Adam shook his head. Fierce tension and remorse radiated from his friend. "This is it."

"No, it's not. Get something else," Jason demanded.

They stood quietly for a moment, glaring at each other. He didn't want to, but he started to feel guilty for putting his friend in this position and understanding hit. Of course his friend wouldn't want him to suffer too much, but he still had to carry out the penalty.

"Fine then. Where's the crowd though?" The pillory was used back in the day to humiliate criminals in a town square. "Who's going to throw stones and veggies at me if there isn't anyone around?" he asked sardonically.

Looking away, Adam said low, "The pack isn't allowed in this area tonight." He cleared his throat then hesitated. "J, I'm sorry…"

"Don't Adam. I should be the one apologizing. I knew how you felt, and I went against your wishes. I'm truly sorry for that. But you know how much I love her. I can't fight it anymore. She's a part of me, and I won't live without her." His chest tightened at his own words.

Staring sadly, Adam found his voice. "I know, J.

182

That's why I'm sorry. I should have never given the order. I'll regret it for the rest of my days, but when Serena came back...I panicked. I didn't think anyone would be able to take care of her as well as I can. I was foolish."

Jason only nodded.

Adam seemed to struggle with himself, his eyes everywhere but on him.

Before his friend lost it, Jason said, "Let's get this over with." He strode to the pillory, stepping on the tiny platform and placed his wrists and neck on the bottom board. "Come on, bro, hook me up."

Adam's knee bounced nervously before he turned to him. Sniffing loudly, he reached up to the top board and brought it down over his head and wrists.

At this close angle, Jason could see the veins throbbing on the side of his alpha's face, the tiny bead of sweat at his temple, could hear the raging of his heart. "Relax, Adam," he said, soft and calmly. "I'd walk through fire for her. This..." He pointed at himself, indicating the boards around him. "...is nothing."

Eyes secured on fastening the lock, Adam murmured, "You're going to phase, J." His jaw twitched. "These gaps are gonna get tight on you. If you..."

"Don't even say it! I swear to God, if you come near me tonight, Adam..."

Raising a calming hand, he said, "All right," then met his eyes when he finished locking him in. "I'm not going anywhere though. I'm here with you. All night."

Shit! He prayed his buddy didn't pick up on his sappy emotions now. Trying to swallow past the lump in his throat, he muttered. "Okay."

The sky blackened over them as Adam backed away, his bloodshot eyes never leaving him. He wanted to tell him to stop being so dramatic. He was fine. In fact, he felt stupid really. With his head angling forward, his long hair tickled his cheeks, and the only thing painful at the moment was the kink in his neck from bending this way. What he really should be doing is bitching out his friend for giving him such a pussy punishment.

Off in the distance he could just make out footsteps on the forest floor. Someone was running this way. Adam jerked his head to the east, hackles raised. He hoped it was a human being nosey or else there would be another wolf joining him in his "torture."

As their visitor grew closer, he sniffed the air, a familiar scent wafting around him.

Damn it!

From the corner of his eye he watched Serena skid to halt between two oaks on his right, her hand covering her mouth. Shutting his eyes, real humiliation flooded him. He'd rather be flogged than have his girl see him this way.

"You can't be here, Serena," Adam ordered.

Without sparing her brother a glance, Serena walked determinedly toward him. "I'm not going anywhere, Adam, so either get another one of these contraptions for me or shut up."

The fight had left his buddy. With his shoulder's slumped, Adam turned, giving them his back and a little privacy.

When Serena's precious hand slipped into his, he opened his eyes. Giving her a small smile, he said,

"What are you doing up, little one?" In the past, Serena would occasionally run with the pack during the full moon, but often times, she'd sleep right through it.

Her other hand gripped his, her eyes roaming around the pillory. "Does it hurt?" she asked, her expression sad, yet somehow resigned as if she understood how painful this was for all of them and didn't want to start any unnecessary arguing with him or her brother.

He snorted. "No, my love." He jerked awkwardly when he tried to move closer to her. Now this was torture. Not being able to hold her when she was so close was agony. "The only first aid I'll need tomorrow is a massage."

Her face fell even more. "You're trying to make me laugh."

Smirking, he said, "Well, now my pride hurts. I can't even make my future wife laugh?"

Wide brown eyes met his. "What did you say?"

Gripping her hands tightly in his, he said, "This isn't how I pictured it, but now is as good a time as any." Flushing, he thought of the times he'd imagined bending on one knee professing his love for her with a diamond in hand.

He didn't know why he'd blurted it out this way, but he'd wasted enough time trying to stay away from her. Now that they were together, he didn't want to waste a single moment. "Will you?" he asked, gently, peeking up at her in his crouched position. "Will you make me the happiest man alive and be my wife?"

In answer, her mouth claimed his in a fierce kiss. As she pulled away, she ran her fingers through his hair, brushing the strands away from his face. "You know I will," she said, sweetly.

Melting underneath her touch, he felt the shudders run through his body and knew he was about to phase. Their eyes shifted in unison, Serena's burning a bright gold as she stepped back. "You should go," he said.

Shaking her head, she said, "I'm not leaving you."

He tensed. Adam was right. The minute he changed he wasn't going to fit in these holes. If he really wanted to, he could try and break free, but there was no way he was going to do it. He'd take the pain, but he didn't want her to see him struggle. "Please, Serena. Go run."

His body stretched, his neck contorting within the boards as the wolf fought to be released. Serena stripped down before him, and he watched with searing eyes as his girl phased into a magnificent wolf girl, rising up in the air with grace and fluidity. The hairs over her skin sprouted and grew, quickly and elegantly as if she'd rehearsed how to phase with dignity over the years. Covered in brown fur, she was still small for their kind, but magnificent, nonetheless.

As his wrists snapped, engorging between the boards, he felt the splinters at his neck and the wretched choking at his throat. Growling, he fought with his wolf side to stay still, but it was useless. His body could only thrash under the pain and resistance. The wood squeezed the hell out of him, piercing through the fur, right down to his skin.

Standing before him, he felt Serena's need to free him, but he stayed her with a sharp glance. Grunting, he begged her to run away from him.

Whining, she crouched on all fours and kicked up the dirt at her feet, reluctant to leave.

Just then, the hushed night was broken by a series of howls. They froze, ears pricked, as they listened to first one, then two, no four. *Oh wow*, he heard eight Weres howling in the night. They were joined by several more, until the woods was filled with the earsplitting song of his pack's call.

His eyes landed on his alpha far off at the edge of the clearing, his wolf form standing just beneath the full moon. He turned this way and that, listening to the call of the Blacktails. It was howl of respect, of admiration for Jason's willingness to defy his master for the love of his life. His heart slammed in his chest, not for the pain, but for his pack's support.

Serena carefully moved toward him, nudging her snout gently over his, circling him in a sweet caress. Despite the pain, he felt her calming him, soothing. Then, with pure devotion in her heart, she ran to meet her pack and join them in their arduous salute to him.

When she was out of sight, he turned to Adam, who stared through yellow focused eyes. And miraculously, the Blacktail alpha crouched low to the ground, his front claws digging in the earth, bent his head back and howled at the moon for his beta, his friend.

With renewed strength, Jason stilled, welcoming the pain, knowing without a doubt he'd endure anything for not just Serena, but for every one of the Blacktails.

****

Jason opened his eyes to a brightening sky. Somehow, when his body could no longer take the choking and crushing sensation, he'd slipped into a kind of an wakeful sleep. As exhausted as he was, he couldn't quite knock out under those conditions. Back in human form, he was now just uncomfortable. He'd been joking about the massage, but he could really use one right about now. Every muscle in his body ached, and he was drenched in sweat.

He jerked when Adam came around him and unlocked the boards. His friend looked like he felt. The dark circles under his eyes matched the bruising around Jason's wrists. In a scratchy voice, he asked, "Are you okay?"

Standing up straight, he heard the cracks in his neck and back and moaned. It was difficult to stand, let alone keep his eyes open, but he smiled lazily at his alpha. "I'm good."

Evangeline teleported right next to them, Serena running into the clearing at the same time, a white towel wrapped around her. Evangeline handed him a bottle of water, her worried eyes looking him over.

Stepping off the platform, he reached for the towel she held out for him and wrapped it around his waist. "No, Eva," he said, sternly.

"I didn't say anything," she said, innocently.

Jason took a swig from the bottle then capped it. "I know what you want to do, and you can forget it. I'll heal in no time."

Biting her bottom lip she looked to her sullen mate. How much this night had affected him was written all over Adam's face, and she was wise to let her anger drop. Instead, Evangeline quietly stepped to him and held his hand in hers.

"Will you guys lighten up? I feel like I'm at my own funeral," he said, reaching for Serena and holding her tight to his side. He kissed the top of her head and tried to hide his unsteady gait as he led her through the trees and to the street.

Jason insisted on taking Serena home to her place since she had no clothes at his apartment aside from the lovely black number she'd surprised him with and her coat. As he'd left his truck at home, Adam drove them in his SUV.

Sitting in the back, Serena fussed with his cuts around his neck and wrists. He should've told her to stop, that he could take a few gashes here and there, but hell if he didn't love the attention. Resting his head back, he smiled lazily at the little crease in her forehead.

"Stop it," she scolded, when he playfully bit her hand.

He chuckled. "You're fussing for nothing. I'll be healed by tonight.

"But you're hurting now."

"I'm not. Really," he murmured seductively, pulling her closer into his side.

She glanced nervously at the back of her brother's head. Adam hadn't said a word since leaving the woods. He suspected his friend still struggled with the fact his beta and his sister were together, but Jason was through holding back. His soon-to-be wife and mate was in his arms, and there wasn't anything anyone could do about it.

I love you, he mouthed to her.

Smiling, she responded in kind, all worry for the moment abated as she thrilled at his words.

****

Leonardo Russo's hand burned excruciatingly when, like an idiot, he'd used it to bang on the hotel room door. Cursing under his breath, he lifted the collar of his leather jacket to cover the marks and bruises on his skin as he scanned the hall he stood in. Down at the end, a mirror hung a bit lopsided and he caught his reflection. *Damn.*

The man looking back at him looked nothing like the arrogant boy who'd been the Blue Demons' best shooting guard at DePaul University on his way to begin his career in the corporate world. With exotic good looks and charm even his female professors couldn't resist, he'd landed the hottest girl on campus and in a blink of an eye...it was gone. Just like that.

Cassandra had found him and turned his world upside down, introducing him to a whole new one. He'll admit, the orgies were pretty freaking amazing, but the past few weeks were pissing him off. He didn't know how much humiliation he could take.

At first, being at the mercy of Cassandra and her sisters was a dream come true. Sure he'd been tortured a bit. It was the torture that excited him, but now? Things had certainly taken a turn for the worse. Every time he laid eyes on Cassandra now, the urge to wrap his hands around her throat was way too appealing.

He looked away from his reflection. The pale, thinned out man looking back at him was not the Leo he used to be. What had become of him? Why was he still under her spell? He knew he must be because otherwise he wouldn't be doing what he was doing right now.

The power Cassandra had over him was so insurmountable that the thought of leaving this hotel and driving as far away from the witch as possible gave him a blinding headache. No matter what he thought, no matter how he felt, he couldn't leave her. Never would. He would die her slave, and the thought sickened him.

The door opened, and an old man answered rubbing his eyes in a white undershirt and flannel pajama pants. Speaking in a gruff voice having been woken up by Leo's knocking, he said, "Can I help you, son?"

Leo's hand shot out, seizing him around the neck. Kevin Goode shouted in pain, gripping Leo's hand, trying to fight him off. "Why, yes you can," Leo responded, uttering the incantation rapidly under his breath. "Ah ah ah…Look at me, pops. That's it." Taking his hold off the man's neck, he spoke fast. "Keep your eyes on me." He knew the spell Cassandra had given him would work better on humans than it did with the Weres.

"Looks like we have someone in common. How do you know Serena Perez and what do you want with her?" Leo had been monitoring the Blacktail pack for weeks. Wasn't easy, so he'd had to enchant a few pack friends into giving him details. During his surveillance he'd spotted the old man lurking around the library she worked in, then again around her house. He thought the creep might be able to help him.

His expression glazed, Kevin responded automatically. "I'm her father. I want to get to know her."

Leo's brows shot up. *No shit.* He wondered if Cassandra knew they were making Nightwalkers with a half-breed's blood. "Are you going to see her again?" he asked, already planning as he waited for a response. This might be easier than they'd hoped.

"Yes. We're going to have lunch today."

Smiling, Leo thought of the reward he'd receive for bringing back the werewolf. There was only the tiniest sense of remorse, but the spell he was under washed it away. With a gleam in his eyes, he asked, "Where?"

****

Serena's tongue glided over Jason's skin in gentle laps as she attempted to heal the already mending wounds scattered about his neck. Tasting his hot skin was a feeling so new to her it didn't seem real. She'd never healed someone before, never tasted a man the way she did now, but knowing it was Jason beneath her sent an incredible sense of pleasure straight to her belly.

She felt the moment he awoke, his body tensing slightly, then stirring, heating up under her. The smell of his arousal wafted into her senses awakening her own body in ways only he could induce.

"Don't stop," he murmured low.

Peeking up at him, she saw his closed lids, his head tilted to the side giving her a lovely view of his sexy jaw. Continuing her ministrations with a bit more vigor, Serena ran her tongue down the length of his shoulder, journeying along his arm to his swollen wrist. She lapped at the faint scrapes, her own eyes lowering, thrilled at the power she felt.

With a swipe of his arm, Jason tossed the sheet off his hips. Pausing, Serena watched in amazement as his golden member swelled before her. Growing tall and thick, the tip soft and smooth came to rest on his stomach. "Oh," she uttered, completely enthralled.

Letting out a light laugh, he asked, "Did I shock you, little one?"

Her stomach tightened at the sound of his voice. He could so easily undo her with the simplest of words.

"Just a bit." Looking up at him, she saw him smirking seductively at her. "Feeling better?"

"Hell yeah." Moving over her, he flipped her onto her belly, his own mouth now exploring her skin at her back.

"Ah Jason, no. I have to go soon," she pleaded, not really wanting him to stop in the slightest. She felt his apprehension, but he didn't move away, his soft kisses moving upward to the base of her neck.

"Where do you think you're going?" he moaned, slowly rubbing his thick length at the juncture of her thighs, his silken lips sending shivers down her spine.

Her mind so far from her lunch date, she murmured, "Mmmm?"

"That's what I thought," he answered. His hand curved around her waist, sliding between her stomach and the mattress, traveling down to cup her sex. "You started this. You're going to finish it."

Serena pressed her cheek further into the pillow, her eyelids lowering at the feel of his body against her. She felt his hard shaft poking at her back.

Jason straddled her hips. "Close your legs," he demanded.

She complied, not sure what he was going to do. If she wasn't mistaken, her legs would have to be open to accept him inside her.

Lifting his hips slightly, he squeezed his manhood between her upper thighs and backside, impaling her from behind when he found her hot entrance.

"Oh God, Jason," she moaned, her cries slightly muffled from the pillow. Wet with need, he fit perfectly, filling her completely. His hand at her sex moved, his fingers finding her sensitive nub, rubbing

enticingly as he slid in and out of her.

"Do you like that, my love?" he whispered in her ear.

Unable to speak, she nodded, her moans growing louder the closer she got to her release.

"You feel so good this way, honey. Fuck, Serena." His fingers circled her moist pearl faster, just the way she wanted. "Mmmm...Tell me you love me. Tell me, so I can come inside you."

Eyes closed, she smiled, loving how her mute lover became so talkative in the bedroom. "I love you, Jason. *Ah...Come with me*," she moaned, breathlessly, unable to control the spasm running through her. Jerking beneath him, Serena rode the fiery sparks coursing through her body as Jason breathed heavily in her ear, pumping his seed into her.

An hour later, they were dressed and saying their goodbyes at her door. Standing on the porch, Jason held her in his arms, looking down at her as he lectured her on being aware of her surroundings and going straight home after her lunch with Kevin.

"I'll be fine, Jason. Besides, Ram will be right outside the restaurant."

He still looked worried as he regarded her. "I'd go with you, but I need to meet with this contractor. I've been putting him off for too long."

She wondered how behind he'd gotten on his work because of her and felt slightly guilty.

Shaking his head at her, he said, "Don't you dare feel bad. Business is fine, and you're more important." His phone vibrated in his pocket and he rolled his eyes.

Pulling back, he slipped his hand in his jean pocket and took out his phone. His brow furrowed the instant he read the text message.

"I've got to go," he stated firmly.

She flinched.

"I'm sorry, honey," he kissed her quickly on the lips and let her go.

"Is everything all right?" she asked, suspiciously.

He took one step down the stairs, then hesitated, looking back at her. With an odd look on his face he said, "Text me Kevin's number. I'm not sure Ramo's gonna be able to go with you."

"Okay," she said, taking out her phone, her eyes leveled on his face. "Jason, is everything…"

"It's fine. Just don't go anywhere else. Meet Kevin and go straight home. Set the alarms as soon as you're back." With that, he reached forward to give her one last kiss, then raced down the stairs to his pickup, peeling off down the street.

Serena watched him go, wondering if life with the beta would always be filled with exquisite joy and constant fear.

Chapter Fifteen

Jason tossed his jacket on the seat as he alighted the pickup, leaving it in case he needed to phase. The meeting with the contractor all but forgotten when he'd received the text from Alex. *Humans spotted a jackal by Milken Lake. Phasing and headin over with Nick.* Adam had responded in the thread. *All hands on deck. ETA 15 min.*

Jason was the last to arrive, choosing to position himself on the west bank of the lake as his pack members lurked along the perimeter on the north, east, and south. Scanning the area, he made out Nick's wolf form just across the lake, moving slowly among the dense trees.

As Milken Lake was only about twenty-two acres, there wasn't much surrounding land to cover. Peering a moment into its depths, Jason noticed how shallow it was. Staying in his human form for the time being, he made his way along the still water, his senses on high alert.

They all patrolled for a while, zigzagging from the edge of the lake and out. Jason trotted back toward the water after going a hundred yards out for the fourth time, spotting Adam doing the same in his wolf form on the south bank.

Ramo made his way toward him from the north in human form, shirtless and barefoot. "Ran into the humans. A bunch of teenage kids high as shit said they saw the jackal on the northeast corner of the lake." He pointed in the direction across the water where the trees thickened.

"One of them ran to his car and drove off. They told me it was about the size of a jaguar, huge and long. Scared the crap out of them. The boy who ran called his dad. Dad just happened to be on our payroll. Called headquarters, and Alex picked up." Ramo answered his unspoken question, giving him a sidelong glance. "Adam and Eva were in the woods…making up."

Jason was happy to hear his friend and Evangeline weren't fighting over his punishment, but this lake was way too close to home. "Any sign of it?"

Ramo shook his head peering around, his forehead furrowed. "Nada. Just an odd stench where the kids saw it."

"Could they have been mistaken?" Jason asked, his eyes still searching the surrounding area as well.

Ramo shrugged. "Who knows? They're stoned enough, but what are the chances they'd hallucinate the very creature that's trying to kill us?"

Jason didn't know what to think of it. They stood silently for a moment in the afternoon quiet. A few nearby ducks quacked, the echo dying in the cool breeze. Jason cast his eyes across the lake, his gaze panned from Nick to Alex to Adam, a knot forming in his stomach. The hushed sound around the lake was unnerving. He had a sinking feeling about this whole situation. Something was off. The hairs at his nape stood on end. He felt as though a storm was coming; only the sky was clear blue.

"What?" Ramo asked, picking up on his anxiety.

All he could do was shake his head, the sinking feeling in his gut building. His pack members felt it too. Nick howled at him, wondering what was wrong. Adam joined in, their message clear: The area seems secure. Why are you worrying?

"No," Jason uttered.

"What J?" Ramo asked again, louder.

His body hummed now with fear as reality hit. *This* area was secured, but Wilmington wasn't.

In their haste to find the jackal, the Fighters had left their town defenseless. The Chicago crew was back in the city. Fear of their species' new enemy had brought the five remaining Fighters to a secluded lake, miles outside of Wilmington.

"Fuck," he heard Ramo utter, as they all understood.

There'd been no sign of the jackal aside from the smell because it was a goddamn decoy.

"Move out," Jason shouted, as he raced back to the pickup, a pain stabbing through his heart, hoping to God the horrible thoughts running through his head weren't true.

****

Kevin held the door for Serena as they stepped out of the diner into the cool fall afternoon. Smiling nervously, she wrung her hands, her mind filled with images of her mother and Kevin falling in love and carrying on an affair for roughly two weeks. She'd outright chided Kevin for preying on a married woman, but she was delighted her mother found some semblance of happiness even though it had been short-lived.

"Thank you so much for meeting me today," Kevin

said, pausing next to her car.

"Of course. How long will you be in town?" she asked, anxiety overcoming her at the thought of him leaving. She was just getting to know him.

Smiling hopefully at her, he said, "For as long as you'll have me, my dear."

Without thinking, Serena swung her arms around him, whispering in his ear, "A long, long while then."

Kevin chuckled as they pulled apart and she noticed his eyes glimmered with unshed tears.

Holding his hand in hers, she said, "Come to the library tomorrow afternoon. I'll show you what I do."

"I'd like that. Thank you, Serena."

He stepped around to open the door for her as a black van came peeling down the street, the engine roaring noisily disrupting their peaceful afternoon. They both peered at the speeding vehicle, wondering if it would slow down at the stoplight. Surprised, it came to an abrupt stop right next to them, the wide hood of the van lurching forward as the driver slammed on the brakes.

Just as the side door slid open, Serena's vision was cut off as someone grabbed her from behind. A dark cloth covered her entire face as a commotion grew around her. The feel of string tightened around her throat at the same instant she heard Kevin shout, then a loud thump, and someone hit the ground.

Kevin's shouts were no longer audible as she was hurled into someone's arms and knocked back onto some sort of metal, her teeth chattering on impact. The wind was knocked out of her, and she fought for breath, coughing into the suffocating hood. Head swimming dizzily, her body began to tremble, her limbs contorting. *Please phase, please phase. Hurry!*

A familiar pain shot through her arm, and real panic set in as she screamed, her body flailing wildly in the confined space they'd flung her in. She felt her body, which had begun to grow, shrink back down. The few seconds of power she'd felt gone as the serum began coursing through her veins.

She fell to her knees, bringing her captor down with her. "No, no, no!" she screamed, her hands hitting every part of Leo she could manage. She'd recognize his filthy stench anywhere. "Please, please, let me go. Don't take me back there! Please!" she cried desperately, aware now she was in the back of the van and it had begun to move again.

He gripped her wrists, and shook her hard. "Don't bother fighting. It'll be worse if you do."

Leo's snide voice sounded different to her ears. His usual cool and self-assured tenor was now low and subdued, but she didn't care what he said. She'd been too weak to fight the last time, but not now. There was too much to fight for…Jason, Adam, her nephews. She'd just found her real father. *God no!* She had to fight!

"Don't do this, Leo, please," she begged, struggling blindly under his hold. "The Fighters are always on patrol. They're watching me. When the alpha and beta find you, they will kill you," she added forcefully, saying anything that'll get to him, yet knowing her words were very true.

"Nah," he said, his voice tired and groggy. "Showed some kid one of the Nightwalkers…one of yours in fact…Enchanted him to call his dad and low and behold, it worked. Dad works for your big bro and called headquarters. Your Fighters aren't around, sweetheart."

Cold dread slipped down her spine. The text message Jason had received must have lured him far from the area of the diner. Oh God. A Nightwalker? Were the Fighters able to kill it? She prayed no one was hurt. Standing, she lurched at him. "You bastard!" she uttered through gritted teeth, her head thrashing as she tried futilely to get the cloth off her head.

As the van sped down the road, she continued to punch and kick, her hands and wrists throbbing from the impact. Leo tried in vain to keep her off, until she managed to land a swift kick right between the legs. His curse was the last thing she heard before a heavy object hit the side of her head, knocking her out cold.

****

"She can't be far, J. We'll find her," Nick's calm tone barely registered. "The whole pack is out looking for her. There's bound to be…"

Jason strode into the round house and into the dining room completely numb with Nick on his heels. Nick went on, but he couldn't listen to his positive words. He couldn't hear anything but Serena's voice telling him she loved him earlier today.

They were not the last to arrive at headquarters. Aside from Ramo, the entire pack, including the Chicago crew was crammed in the room looking the worse for wear. Most of them half dressed as they'd only just phased back after searching for several hours.

When they'd reached the diner, they'd found an unconscious Kevin on the ground, a deep gash along the side of his head.

The instant Jason saw Serena's father, but no sign

of his girl, his heart plummeted. He'd gotten out of the car, faltered, falling back against the door of the truck, dizzied with grief. *Not again. Not again*, he'd chanted in his head. His body humming with shock, his hand automatically rubbed the ache in his chest as he tried to breathe through the lump in his throat.

The Fighters had paused for a moment, not knowing whether to go to Kevin or Jason. His body quivering with anguish, he balled his fist in a blood-curdling grip and smashed the driver's side windshield of his truck. "Noooooooo!" His agony ripping through the pack. His very skin had felt as though it would burst into flames, and the longer they'd searched, the more turbulent he became.

The instant Kevin came to, they'd drilled him for information before splitting up to search for Serena. Her scent had been cut off near the street where Kevin said a black van had stopped. They could only assume the inside of the van was enchanted to cover her scent so they couldn't follow.

Adam had not only called the Chicago Fighters, but in his desperation, he'd called out to the rest of the Blacktail pack, ordering them to phase. The mayor of Wilmington was already blowing up headquarters at the mass of werewolves running around town in search of Serena.

Even now, the civilian pack members continued to search for her, their loyalty to their alpha and their admiration for Jason's famed love for Adam's sister driving them on. Jason would still be with them had he not been called to headquarters.

He pinned Adam with a glare the instant he entered, shirtless and barefoot, perspiration running down his chest. Everyone tensed the instant they saw him.

Adam stood next to the table, his t-shirt flung over his shoulder. Raising a calming hand he said, "We'll be back out there in a minute. It only makes sense to discuss tactics."

Jason didn't say a word. He was afraid to even speak, barely having the energy to breathe. With his chest heaving rapidly, he looked to Alex who was typing away on a laptop. He didn't need to ask his question aloud. The Fighter knew what Jason wanted.

"I'm running schematics from the place you found Serena. From there we can fan out and continue searching. I'm also looking at every building around the area where she might have been housed the last time." They'd done this when Serena returned, but with no leads. The only chance they had was to search the area again and hope the witches unknowingly left some clue.

Jason's stomach knotted for the umpteenth time as he thought of the place Serena had described. His chest ached, a stabbing pain piercing his heart. They needed to hurry up. He couldn't stand here much longer.

Ramo finally joined them, strolling in with car keys in hand. He'd gone back to speak to the kid who'd seen the jackal. They all looked to him expectantly. Shaking his head, he said in a serious tone, completely out of character for the guy who treated life as if it were a big joke. "The boy doesn't remember a thing but the jackal. He described it to me, and it looks like we're dealing with something bigger than we thought. It's not the size of a regular jackal. These Nightwalkers are huge."

Everyone in the room tensed even more, on top of losing Serena again, they had to watch out for a species completely unfamiliar to them.

"I searched the entire area and came up empty," Ramo finished.

Alex sat back roughly in his chair, dropping his hands in his lap as though the Internet was letting him down. "Jason, there's got to be something Serena mentioned, something she didn't tell Eva, but to you in confidence."

He glared at Alex, thinking of the witch's torture, something he knew Serena would not want him to share with the rest of them, but he knew the Alex was just looking for any helpful information.

Evangeline entered the room with Kevin at her side, a thick bandage over his right temple. She looked to him, and he felt her thinking long and hard about everything Serena told them, worry plastered on her face.

Finding his voice, he uttered, "Eva described the ballroom and the hallway and everything else. I can't think of anything you don't already know."

Danny Amato sat in a chair near the window, dressed as if he'd just gotten off work in shirtsleeves and slacks with his duty belt, badge, and vest strewn across the table in front of him. "Walk us through her escape," he said, looking to both Jason and Evangeline. "I know it's rough, but we need to hear everything again."

Thankfully, Evangeline started retelling them how Serena and Benjamin began sucking out the serum when they were injected...Ben phasing and attacking a male witch and getting him to open Serena's cell. He knew it was helpful to go over it again, but he couldn't handle the thought of Serena going through all of it on her own.

He kept picturing her scared and hurt trying to escape, wondering if she'd be caught or not and his stomach turned. And now she was back there. Pain sliced through his skull just thinking of what they might be doing to her.

"Serena said Benjamin found a tunnel which led outside, but it was only big enough for a human not a werewolf so she went ahead of him," Evangeline was saying uneasily. He could feel her apprehension, wondering if she was remembering correctly.

Alex asked, his tone business-like, "I can't picture this tunnel in a basement. Doesn't make sense."

Evangeline shrugged nervously, looking to Jason. They were all counting on him to remember something. Serena was counting on him and he could barely focus. How scared had she been trying to escape with witches and Nightwalkers on her heels? How scared was she right now? Was he picking up on her panic at this moment or was it his?

Pinching the bridge of his nose, he closed his eyes. Then, crossing his arms over his chest, he took a deep breath. With his eyes still closed, he was able to picture the place where she was held. "They were usually brought up to the ballroom from stairs to the left of her cell. Serena said they went right, hoping to find an alternate exit, with Benjamin in his wolf form leading the way. When they got to the end, there was tunnel in the wall. There were a few rooms like hers down there on either side of the stream. They'd walked about …"

Alex cut him off. "What stream?"

Caught off guard, Jason opened his eyes to meet Alex's. "There was a stream running the length of the basement." He glanced at Evangeline, who looked as though she hadn't known about the stream. Thinking back on those heart-wrenching conversations when Serena was healing, he remembered her briefly telling him about crawling in the stream into the tunnel.

At the time he hadn't paid much mind to the stream part of the conversation. He was trying not to breakdown at the thought of her getting caught trying to escape. "The stream led outside through the tunnel."

Alex sat up straight again, typing away on the keyboard. "This would have been useful weeks ago."

"Why?" Adam asked, his face concerned, evidently wondering why they were discussing a stream.

"Narrows it down. There are not a lot of rundown places near where she was found with a ballroom and a...stream..." He trailed off, his eyes narrowing as he read the screen. "The Sweetin House in Hillview," he said, triumphantly. "Motherfucker! That's only an hour run from here."

Heart leaping to his throat, Jason stalked across the room to the laptop, turning it in his direction. An image of an abandoned building in ruins covered the screen. The bits of limestone left on the land scoured and crawling with ivy. "This place doesn't even have a roof. How the hell could she have been held here?" He didn't want to lose hope they'd found where Serena could be, but he couldn't help but think logically. This place was not livable.

No one said a word as he read more about the old home until he felt Evangeline's excitement. They all turned to her at once.

"There's a charm which can recreate the physical aspects of the past in a certain place. It's a difficult spell, not many can do it, but I'm sure Cassandra was able to work her way around it.

"It may not have been perfect as Serena described the ballroom's interior in a dilapidated state, but certainly would have been useful. If I'm right, the Sweetin House would look almost the same as it did back then."

They all stared thoughtfully at her. No one really knew much about witches' spells. This sort of magic was unsettling. What else could these witches do?

She answered their unspoken question. "My mother's been telling me what she knows about the witch culture," she said uneasily.

Before they all harped on the fact Evangeline was a witch as well, Adam said authoritatively, "Okay. We need to scout the place first before going in. Jason, Alex, and Ramo will head out now. We'll be right on your tail. When you've reached the perimeter, Alex call Viola and Cameron." He turned to the two Weres. "You'll take a vehicle. We may need another form of transport, especially if they've given Serena the serum that keeps her from phasing. Then call me, we'll continue tactics from here and head out in ten."

Just as he, Ramo, and Alex made to move, Evangeline stepped closer into the room toward her mate. They all paused. Adam looked to her questioningly. "Alex says it's an hour run from here. Hillview is about a four-hour drive. You'll be lacking numbers if two of you are driving."

Narrowing his eyes at her, Adam said, "They'll leave now. Don't worry, Eva." He turned away from her to address Jason. "Go now. I expect a call in an hour."

"Adam…" Evangeline interrupted again, stalling them. "You'll lose time. I can teleport there right now. Take a picture of the place and the surrounding area and be back in less than a minute."

Adam froze, the sound of his pulse beating loudly in all their ears. "Absolutely not! Out of the question."

"Why? It's a simple solution…" Evangeline argued, but her words were cut off by the collective growls emanating from eleven werewolves. Jason's eyes shifted, his teeth baring as he glared. Kevin Goode took a cautious step back toward the wall as the Fighters rose to their feet, arching their backs as they hunched forward, every yellow eye glued to the dining room entrance.

"My…what a gracious welcome," came the cocky voice of Cyrus Stewart, the vampire king. He stood with his beast of a manservant behind him, eyeing them all with an arrogant smirk. His black eyes landed on Evangeline, his face softening for an instant before meeting Adam's glare.

"What the fuck are you doing here?" Adam growled.

Cameron O'Connell seethed. "How the hell did he get in here?"

Danny stealthily went for his gun in the holster of his duty belt, his fierce eyes never leaving Cyrus' face.

"Relax, dogs," he said in a bored tone. Rolling his eyes, he held his hands up, "I come in peace." He took a cautious step forward, then smiled as they all hunched over more, ready to phase and pounce on his ass. "I was invited in months ago when I saved your alpha's mate." He said this slowly, looking around.

Evangeline put a calming hand on Adam's arm

then stepped to the king. "What are you doing here, Cyrus?" She was trying to ease the situation, but they all knew she was putting herself between the vampire king and eleven angry werewolves.

"Mayor Boyle is in a tizzy over all the activity today. Called to see if I knew anything. I'll be honest, I didn't give a rat's ass what was happening in the Blacktail community, but you did mention these pesky Nightwalkers are after our kind too, so I thought I'd find out what all the fuss was about."

"You couldn't send your human to do it?" Adam asked. His lips curling as he clenched his fists.

"I could have, yes," he said, nodding, his face and tone becoming humorless. "But my *ward's* anxiety was too much to ignore." Cyrus looked to Evangeline. "What's going on and where is it you want to go that has your fiancé ready to bust a nut?"

Evangeline explained quickly, her words coming out fast and nervous as several Fighters muttered under their breath at the audacity of the vampire king entering their alpha's home.

"…It'll be faster if I just go right now," Evangeline was telling a thoughtful Cyrus. She turned away from him to face her mate. "I won't get too close. I'll come back with a description, but you're going to need me there anyway. With the Nightwalkers, you're outnumbered. I can help."

Fighting for control Adam said, "I can't fight, find my sister, get her out of there, and protect you at the same time. Neither can the guys. I'm going to need their focus."

"You won't have to. I can take care of myself. My mother's been giving me lessons. The Transition

Facility is teaching me to fight. Trust me. I'm useful."

"Damn it, Eva. You're also impulsive. I won't risk you getting hurt," Adam shouted.

"I'll take care of that," Cyrus said evenly, his face more somber now than ever.

Adam's brow crinkled as he glared at the king. "You think you're coming too?"

"Don't misunderstand. I'm not fighting your battles, but if you think I'm going to let a species after my own kind sit pretty only miles away without checking it out you're sorely mistaken. Besides, if my ward is going, I'm going."

Evangeline rolled her eyes, frustrated.

Cyrus ignored her and continued to address a red-faced Adam. "She won't be in harm's way because I'll order her not to be."

Growling, Adam said, seething, "She's not going."

"Growl all you like, but you must see the advantage here. Victor and I will be on her like white on rice. You need her to get your sister out safe and sound." Cyrus glanced at Evangeline, his black eyes twinkling slightly. "She's faster than your lot. You and your Fighters will be busy.

"Eva's your best option to tend to Serena. She'll get the girl and leave. I know she'll want to stay and fight, but with me at her side she won't be able to do anything impulsive." He let out an exasperated breath when Adam snarled at him for flaunting his power over Evangeline. "Her safety far outweighs your hatred for me."

A long, odd silence ensued as every eye fixated on Adam and Cyrus. The Fighters all jerked as they picked up on Adam's sense of hope, then regret, straight back to anger. They all looked back and forth from their alpha and the king in confusion.

"Her safety is a necessity," Adam suddenly said as if in answer to some unspoken question.

Everyone stared at Adam, wondering why he was speaking out, till Jason remembered vampires could speak telepathically.

Evangeline tensed and crossed to her mate. "What did he tell you?" She turned angrily to her maker. "What are you telling him? Speak up!"

Cyrus simply glanced at her, his stony face impassive. When she turned to Adam, he looked like he was ready to vomit. "Fine," Adam said. "Don't let her out of your sight."

Swiftly, the vampire king's mood shifted as though he and Evangeline were about to go on a picnic. Buttoning his sport jacket, he gave her a brief nod. "Very well then. Shall we, my sweet?"

Evangeline turned a grave face to Adam. Then, without hesitation she went to him, held his face in her hands and kissed him fiercely on the mouth. Jason's eyes flicked to Cyrus' when he felt searing jealousy wash over him. When she pulled back, their alpha's mate whispered, "Thank you. I'll be right back, baby." Adam leaned his forehead to hers, gripping the back of her shirt, his veins popping then let go.

Turning to Cyrus, she said, "Ready." In a flash, Evangeline, Cyrus, and Victor, the king's manservant disappeared from the room.

Pursing his lips, Adam stared at the place his mate had stood, a haunting look in his eyes.

Danny spoke then, breaking the icy silence. "All right. Viola and Cameron, I think you can make your way out now. Once they get there we'll have fourteen. Not ideal against a coven of thirteen and fifty or so jackals, but it'll do.

"Fifteen," Kevin said, speaking up from the side of the room. "I can drive. That way you'll have all your Fighters on hand in an hour and the transport you'll need."

They stared, dumbfounded for a moment. Jason had forgotten the old man was still in the room.

Stepping closer to the table, he looked around at all the questionable looks in his direction. "I can hold my own," he said, his chest jutting out as he slid the sides of his jacket back, resting his hands on his hips.

Anthony asked, a look of incredulity and humor on his face, "You pretty handy with that pistol there?" They all eyed Kevin's early Smith and Wesson.

Kevin gave him a stern, no-nonsense look. "Let's just hope I don't have to use it." Then he looked to Adam. "I'm going, son. Let's get on with the tactics."

Chapter Sixteen

Ramo rolled his shoulders back a few times to ease his taut muscles. It didn't work. The longer he kneeled on the ground hunched over as he was, the more uncomfortable he became. Although, if he were honest with himself, he'd realize it wasn't the cold ground making him tense. Hell. It wasn't even the fight sure to come which caused his anxiety. He shook his head; trying to forget about the conversation he'd had with Adam the day of the moon heat.

"Where's Eva? Shouldn't she be around here? And why the hell can I smell humans and those animals, but can't see shit?" Alex grumbled next to him, stirring him out of his musings.

He, Alex, and Jason were spread out low to the ground where the grassland sloped downward, a few nearby trees providing added coverage. They were positioned about fifty yards from where the Sweetin Home should be…only…there wasn't anything around for miles. They each crouched behind a tree, staring at a wide clearing with dried grass but little else.

Ramo spoke low, but knew the guys would hear him. "Eva said they didn't find anything, but the stench of Nightwalkers." His eyes scanned all around them. It was an odd feeling to smell and feel the emotions of the enemy nearby, but not see them. Could witches make themselves invisible?

He was antsy to get the fight started. The sooner they made their move, the sooner he'd be out of his head. Hope flared as he thought of how distracted his alpha had become, first with Jason's punishment, now this. He wasn't an asshole, he knew they were pretty terrible things, but they would have surely put Adam's mind off his earlier concern with the Grayback wolf pack.

Most of the Graybacks lived in Chicago, and according to Adam, they'd suffered two unusual deaths in the past two weeks. The Grayback alpha described his pack members' killings, which pointed to the Nightwalkers, confirming their suspicion other *convenios* were creating these species or Cassandra was sending them on their merry way to the city.

As packs went, the Graybacks were all right, respectful enough to keep their distance, but always checking in to keep the Blacktails and other packs abreast of what was going on in the city. Different packs usually didn't socialize. It just wasn't in a wolf's nature to buddy up with a were from another pack unless it was for alliance purposes.

Ramo's jaw flexed, his eyes hard on the vacant expanse of land in front of them.

Fucking alliances.

The image of the dark-haired girl sprung in his mind, her face was still blurry, but he couldn't forget the long dark straight hair of his wife.

Adam's words from a few days ago played in his head. "You married her for a reason. We have to keep the bond tight, especially now. You're going to the city, so deal with it."

As if it weren't bad enough he'd had to marry

outside of the Blacktails, but now he had to go make nice with this pack? *I married the alpha's daughter. Isn't that good enough?* Ramo thought angrily. Nope. Not according to his cousin. Adam was sending him to Chicago as soon as the smoke settled here.

"Hey," Alex whispered. "Look."

Ramo glanced his way. Alex's dark eyes were focused on something high in the sky, jerking his head toward the top of a leafless tree, just about where the home should be.

Finding the spot Alex was so fixated on, Ramo stared dumbly at a cluster of thin branches at the top of a tree. He was about to make a smartass comment when he noticed one of the branches disappear as the wind picked up then appear again out of nowhere.

What the hell?

They all watched as this same branch disappeared a few more times, sometimes taking another one with it the more the wind picked up.

"The house is surrounded by a concealment charm."

"Fuck!" Ramo flinched as Evangeline's voice spoke in his head, freaking him out. "I keep forgetting you can do that shit. Where are you?" he whispered heatedly, more than ready now to get his cousin out of here and face off with these fuckers.

"Just east of where you are. You three are facing the front of the building. The charm isn't impenetrable. It's just meant to hide it from view. As soon as you're within twenty yards of the house, you'll hit it. I just texted you pics of the four entries."

He heard Jason speak low, knowing Evangeline's vampire ears could pick up just about anything in the vicinity. "Got it," he said, flicking his thumb over his cellphone screen, his face illuminated by the small light. "You three take the east entrance. We'll take the west through the tunnel. Be careful."

"You too."

In unison, they stood up smoothly, Ramo and Jason reaching into their back pockets for their Glocks as Alex phased. The rush of the impending fight running through him, Ramo made his eyes shift, his mind completely clear now. The three of them moved silently in a V formation toward the concealment barrier with Jason at the lead, weapons out and at the ready.

They all felt the magic of the barrier when Jason neared it. There was a slight humming sound in the air, and Ramo heard static when Jason stepped through it.

Not too keen on letting his beta step into the unknown alone, Ramo was right next to him in an instant. He felt his body sucked into the invisible wall and in a second, he was through, staring straight at the front door of the Sweetin Home. It was like stepping back in time. The limestone building actually looked pretty decent compared to the photo on Alex's laptop. Looking around, he half expected a horse and carriage to come down the dirt circular drive.

Catching Jason's signal to move left, they fell back into formation, listening out for any sounds of activity.

In an instant he felt the rest of the Fighters break the barrier on the other sides, Viola and Anthony sending an encouraging vibe, which told them they were covered with .50 caliber sniper riffles aimed at the house.

The sky darkened above them as they made their way along the side of the house. Neither of them made a sound, their light footfalls barely above a whisper. Jason found the small stream and the arch, which led into a tunnel. He felt his friend stiffen, his heart racing wildly and knew he was thinking of Serena escaping through this very tunnel weeks ago.

Without another moment's hesitation, he went in with Ramo right on his heels.

****

The pounding in her head was nothing compared to the familiar pain burning down the front of her thigh. This couldn't be happening again. No. She was dreaming. She was dreaming and any minute now she was going to wake up in Jason's arms. He'd hold her and whisper soothing words in her ear.

Opening her eyes, she cringed, knowing damn well it wasn't a dream. The side of her face throbbed, and her left eye was practically swollen shut. What had Leonardo hit her with? There was no way the idiot could pack a punch good enough to knock out a werewolf. She could only spare her thigh a quick glance, too angry to even care what her condition was. The most important thing now was to get the hell out of here.

Looking around the ballroom from the same wall she'd been strung up so many times, the witches all knelt together on the floor around Cassandra, Serena's blood dripping off her bony fingers. The smell of the carcass on the sarcophagus wafted toward her, and she gagged.

Refusing to fall into the numb existence she'd succumbed to so many times before, Serena searched the room for anything to aid in her escape. With Cassandra preoccupied with her spell, she wouldn't be looking into her mind.

As she turned her head left, her body jerked, heart slamming in her chest and she cried out, horrified at the sight blocked by her swollen eye.

Ben's lifeless body hung naked, limp, and grotesque next to her.

Shutting her eyes, she spun her head away, her body beginning to shake as the sobs she was incapable of containing rocked through her. Bile rose in her throat as the image of her boss's' decaying form flashed in her mind. It would forever haunt her, and the agony she'd felt the night he died resurfaced, overpowering her.

Fury and loathing, the likes of which she'd never known surged through her. Forcing her swollen eye to barely an open slit, she glared at the witches before her. "You sick bitch!" she cried out so forcefully, her throat actually ached.

Cassandra smirked, but didn't pause from her chant. The others didn't dare look her way. Serena stared at all of them, wishing she could phase. For the first time in her life, the need to kill overcame any other thought. There was nothing but vengeance in her heart, and it mingled with the sudden sense of wrath and revenge she felt the moment her pack drew near.

Hope flared in her chest. They were near and they were coming for her. Angling her neck back, she found the cherub in the ceiling and said a silent prayer for the Fighters, then cleared her mind. Her sole focus now was to remain calm and help her pack in any way possible.

****

Jason stormed the damp bowels of the Sweetin Home with Ramo behind him, Alex taking up the rear, back in wolf form. He and Ramo chose to stay human in case they needed to access a section of the house like the small tunnel in an instant and to carry their weapons. They decided back at headquarters to enter this way, with some Fighters carrying weapons and the others phasing.

He faltered as they came to a door on their left, his heart tightening as a familiar scent filled his senses. Staring at the floor, he couldn't help but picture Serena huddled inside the god-forsaken room and didn't have the courage to look inside. He felt a tap on his shoulder and turned to see Ramo point with two fingers up ahead.

There were steps a few feet in front of them that led upstairs. Serena had said the stairs led to a hallway and ballroom. She must be in there as every room they'd come across had been empty.

Jason charged on, only pausing once when a shout reached them.

Serena.

Anger filled him as her raging emotions reached him. She was shouting at someone. He felt her readiness to fight and panic set in. Hoping to God she wouldn't be punished for her outburst, they surged on, ascending the stairs into a dark hallway.

Light spilled out of a room up ahead and they pressed their backs to the wall, their eyes going in every direction, waiting for an attack from a witch or Nightwalker.

Stopping just before the door, Jason leaned his head back against the wall for a second and took a deep breath, preparing himself for the horror he was about to witness. His body tight with tension, he angled his neck to look inside.

The first thing he saw was a cluster of witches on the ground, surrounding a woman at their center. Ignoring this, he scanned the room till his eyes landed on a sight that would forever haunt his dreams.

Serena, naked and bleeding hung on the wall by her wrists and ankles.

Wolf eyes stung, his body trembled, as he stared fixated at his girl writhing in pain. Someone stepped on his foot, whispering for him to wait until they were all in position, but he couldn't even find the energy to read his pack members in the other parts of the house. His sole focus was Serena. Jesus Christ. He had to get to her. Why was he still standing there? Suddenly he noticed Ramo and Alex whose clawed hands dug into his shoulder, restraining him.

"Not yet, bro," Ramo whispered in his ear.

They pulled him back, his view of Serena now blocked by the wall. He was about to shove his pack members off him when the distinct sound of light footfalls hit the floor at the end of the darkened hallway.

They all sniffed loudly, guns outstretched as two pair of glowing amber eyes appeared out of the darkness, making their way in their direction like four tiny bright orbs dangling in midair.

The Nightwalkers advanced slowly with cool calculated strides, preparing to attack.

"I got this." Ramo made to move toward the Nightwalkers when Alex put a furry arm out, pushing Ramo back.

He watched, with a sinking feeling in his gut as their pack member headed straight toward a species that could kill them in just one bite. They were strong in their human forms, but Alex had more strength in were form. Still, they held their guns out.

They knew Alex didn't want them using their weapons and alerting the witches just yet when the others weren't in position. But fuck, the closer the Nightwalkers drew, the bigger they became. These were no ordinary jackals.

They were mutations of jackals with fierce eyes and teeth, which rivaled the Weres. He gaped as Alex risked his life to keep them from being discovered sooner than they should. Fear for their friend held them frozen. Jason didn't know if he should intercede or not. He didn't know what move Alex was about to make, and he could quite possibly put him in more danger than he already was.

Jason's heart leapt to his throat when, simultaneously, the two Nightwalkers bowed low to the ground, then pushing off the floor, soared high through the air straight for Alex. Before he or Ramo could get a good angle for a shot that would miss Alex, the Fighter reached out catching them in midflight, clamping his ginormous claws around the necks of each Nightwalker. Squeezing with all his might, he choked the fuckers before knocking their heads together. Each fell limp in Alex's grip.

Well…there's one way to kill a Nightwalker. Nice.

Alex brought them down, quietly to the floor just as someone spoke from inside the ballroom.

"Did you hear something?" someone asked.

"I thought I heard a yelp," another said.

Jason felt Adam, who was at the north end of the ballroom at a door leading into the kitchen send them

Julia Laque

an affirmative. Ramo and Jason met Alex's eyes for a brief second and they all nodded.

Holding his Glock out in front of him, Jason stepped into the ballroom.

****

Cyrus stood impatiently as Evangeline spoke to two Weres telepathically. Having discarded his coat outside, he rolled his shirtsleeves up to his elbows as they waited. The plan was to get the girl out with these two Weres covering them from behind.

They hid behind an open door at the east entrance of the ballroom, watching through the crack for the signal to make their move.

His eyes landed on the girl he'd been accused of kidnapping months ago and cringed. Werewolf or not, no one deserved such depravity, and Cyrus felt anger rush through him for what was about to come.

Do you remember Leonardo Russo? Evangeline asked him in his head.

Cyrus crinkled his brow. Why was she bringing up her ex-boyfriend at a time like this? *Yes. The boy you first fornicated with. How can I forget?*

Letting out a frustrated breath she said, *That's him. In the leather jacket.* She inclined her head toward the circle in the middle of the room.

Cyrus angled his head over hers to peer into the room. A man in a dark leather jacket knelt with his hands behind his back, looking the worse for wear. *We need to have a serious discussion on your taste in men, my sweet. Guess we know where he disappeared to…*

Just then, one of the witches said something about a noise. They too heard the soft yelp at the other end of the ballroom and wondered what was going on. Eager to move and get Evangeline the hell out of there, he held a hand out to Victor who stood behind him with a Remington 700 firmly in his grip. His man took out a Springfield and placed the pistol in his hand. Cyrus gave him a derisive look as he checked the measly 9-millimeter, then glanced at the massive weapon Victor held. *We're going to discuss who carries what in combat when we get home.*

They all braced themselves the second Jason entered the ballroom and before he could stop himself, he gripped Evangeline's arm. Her back was to him, her gaze on Serena in the ballroom, but he was sure she understood what his grip meant.

His heart in his throat as his ward prepared herself to enter into the lion's den, he told her quietly, *Stay alive.*

Evangeline nodded, *I will.*

****

On impulse, Jason stormed the ballroom, going straight for Serena with the others entering at the same time from the other entrances. He knew the plan was to cover Serena and Evangeline so they could make their escape, but adrenaline, rage, and pure terror drove him toward Serena.

Relief washed over her stricken face at his approach, his hands immediately reaching gently to cup her cheeks, careful not to put too much pressure on her left side. Grief and fury squeezed his insides as he pictured one of these pricks putting his hands on her sweet skin.

Pressing his forehead against hers, Jason was speechless. He let out a breath of relief, relishing the feel of her, telling himself she was okay. There were no soothing sounds or words of encouragement.

He'd come to save her, but it seemed as though she needed to rescue him, rescue him from the turmoil surging through him, the burning ache in his chest. He felt completely useless.

"We've got her, Jason!" Evangeline shouted, desperately trying to move him aside, her eyes wide as the room grew louder.

Jason nodded, breathing deep through his nostrils. "Get the hell out of here," he uttered to them both, then turned to join the others as Evangeline cut her loose. With vengeance in his eyes, he unleashed his rage on the enemy.

****

Amid the fury running through his veins, Adam Perez felt jealousy pull at his gut the instant he felt Cyrus' emotions toward his mate. Ignoring it for now, he turned when James and Cameron approached from behind, weapons secured in their hands. They both nodded at him, letting him know their business outside had been completed. Standing in the small entrance leading into the kitchen from the ballroom, they readied themselves for the attack.

In his wolf form, Adam led the way inside, his eyes immediately going to his sister on his right. Anger burned like wild fire through him. Growling, he made his way toward the witches in the middle of the room, intending to distract them away from Serena so Evangeline could teleport to his sister.

"It seems we have guests," Cassandra said casually, looking about the room as the Fighters surrounded the ballroom on all sides. Jason, Danny, James, and Cameron remained in their human forms while Adam, Samantha, Ramo, Alex, and Nick, who'd entered alone at the front of the house, advanced as wolves crouched low on all fours, ready to spring into action.

The witches on the floor stood slowly, their heads panning the room with looks of terror on their faces.

Danny spoke loud and menacingly with a gun aimed at Cassandra. "You're completely surrounded. Whatever you're planning, I'd think twice about."

Cassandra laughed, "Do you honestly think guns and your vicious pups scare me?"

"You're not bulletproof, bitch," he answered back.

"Ah, yes, but I encompass something you buffoons lack." Cassandra said, then raised her hands in the air. Her red eyes falling back into her head, she spoke in an odd high-pitched voice. "*Venio meus Nightwalkers quod pugna ut nex.*" She met Danny's eyes again. "Skill."

From all points of the house, they heard the sound of paws hitting the ground, making their way toward the ballroom. The roar of the stampede held everyone still for a moment till Adam gave the deafening growl to attack.

A shot rang out from Danny's gun. Cassandra disappeared in smoke before the bullet struck her. It hit the far side of the wall where Ramo and Alex were crouched. The two Weres sprung into action, attacking the nearest witches who tried to waylay them with glowing white lights shot from their hands.

Just then, Adam saw Evangeline teleport in front of Serena, Cyrus and Victor standing with their backs to them, sending shots around the room at the scattering witches. His beta moved away from his sister, advancing on the chaos within. The scraping sound as the Nightwalkers drew closer rang loud and ominous throughout the ballroom.

He saw Jason firing bullets around the room as he tried to deflect the onslaught of the white light the witches were throwing out, making his way toward the middle of the fight. His pack had nailed a couple witches, but the white light was blinding and each of the Fighters kept a watchful eye on the doors, waiting for the jackals to enter.

They appeared in an instant, charging in from three of the doors, their massive forms bouncing as they attacked. They leapt with agility and precision that matched their own skill. As big as they were, they were nowhere near the size of a werewolf.

The sight of Ramo crashing into a Nightwalker on the fly was something he'd never forget. The room sprang into action with dizzying speed. Growls echoed loudly, blood splattered the walls, and Adam could hear groans from a few Fighters as the witches fought back with their magic.

It was evident only Cassandra could appear and disappear at whim. She moved about the room, also sending shocks of white light at his Fighters.

Trying as hard as he could to focus on the fight and not on his sister and Evangeline standing so precariously close to the gruesome battle, Adam leapt onto the nearest witch, a male with deep sunken eyes. He pinned him to the floor and sank his teeth in the fucker's throat.

Behind him, he heard the commotion as Evangeline cut Serena down. He checked on them when he was through with the jackal beneath him. His mate was throwing a long white t-shirt over Serena who shook visibly, her eyes never leaving Jason.

"Please," Serena said, shakily to Evangeline. "Cut him down."

Adam bit down hard at the sight of his pack member's mangled body on the wall next to her. Surprised, he saw Victor instantly move toward Ben and cut him down in a flash, flinging his lifeless body over his shoulder. He spun around fast for a man of his size and hanging onto Adam's pack member, aimed his rifle with his free hand at a Nightwalker slinking into the room.

It was an odd feeling to know he'd forever be in Cyrus and Victor's debt for doing this for the Blacktails when they could have easily stayed out of the fight.

Even now, Cyrus inched closer to join in, shooting as Cassandra's beasts swarmed into the room. Spinning around, the king's eyes landed on him. *Coming up your left flank, dog,* he told him in his head.

Adam whirled around just as a Nightwalker sprung at him, its vicious teeth snapping wildly, claws up. Leaping out of the way, Jason landed a bullet from the other end of the room straight through the jackal's head. It plopped down at his feet, and Adam cursed silently. Looking back at the vampire king, he gave him a brief nod, then looked to Evangeline and Serena.

Cyrus knew what he wanted. *They're going. We got them covered.*

"Time to move, Eva," Cyrus shouted at her, as he backed his way closer to the women.

Evangeline had Serena's arm flung over her shoulder as they made their way toward the exit leading to the kitchen.

"Evangeline?" a man in a black leather jacket said, pausing in the middle of the room.

Adam snarled, hardly noticing the man was the only living witch aside from Cassandra in the room. The ballroom resembled a horror flick, with bodies strewn all over the floor. He made a quick count of his pack. They seemed to be okay with only a few gashes from the witch's white lights.

It was then Cassandra noticed her great granddaughter's presence. "You stupid bitch!" she shouted at Evangeline, raising her arms. Adam made to move, but the man in the leather jacket knocked Cassandra's hands down. "NO!" he shouted, then, realizing what he'd done, fell to his knees. "I'm sorry. I'm sorry, mistress. Please. I couldn't help it."

Struck dumb, Adam watched amazed as the fight continued around him, the sound of gunfire a kind of soundtrack to the battle, cracking throughout the room. Nick had been fighting the guy in leather when a Nightwalker jumped him from behind. Nick continued to fight the beast a few feet to where Cassandra and her witch stood.

Eyes blazing, Cassandra looked down at the man. "How romantic," she said, scathingly. "Trying to save your precious Evangeline, little fool?"

Confused as all hell, Adam looked to Evangeline, who had paused near the door staring wide-eyed at the man. Understanding hit as he glanced back at the guy. This was Evangeline's old boyfriend. The one who'd ditched her all those years ago.

"You'll pay for your lapse in judgment, my dear."

Standing tall, she called out to the Nightwalkers, "My pets…kill him. *Slowly*."

The room stilled as five jackals advanced on the man on the floor.

****

Serena nearly vomited as she watched in horror at what the monsters were capable of doing. As much as she hated Leonardo, the sight before her was like nothing she'd ever seen. The Nightwalkers chewed on every limb, digging into his skin, chunks of flesh flailing about as he cried out in agony. Meeting Jason's eyes, she begged him silently to stop it. Despite what he'd done, no one deserved that kind of torture.

Feeling Jason's hatred for the witch, she watched as pity washed over his face. Clenching his jaw, he raised his arm, the gun in his hand jerked as a blast resounded around the room. The bullet hit its mark, landing straight through Leonardo's heart, ending his shouts of pain. Ending his suffering.

Both Serena and Evangeline exhaled loudly with relief. Evangeline shook violently as she half-carried Serena toward a door. "Come on. Lean on me," she whispered. Limping, she moved as quickly as she could, her heart racing as she heard shouts and snarls behind them.

She wanted Jason so much her stomach knotted, but she knew he was making sure they got out of there alive, and he'd never leave his pack members to face off the foray of Nightwalkers continuing to swarm the ballroom.

The minute they entered the kitchen, two Nightwalkers curled their way around the island in the middle of the room, their bright eyes honed on Serena and Evangeline.

Next to her, Serena felt Evangeline pushed aside.

She noticed for the first time they were covered by two vampires and stared for a moment at the king in confusion. Why was he here?

The king shouted at Evangeline as he thrust a gun in her hand, "Take her up the stairs! Go!" He had shoved them toward a long staircase leading up just outside of the kitchen door.

Evangeline lifted Serena at her side and raced up the stairs. "Do you know where this leads?"

Shaking her head she tried not to worry about the two men facing off with Nightwalkers in such a confined space with Ben slung over the bigger one's shoulder. They faltered at a door at the top of the stairs. Evangeline opened it quickly and led Serena outside, shutting the door behind them.

On the roof, they stood for a moment, their gazes searching danger, but all they saw was the dark night sky and the swaying tops of tree branches.

Evangeline reached for her again. "Let's get you to the ledge. We can jump from there. Don't worry. I've got you. Your father should be here by now with Jason's pickup."

Before they could make a move, the door banged opened behind them. Serena fell down hard onto her bleeding leg, as Evangeline spun quickly to catch the springing Nightwalker in her grip, sending the gun flying through the air. Serena screamed as she witnessed the giant beast pin her brother's mate.

On her back, Evangeline fought to keep the Nightwalker's mouth shut with her hand clamped around its snout, struggling to get it off her. Cold fear in her heart, Serena dragged herself toward the fallen gun, hoping her movements distracted the beast.

"Get off her!" she shouted as she moved. Her body shook as she scrambled for the gun. She reached it just as the Nightwalker managed to break free from Evangeline's hold and sink its teeth into her upper arm, its large fangs cutting her skin to the bone. Evangeline's expression froze before she could move again.

"No!" Dread laced through Serena. Staring wide-eyed, Evangeline managed to wrench the jackal off her arm. Fangs bared, Evangeline's eyes flashed silver and with nimble hands held the Nightwalker's neck squeezing with all her might.

Terror washed through Serena as the truth hit her. Her brother's mate, her nephews' mother, bitten by these creatures...these *poisonous* creatures. A red haze filled her gaze. Gripping the gun tightly in her trembling hands, Serena aimed and shot the beast straight through its ribs. The Nightwalker fell in a heap onto Evangeline's chest. In a huff, Evangeline's hands dropped to her sides, all energy knocked out of her.

Serena made her way to her friend, and pushed the huge jackal off her with surprising strength. "Eva? Eva?" Pulling her upper body into her arms, Evangeline met her gaze. Serena watched, terrified, as Evangeline's eyes shifted back to green.

She gave Serena a confused look as though she didn't know what exactly had just happened. Reaching for her arm, Serena meant to lap at her wounds when Evangeline said weakly, "*No.* The venom will kill you." Her sister-in-law looked around them, and she didn't know if Evangeline was checking to see if they were in danger or looking for her mate to suddenly appear at her side. The wretched look of shock and confusion on her friend's face terrified her.

Serena's eyes blurred as tears formed. Oh God, please. This couldn't be happening. She was going to be okay. Panic twisted her insides as Evangeline's eyes met hers again. There were no words, just a look, which spoke volumes...a desperate look telling her to take care of Adam and the boys.

Evangeline's lids fluttered several times before finally closing, her body going limp in Serena's arms. "Oh God, no! Eva!" She shook her hard, forcing her to wake. Closing her eyes, she listened carefully for a heartbeat, then realized as a vampire Evangeline didn't have one, but every fiber of her being told her she was still alive. Noticing how cold she was, she reminded herself that vampires were naturally cool to the touch. It didn't mean anything. It didn't mean they had lost her brother's mate.

They had to get off this roof. Fighting the pain in her leg, bleeding more now than ever she tried to lift Evangeline as she attempted to stand. They could creep back into the stairway and find an alternate exit. The hairs on the back of her neck rose and alarm shot down her spine as a snarl echoed behind her.

The loss of blood made her movements agonizingly slow as she turned her head to meet two more Nightwalkers. Hackles raised, they progressed forward, right at them. Still holding the gun, she shot at them, but to her everlasting horror, the gun only clicked. She was out of bullets on the roof with an injured leg and her brother's unconscious mate. Shaking now with unimaginable fear, Serena found strength she did not know she possessed and lifted Evangeline fully into her arms as she stood. Ignoring the ripping down her thigh, she bolted for the ledge, which seemed to be miles away.

The sound of snarls and large paws hitting the rooftop induced a panic inside her so prevalent she nearly lost it. Gripping Evangeline tighter to her chest she forced herself to ignore the pain running through her and willed her body to move faster.

If she was uninjured, she could make the jump with no problem, even better in her wolf form, but the serum still ran through her. Continuing to run blindly toward the ledge, the roar of wind in her ears, she heard the Fighters falling out of the house below. Her plan was madness, but she had no choice. Spying her brother and Jason in the distance, she screamed as loud as she could, "Adam!"

Agonizing pain sliced down her leg with every pounding step she took. Running with all her might, she tried to focus, her vision made hazy by tears. Cold sweat ran down her back as she sped on, tremulous voices reaching her from below.

"Oh shit!" Ramo shouted.

"She's gonna jump," a female voice said.

"It's too high. Look at her leg."

"Eva?"

"Oh Jesus!"

The terrified voices rang in her ears as she charged on, the jackals closing in on her. She felt their panting breaths at her back, but in her heart she knew they would make it.

They had to make it.

"Adam!" Serena shouted again, knowing her brother wouldn't let her down. "Catch her!"

Chapter Seventeen

Jason raced out of the house, eager to find Serena. He felt the terror she was going through and wondered what the hell was going on. The instant he saw Cyrus and Victor back into the ballroom, fighting off a team of Nightwalkers his heart froze.

The jackals continued to advance on them from every crevice of the house, and Adam motioned for the Fighters to fall out. Danny was still in there with Nick trying to get out while they held off the remaining Nightwalkers.

He panned the front and found his pickup, a pale-faced Kevin standing next to the open driver's side door. When Cyrus came charging out of the house, Jason called to him. "Where are they?"

The king's eyes never looked to him, an odd expression appearing on his face as though he'd been struck by some unseen force. Gazing absently at the ground, his hand went to his right arm, fear lacing through him. Cyrus' head jerked up. "The roof," he said.

Stepping back to get a better look at the roof, he heard Serena's wild cry pierce through him.

"Adam!"

Everyone stared, wild-eyed as two jackals raced toward Serena, who carried an unconscious Evangeline in her arms.

Jesus Christ!

The blood drained from his face, his heart pounding maddeningly. All around him he heard his pack members yell out.

"Adam!" Serena shouted. Her entire leg was covered in blood as she ran toward the edge. "Catch her!"

It was all too fast to have any conscious thought, yet the horrid display seemed to occur in slow motion. With shock rooting him to the spot, the blood left his face as Serena leapt off the edge, simultaneously flinging Evangeline's limp body through the air toward her brother. Evangeline's long limbs hung loose, her back arched as she flew past the trees.

Adam raced on all fours toward her, then, pushing off the ground, soared twenty feet into the sky, catching his mate in his burly arms.

Jason sprung into action. He ran headlong, not sure he'd make it in time to catch Serena who fell to the ground with increasing speed, her hair trailing over her head, fluttering in the wind. Sliding on his knees, he caught her just as she was about to hit.

He held her tight as the Nightwalkers, who'd leapt after them, both contorted grotesquely in midflight when bullets from every able Fighter and vampire caught them in fifty different places. Jason skidded to a halt on the dirt ground a few feet away from Adam and Evangeline.

Jason and Adam's eyes met briefly, making sure the other had safely caught the two most important women in their lives. Relief filled him when he felt Serena's warmth in his arms, her heart raced uncontrollably, but she was alive and with him.

He stood up fast and looked to James, who held a detonator in his hands. "Blow the fucker!" Jason demanded and ran to his truck.

"Aye, aye," James responded, spinning to face the home.

Danny shouted from the doorway, backing out with his gun still out, "Clear out!"

Jason reached his truck and placed Serena in the back. "Get in, Kevin."

Kevin hesitated, staring at Serena. "Is she…is she…"

"We need to move. Now." Jason slammed the door behind him as Kevin slid into the driver's seat.

Adam leapt into the back bed of the pickup, his body morphing back into human with Evangeline in his arms. A naked Nick limped into the passenger seat, holding his side, his face tight, clearly in pain.

Kevin asked, "Anyone else need…"

Nick muttered through clenched teeth. "No. We're good. Go!"

The pickup revved loudly as they peeled away from the Sweetin home.

Jason held Serena's face in his hands for a moment before he went to work on her leg. Glancing out the back window, he saw the house disappear, covered by the concealment charm once again until a blast of red light broke its magic, the booming sound piercing the dead night.

Serena jumped, her eyes wide. Sitting up, she looked in horror at the huge ball of flames erupting into the sky.

"Please tell me everyone was out," she said nervously, praying everyone had made it out of the

Sweetin Home

He held her chin and turned her to face him. "Yes, honey. Those were our explosives." He laid her back against the door. "Lie still."

Cleaning her wound as best he could with a towel, he then slipped off his belt and tied a tourniquet around her thigh.

Serena bit down hard, but his brave girl held it together. Their eyes met, and his heart tightened in his chest.

As much as they wanted to comfort each other, they couldn't ignore the anguished voice of their alpha outside in the pickup's bed. Kevin, Nick, Serena, and Jason didn't make a sound as they listened with heavy hearts as Adam willed his mate to come back to him.

"Please baby, please. Wake up," he pleaded desperately.

When Jason had tended to Serena's leg, they both chanced a look into the back. Adam held his mate in his lap, his red-rimmed eyes wildly gazing at Evangeline. He shook her gently. "Wake up, baby! Wake up!" With his wrist at her mouth, he tried to get her to feed, but she still didn't move.

They all jerked suddenly when a loud thump hit the back bed. Cyrus had teleported to his ward's side. "Is she drinking?" he asked, his voice deadened. He knelt before them, his eyes unblinking on Evangeline.

Adam shook his head. "I don't know."

"Let me try. Please," the king begged. Scouring his wrist with his fangs, Cyrus held it out. Adam hesitated briefly before removing his hand. His wrist was replaced by Cyrus'. No one made a sound as the king fed her, but Evangeline still didn't move.

Serena wept silently as she watched, guilt oozing out of her, blaming herself for Evangeline's predicament. Jason wanted to soothe her, but couldn't find the words.

After a time, Cyrus removed his hand, running a shaky hand over his face. "Give her more of yours." His jaw clenched. "Your blood gives her more nourishment than mine."

Adam did so, continuing to whisper in his mate's ear.

Jason brought Serena's hand to his lips as they both stared out the back. They drove on in complete silence; the only sound was the roaring of the engine. They could barely breathe let alone talk as they waited for some miracle.

Adam suddenly hitched in a breath. Squinting, Jason watched as the wound on Evangeline's arm began to close slowly. She was healing herself. Even now, her skin started to glow slightly.

As Evangeline was a healer, Jason wondered if her body would be strong enough to heal, to fight off the poison the Nightwalkers bite had induced.

The glow in Evangeline's skin faded, but the wound on her arm was now closed. Jason felt a sudden awareness from the two men outside. At the exact same time, their eyes met and in unison, they spoke, "She's alive."

Serena let out a trembling breath, her hand covering her heart with tears in her eyes. Jason kissed her hand softly, relief washing over him.

"Everything all right back there?" Kevin asked, his eyes flickering to the rearview mirror.

Nick let out a sigh of relief and leaned his seat back

a bit, closing his eyes. "Eva's okay."

"How are you, son?" Kevin asked, glancing at Nick's tattered form.

Serena shifted, her eyes closing for a moment as pain shot through her. His chest tightened, wishing he could take the pain away from her. Hands trembling, he rubbed the side of her leg as he held her hand in his. Wishing he were a doctor, he felt completely helpless. He couldn't stand to see her in pain.

"I'll be all right," Nick said in a strained voice.

"Your side doesn't look good," Kevin was saying.

Jason took his eyes off Serena to check on his pack member. There was a deep gash on Nick's left side, just under his arm. "What happened?"

Nick pinched his eyes, his face scrunching up in pain before he answered. "The witch who got mauled stuck me with a knife. He was the only one fighting with a weapon." He angled his head to look at his leg. "Whatever the white light was, three of them got me good in the leg. The cuts are taking longer than usual to heal. Bet that's why they chose the spell."

Jason looked down at his chest where he too had been hit a couple times. Funny, he hadn't felt a thing till now. By this time, they should be healing, but it looked like the cuts the white light made were meant to pierce a supernatural and keep them from healing. He didn't think it was life threatening, just really painful.

Serena reached a hand to rub his chest where the strikes had sliced his shirt. "It's fine," he whispered.

Nick turned his head to look at Serena. "You hangin' in there?"

Serena leaned her head to the side to smile weakly at him. "Yeah," she said meekly.

Nick's hand reached back and caught hers, his brow furrowing as he got a better look at her face, which had begun to heal, but still looked bruised and swollen. "What you did was incredibly brave," he said, squeezing her hand. "It's good to have you back," he finished, the side of his mouth curling in a meager smile.

A sudden weight filled Jason's chest, and it had nothing to do with the lacerations in his skin. He looked from Serena to Nick, her small hand in his, as awareness struck.

Nick was perfect for her.

His stomach lurching, he thought of a hundred reasons why Nicholas Manning would be the best mate for Serena. The man was the nicest guy any of them had ever met. He would never hurt her or raise a hand or voice to her. Nick wouldn't accuse her of having a heat mate like he'd done. He'd keep her out of harm's way and treat her like the goddess she was. He wouldn't whisper obscenities in her ear in the bedroom, but would probably make gentle, slow love to her.

He thought he was going to be sick in the back of his pickup as his stomach knotted. While she gazed warmly at his friend, he realized Serena was just in a measly t-shirt, her upper thighs exposed and she had a clear shot of Nick's ginormous naked form sitting in the passenger seat. Without thinking, he pulled her shirt down as much as he could to cover up her legs.

Nick seemed to notice Jason's jealous nature and smirked a bit before letting go of Serena's hand and facing forward again.

Serena too sensed something, giving him a questioning look. He shook his head at her and carefully brought her onto his lap so she was more comfortable leaning her back on his arm rather than on the car door.

Snuggling into him, Serena soon fell asleep, her soft breaths warming his chest. Jason stared out the window with his lips to her forehead, trying hard not to think, but he couldn't help it. Was he right? Was Nick better for her? And if so, could he let her go? It was a wild notion, but he couldn't help but wonder.

As they'd stared tenderly at each other a few moments ago, Jason tried to feel their emotions toward one another, to see if it went beyond friendship. All he got from Serena was a profound kindness toward his friend.

Nick had stared with deep admiration and a small amount of affection toward her, but how could he not after what they'd all just witnessed back at the house? They all knew Serena would have leapt off the roof had they been out there or not.

The thought terrified him, knowing she wouldn't have been able to handle the fall with her injured leg, especially while holding Evangeline at the same time. But she would have done it, would have risked her life trying to save her brother's mate.

Jason turned to look at the back of Nick's head. He was a great Fighter, but he'd be an even better mate. If he could stomach letting Serena go, then Nick would have to resign as a Fighter. There was no way Jason would ever be able to look at the guy again.

He'd buy them a house somewhere far off in the country where he knew Serena would be safe. Nick would make her happy and most importantly, keep her from danger, the danger that apparently seemed to

Julia Laque

hover over Jason like a goddamn curse.

Shutting his eyes tight, he held Serena closer to him, not believing he was actually considering letting her go.

Jerking awake in his arms, Serena raised her head, her wide eyes on his. Her expression pulled at his heart, as she'd felt what he was silently going through.

No, she mouthed, her body tensing.

Kissing her brow, he shook his head at her then nudged her temple softly with his nose, urging her to fall back asleep. Forcing himself to focus on the love he felt for her and not the choices he was making, he rocked her softly in his arms and prayed he was making the right decision.

****

The next afternoon Serena awoke at home, the dull gray sky outside lighting her room in somber tones. Alone, she felt a hollow sense in her chest and wondered what she could be worrying about. It was over. Everyone had made it out safely. She was home again and the wretched Sweetin Home was now a pile of dust.

Lifting the sheets she examined her leg, which had been bandaged. Dimly, she remembered waking up in the hospital as they'd stitched her leg last night and Jason's whispered request to give her something to help her sleep. Glancing at the clock, she saw it was three in the afternoon. Other than feeling a bit groggy, she felt fine. As she could now see quite well, she expected her face had healed already.

Rubbing at the odd sting in her chest, she was about to lurch out of bed in search of Jason when the bedroom door opened and he stepped in, a steaming

242

mug in hand.

Her body came alive at the sight of him, so magnificently beautiful as he took up the entire room. Barely smiling, he said, "I thought you might want this." Holding the cup out to her, he sat beside her on the bed. "How are you feeling?" he asked quietly, a peculiar look in his eyes.

Taking the cup, she held it in her hands, her gaze never leaving his. "I'm fine. Really." She placed the cup on the nightstand and sat up. "What's wrong?"

He bent his head, curiously. It took all the control she had not to run her fingers through his soft hair. His firm lips were so close and yet she felt as though she wasn't allowed to kiss him. Why was that?

"You're hiding something. Tell me."

Jason looked away, his cheekbones hardening somehow as he stared at the back wall. They sat silently for a long while and every passing second terrified her. What was he thinking? She'd felt him going through turmoil last night on the way to the hospital, and even as they sat now, she felt him slipping away. The pang in her chest increased.

Too frightened of what was about to come out of his mouth she blurted, "How's Eva? Have you talked to my brother? Is she going to be okay?" Her voice came out high-pitched and clipped.

Nodding he said, "She's still out, but Dr. Moros was there earlier and said she was getting stronger." His wide shoulders heaved as he took a deep breath. "Without her healing capabilities, there was no way she would have survived the Nightwalkers bite.

"Out of everyone there last night, she was the only one bitten by those jackals and the only one strong enough to withstand it." He shook his head in bewilderment, then swallowed hard, the cords in his neck throbbing. "Every time I picture you guys on the roof, I…"

"Don't, Jason…" She raised a hand to comfort him, but he caught it and held it in his lap. Frowning, she stared at the sinister look in his eyes.

"You shouldn't have been there. Neither of you," he said ominously.

Wishing he didn't harp on the fact Evangeline and Serena were the only ones seriously hurt last night, she asked, "How's Nick? Did his side heal okay?"

Pain shot through her, and she realized the fierce blast had come from Jason. She froze, her eyes narrowing to slits. "What's going on? Is he okay?"

"He's fine, Serena."

"Then what's wrong with you?" she demanded, her voice more forceful.

Letting go of her hand, he crossed his arms in front of him, finally meeting her gaze. The look on his face terrified and irritated her. He stared as if she'd done something wrong. "I told you this wouldn't work."

She felt as if he'd just slapped her. *"What?"*

"Your brother was right. I'm all wrong for you and last night proved it."

Sitting up, she reached for him, but he stood up swiftly, backing away toward the door. Dread filled her insides as she stilled on the bed.

Arms bulging, he gripped himself tighter to his chest. "I wanted to tell you first before I spoke to Adam. I know he'll agree with me." Jason's voice didn't sound like his. She felt as though someone else were speaking for him.

"What the hell are you talking about?" she yelled as she got out of bed. Barely noticing she was in her own bedclothes, she stared daggers at the man she loved.

Jason wore his all-too-familiar impassive expression. Lips curling as he spoke, he said, "Nick is going to resign as a Fighter. He's going to be in charge of taking you far away from all this bullshit." His eyes flashed yellow for an instant, the vein on his forehead pulsating. "He's going to take you away from *me*."

"No," she breathed. What the hell was wrong with him? How could he say these things to her?

"In time you'll forget about this infatuation you have for me. We haven't officially mated as you are not carrying my child." The indifference in his voice was like ice cutting down her spine. "You'll mate with Nick, making it official so no other were can claim you."

She stared wide-eyed, the pain near to bursting within her. "Are you out of your mind?" She stalked him, but he backed away.

"Don't touch me," he said coolly, arms unfolding, his hands balled into fists at his sides.

Flinching, she faltered. "Why are you saying this?"

Chewing on the inside of his cheek, he said, sardonically, "You know it's true."

"Know what is true?"

"Nick," he said, by way of an answer. "He's the best person to take care of you. What we had was nothing. It's over. It's time the Blacktails did something about your welfare. You've been living for too long on your own."

Anger raged within her. "You have no right. My

brother will never agree to this."

"He was the one to order me away from you in the first place. Of course he will. Especially if Nick is the one mating you."

Her arm moved faster than she could think, and before she knew it, her hand made contact with his cheek. The slap echoed around the room.

Nodding slowly with his head to the side, Jason's jaw throbbed, the skin reddening his perfect cheek.

"Get out!" she screamed, and pushed at his chest.

He stood, paralyzed for a moment, staring at the floor.

"Get out!" she cried again, tears blurring her vision.

With a final, agonizing glance, he left. The front door closing was like a blow to her head. Falling to her knees, Serena wrapped her arms around her and let the sobs claim her.

Chapter Eighteen

Owen Hunter glared at the email on his laptop. Sitting in the back office of his sports bar in Chicago, the Grayback alpha mulled over the Blacktail's message, his thick fingers drumming the top of his desk.

A notice had come in earlier from the Fighter Alex Suarez describing the fight they'd undertaken with a *convenio* in Hillview. Things were getting way out of control.

Two of his own pack members were found dead on the outskirts of the city. Owen hadn't known them too well, but it didn't matter. They were his responsibility and now the Graybacks were in a bit of a panic. This kind of discord didn't sit well with him.

Their pack didn't have Fighters like the Blacktails. Having been too blind or stupid to realize not all werewolves were up to or strong enough to fight, he and the past alpha had not deemed it a priority. Most of the Graybacks, however, were young and naïve and had no clue what to do in the face of danger.

Their natural extinct as Weres would be to attack, but the Blacktail Fighters were trained in combat. He flinched at the thought of his pack going through a battle like the Sweetin one with a team of mutated jackals.

Sitting up, he clasped his hands together tightly on

the desk, and reread the new message from Adam Perez, alpha of the Blacktails. Although it was their jobs as leaders to keep the other informed of certain business, Owen wasn't so thrilled with the guy's counsel.

Two alphas. Not good.

Especially when the cocky prick basically told him what he should be doing. The Blacktail was right, of course. They needed to form Fighters, but hell if he'd ever admit it. He was also right in stating they needed to band together to fight off the mounting number of Nightwalkers the witches were apparently breeding.

A part of him admired the fact the Fighters had managed to leave the battle with no casualties; the other part was irritated they hadn't captured the witch, Cassandra. They were unsure if she was still in the house when the bomb went off. The Fighter Alex was following the investigation of the explosion on the down low, but there was no concrete way to know for sure if the witch was dead or alive.

Pursing his lips, he read the last few lines of the email, fists tightening together, his massive biceps rippling from the effort.

My cousin and Fighter, Ramo Perez, will be in the city next week. He'll be joining his wife, Grayback member, Elizabeth Vitali. Their union several years ago was a testament to keep the peace between our packs in the hopes when we found it necessary or in times of peril, the Graybacks and Blacktails would unite.

Their alliance was approved by the previous Grayback alpha and myself. I suggest you make good use of my Fighter and allow him to train twelve or so members of your choosing to become Grayback

Fighters. He is a valuable member to the pack, and I expect his support will be met with cordiality and respect.

Owen's nostril's flared at the last line, which he read as *You better not fuck with my boy.* Really? Was this the best option for his pack? To have an outsider come in and tell his pack what to do...He didn't like it. Not one fucking bit.

And now Elizabeth would have to confront the husband who'd abandoned her years ago. Releasing his tight grip, he rubbed the stubble over his chin in agitation, leaning back in the leather office chair. She was going to go ballistic. The thought of the dark-eyed, voluptuous beauty heated his blood, making his length thicken in his slacks. He gripped the arms of the chair, trying to cool his raging emotions.

Does this guy actually think he'll be "joining" his estranged wife? Was he stupid? He didn't even know Elizabeth. Didn't know she'd have him flat on his ass outside her door if he dared to go near her. There was no way she'd welcome him home after leaving her for years without a word.

Idiot.

Not looking forward to having this discussion with the fireball, he made a mental note to send notices to everyone in his pack, but her. News like this should be delivered in person and as her alpha, it was his job to help figure out how she wanted to handle this.

He ought to send the douche packing, but, as pissed as he was about this whole business, Adam's message had hit the nail on the head. The Graybacks needed this alliance more now than ever.

Hitting the keys on his laptop, he searched for files

on every member of his pack, then picked up his cell. He and his beta had a long night ahead of them. Deciding just who was capable and willing to fight against Nightwalkers wasn't going to be easy.

****

Tanked, blitzed, plowed, shit-faced, blasted, juiced…these were just a few names for what he actually was at the moment. Sitting on the floor of his apartment, Jason leaned up against the kitchen counter facing the television on the far side of the wall, which was turned off. Everything in sight bugged the hell out of him, so T.V. wasn't an option. In fact, being here was a bad idea. Everything reminded him of Serena. The front door, the windowsill, the bedroom…God, he was pathetic.

Looking around his place, he thought he'd ought to blow it up too, since he'd trashed it a week ago. He didn't have much to begin with, but he knew the stool, chair and bottles didn't belong where they were. His poor cell had been smashed on the far wall days ago when Serena left him a gut-twisting message.

I know why you're doing this, but it won't work. Adam will not force me to move, and you know it. I'm staying here, Jason. Please. I love you and only you. Come back to me.

The womanly voice she spoke in pierced his heart. After everything she'd been through, how could she still be so calm? Why wasn't she running away from him? Didn't she know this was the best option for her?

Palming the bottle of Johnny Walker Blue at his side, he thought of his brief convo with Nick. Taking a swig, he welcomed the fire burning down his chest as angelic Nick's face seared into his brain. The guy had been completely thrown off by his proposal. Adam had tagged along to give him the news, not agreeing to the plan, but not disagreeing either. The alpha knew his plan was solid in the long run, but he flat out said he wasn't forcing it on Serena and Nick.

Now that the seed had been planted, it was up to Nick and Serena to do whatever they liked. Jason was taking care of the bill for a place deep in the mountains in Colorado Springs so they could live happily ever after together.

Hunching over, he placed his elbows on his knees, head in hands as the pain laced through him again. He gripped a handful of hair, biting down hard. Does the pain ever end?

If it's an order, then I have no choice. I'll do the best I can to make her happy, but I won't force her.

Nick's honorable speech filled his mind.

I'm sorry you feel this is the best option, but I have to be frank now...What the hell is wrong with you? We're not in love. She loves you. Get your head out of your ass and go to her.

He'd ignored this, of course, heading to his place instead where he's been curled around bottle after bottle since.

The front door opened suddenly, and with surprising speed, Jason reached for his gun at his side aiming it at his guests.

"Watch it," Adam murmured, darkly.

Lowering his weapon, he shook his head. So far gone, he hadn't sensed his own pack members' presence in the building.

Nick had come along for the visit and stepped to him, snatching the gun from his hand. Growling, Jason glared up at him, eyes narrowing at the man who he'd made his enemy.

"You can knock it off," the blond angel said, clearly pissed. The guy's soft features were now hard, his face flushed. He looked to Adam. "There should be a new law about Fighters throwing their fellow Fighters under the bus. This way I'd get to watch him all night in the pillory."

Rubbing his brow like he had a migraine, Adam shook his head tiredly.

"You look like shit, J."

Leaning back against the counter, he sat lazily eyeing the two with heavy lidded eyes. Having no will to utter a word, he raised a wobbly fist and flicked off his alpha then let his hand fall in his lap.

Growing angrier by the second, Nick said, "Please tell me there's a punishment for giving your alpha the finger?"

Scowling at the Fighter, a low drone sounded from deep inside him.

"Shut up, Nick." Adam moved closer to Jason, his blue eyes trained on him. "Look at yourself. You're fucking useless. You really think this was the best option when I've lost my beta? Is that what you want? Cuz at this rate, you'll be asked to resign. I need my Fighters in tip-top shape, not a drunken mess on the floor."

Continuing to glare up at Nick from the floor, Jason barely heard a word his alpha said. "Have you seen her?" Jason asked Nick in a chilling voice he hardly recognized.

Nick smirked, uncommonly snide. "Yeah, I did. We had a nice *long* talk." Pursing his lips he let his words settle in the air.

Jason whipped the bottle at his face.

Ducking just in time, Nick continued to smile bitterly after the bottle smashed against the door. "You're an idiot." Bending forward he gripped Jason by the throat and hulled him to his feet, pushing him up against the counter. "You really want to fight me, man?" he asked in a disgusted voice, his face inches from his.

Too trashed to pull him off, Jason stammered back, "Go ahead. Hit me."

Nick's look of disgust grew and he let him go, stepping back. "I'm not going to fight you. Yeah, we talked. It was a moot conversation when neither one of us plans on going anywhere. She's not into me. Never will be. Stop being an idiot and go protect her yourself."

Nick's face blurred in and out of focus. Leaning his elbows on the counter, Jason swayed a bit where he stood. "Not good for her…" he stammered, then pointed to his chest, "Cursed."

Closing his eyes, he let the terrifying details of the Sweetin fight creep into his head. He'd failed her twice. Twice! He couldn't keep her safe because he was a goddamn curse.

His cheek stung as someone slapped him. The memory of Serena's delicate hand coming at him warmed him a bit. God, he'd give anything to watch his brave girl land one on him again. Opening his eyes to mere slits, he saw Adam's face up in his grill. "Sober the fuck up. You're at the site tomorrow at six and on rotation in the evening."

The last thing he remembered before hitting the

floor was Nick's pitiful expression right before the Fighter coldcocked him.

****

Jason was still with her.

Aware that he was dreaming, he lay on his back completely naked over the covers, watching her over his large pecs as she worked her mouth over him. His blood roared, shooting straight to his shaft. Her dark eyes met his and smiled seductively. Moving over him, her lithe bare form straddled his hips, taking him inside her.

Ah! He moaned, lifting his hips to move deeper. Watching her breasts rise and fall before him, Jason caressed her chest, her breasts, down to her belly, bringing his hands to cup her ass, impaling himself slow and deep within her sex. She moaned delightfully, her head thrown back, moist lips parted. Damn, she was so beautiful. If he couldn't have her in life, at least she'd forever be with him in his dreams.

In his fantasy, it was dusk and the setting sun shown bright on his girl. Her skin glowed, an angel giving him the pleasure he needed, yearned for. This Serena was not pale or thin, but supple and strong, her golden skin damp with sweet perspiration.

Bending her head forward, she gazed at him as she continued to plunge up and down on his shaft with deliberate strokes. Jason's depraved mind couldn't control his mouth when he was inside her. "Keep fucking me, honey. Don't stop."

His fantasy Serena, smiled again, gripping his thighs as her sex squeezed him. Bits of reality surfaced and he flinched. *No.* Picturing her doing this for his fellow Fighter incensed him. She was his. All his. His eyes hooded, he licked his fingers, blocking out the horrid image. His damp fingers reached her center, rubbing the swollen nub tenderly as she moved. "This is mine," he uttered possessively.

Dream Serena nodded as sighs escaped her lips. Closing her eyes, she climaxed over him, her fervent thrusts driving him to the breaking point. He cocked his head into the pillow, squeezing his lids tight, his body ablaze as he filled her.

Eyes shot open as his breath caught, chest heaving violently. "Serena!" he uttered breathlessly, completely spellbound.

Sitting atop him, Serena's naked body glowed like his dream Serena. Only…it hadn't been a dream.

She was here.

Serena had him in between her legs, hovering over him as if staking her claim. It had only been a week, but she'd gained more weight, the olive color of her skin was back, even her breasts appeared fuller. She was healthier now than she'd been before. And more beautiful and confident than he'd ever seen her. The scared girl he knew so long ago was gone. Here was a woman who knew exactly what she wanted and took it. She'd literally just *taken* him, woken him from his deep slumber and had her way with him.

Jesus Christ.

Taking her wrists, he pinned her with a glare. "What the hell are you doing?" Half sitting up, he was about to let her go to get her off of him when she twisted her hands and caught him by the wrists, placing his hands on the bed over his head. Leaning over him, her hair draped over her cheeks.

In a demanding voice she said, "Listen well, Jason.

Nothing you do or say will ever keep us apart. As I said before, you're mine." She kissed him, softly. "And I'm yours."

This whole scenario was almost comical. His sweet and tiny Serena splayed across his enormous frame, holding him down to the mattress. As a werewolf she was strong, not stronger than him, but pretty damn sexy-as-hell strong.

"I told you…" he started, but she cut him off.

"You told me you were going to marry me. Now, do I need to take this up with the alpha because as beta your word is binding?"

"Serena…" He tried to get up, but she let go of his wrists and pushed his chest down with her delicate hands.

"Tell me you don't love me, and I'll leave." Her eyes were hard on his, her mouth firm as she waited.

Shaking his head, he let the fight go. For years he'd fought his feelings. He let go for a couple of days and he'd fucked up again, putting her in danger. He thought what he was doing was the best option. Still did every time he thought on it.

She'd be away from him, away from the chaos surrounding their town, safe and secluded. He'd be a miserable fuck for the rest of his days, but so what? No. Not miserable. Dead. For the first time in his life, he'd felt the icy coldness in his heart as he pictured a life without her. Hell. He hadn't been able to function. Going a week without food, water, working…Jesus. Did he still have a job? Was he still a Fighter?

Brown eyes penetrated his soul, filling him up with warmth once again. "I'm an idiot," he said, utterly defeated. Smirking, he thought of Nick saying those exact words before he hit him. Shit.

He'd almost ruined his relationship with a member of his pack. Nick was like a brother to him. Not blaming the guy for the sucker punch, he wondered if his pack mate would forgive him for putting him through this.

"Yes, but you're my idiot," she said, leaning forward and gripping his cheeks in her soft hands, kissing him again. When they broke apart she asked, worriedly, "How do you feel?"

Furrowing his brow, Jason wondered how the hell he got to his bed. "Strange, I was sure I was going to have the mother of all hangovers."

Laughing she asked, "You really don't remember a thing, do you?"

"What?"

Placing her chin on her hands, she rested adorably on his chest. "Adam called me after he left. Don't know if you realized, but you were drunk at eight o'clock in the morning. I came over and found you passed out on the floor."

Shifting uneasily, Jason flushed. "I really wish you hadn't seen that."

She giggled. "It was rather interesting. When you came to you kept talking about curses and Nick…I don't know who you thought I was, but you kept talking about me too." An awed expression flitted across her features. "You remembered some of the strangest things this morning. You kept telling me I had to take care of Serena. To make sure I had the jasmine soap she liked and to keep string cheese and saltines in the kitchen." Her eyes glazed over him lovingly. "You made me promise to bring her favorite sweater and to be sure I locked the doors at night."

Even trashed he still worried about her. He guessed this wasn't too embarrassing. "How'd you get me cleaned up?"

"Once I got you off the floor you were pretty easy to manage. You chatted on about one thing or another, then I got you in the shower. You were quiet in there, just staring thoughtfully at me. When I helped you into bed, I made you take about four ibuprofen before you knocked out."

"Damn. I had you in the shower, and I just stood there?" he said, his heavy lidded eyes fixated on her. Still embarrassed, he thought it was kind of funny hearing Serena retell his dumb antics.

"Well, you were definitely *excited* I was bathing you, but you were a complete gentlemen."

Stroking her back gently he asked, "And right now? Did you initiate this?" he asked smoothly.

Eyes smoldering, she smirked. "You were moaning my name in your sleep. As I couldn't get you under the covers, I could see you were…*up*."

Trying to give her a chastised look, he asked, his cheeks flushing, "And the other thing…" He gave a brief nod to subtly indicate his swollen sex still inside her. "Did you really…" His eyes flicked to her supple mouth. "…or was it part of my dream?"

It was her turn to blush. Stammering, she said, sweetly, "I was curious. You touched me there with your mouth, and I thought I'd return the favor."

His thick length twitched inside her, and her mouth fell open, sucking in a deep breath.

"Did you like it?" she whispered.

Nodding, his face grew stern. How in the world did

he ever think he could let her go? His new nickname should be Jason "the idiot" Linus.

Brows lowering, she said earnestly, "Don't ever push me away again, Jason."

His chest expanded at her words. Rolling her over onto her back, he said, slowly moving once again into her hot core, "Never, Serena." Surging back and forth, he leaned his temple to hers, moaning, "*Ah, Serena, you're mine.*"

A word about the author...

Julia Laque holds a B.S. in Education and an M.A. in School Administration. As much as she loves teaching, her true passion has always been the written word. An avid fan of love stories, Julia writes gripping romance. She lives in Chicago, Illinois with her family.

~*~

www.julialaque.com